This ain't no place for gettin' shirty.
—Absolution's station attendant

ADOBE FLATS

A RESURRECTION MAN NOVEL

COLIN CAMPBELL

MIDNIGHT INK
WOODBURY, MINNESOTA

FIRST EDITION
First Printing, 2014

Cover design: Kevin R. Brown
Cover illustration: Steven McAfee, iStockphoto.com/23910207/©Mordolff

Midnight Ink, an imprint of Llewellyn Worldwide Ltd.

Library of Congress Cataloging-in-Publication Data
Campbell, Colin, 1955–
  Adobe Flats : a resurrection man novel / Colin Campbell.—First edition.
    pages cm— (A Resurrection man novel ; 3)
    ISBN 978-0-7387-3633-4
  1. Police—England—Yorkshire—Fiction. 2. British—Texas—Fiction. I. Title.
PR6103.A48A46 2014
823'.92—dc23

                                                                    2014009823

Midnight Ink
Llewellyn Worldwide Ltd.
2143 Wooddale Drive
Woodbury, MN 55125-2989

www.midnightinkbooks.com

Printed in the United States of America

For my daughter, Ann.
One thing I definitely got right.
I love you.

THE PRESENT

That's a neat trick, that balancing thing. You should be in the circus.

—Jim Grant

ONE

Steam hissed up from Jim Grant's lap as scalding hot coffee shrivelled his nuts and turned the front of his jeans into molten lava. At least that's what it felt like when his efforts to peel back the lid of his latte tipped the king-size paper cup over his nether regions and threatened to melt his gonads. Hot coffee in his lap and a swirl of white foam down the front of his T-shirt like a question mark. Not the best start but par for the course considering his reception since arriving in Absolution, Texas. About as friendly as the one those Mexicans got who visited the Alamo.

Grant's frosty reception began even before he arrived. On the train from Los Angeles—not the main line express but the third change after leaving the city of angels. The parched scrubland passing outside the window reminded Grant of that other place, the one where devils ruled and angels feared to tread. When he had asked the conductor how long before they stopped at Absolution, the conductor's reaction had set the tone for all that was to follow.

"This train don't stop at Absolution."

"That's not what my ticket says."

The conductor examined Grant's ticket. The printout gave his journey as Los Angeles, California, to Absolution, Texas. The railroad official frowned and scratched his head.

"We ain't never stopped at Absolution. That's a request-only stop."

"Well, I'm requesting it. How long?"

The conductor handed the ticket back.

"Next stop after Alpine."

He pulled a pocket watch out of his waistcoat pocket, more for effect than necessity. Grant reckoned this fella knew exactly how long before they arrived at the place the train never stopped at.

"Half an hour. Bit more, maybes."

"Thanks."

Grant settled back in his seat and watched Texas drift by through the window. Dry and brown and dusty. He couldn't remember the last patch of greenery he'd seen since changing trains. He didn't expect to see any more up ahead. Considering why he was here, that seemed appropriate. He glanced at the leather holdall in the overhead rack and thought about what was inside. Then he turned his attention to the scenery again.

Absolution wasn't anything he was expecting either.

STEAM DIDN'T RISE UP from the engine as the train pulled in at the one-stop bug hutch of a town. It wasn't that kind of train. This wasn't the iconic steam engine of the Old West, with its cowcatcher grill and enormous chimney; it was the squat, bulky diesel of the Southern Pacific that hadn't changed shape since the '50s. Grant felt like Spencer Tracy stepping down from the streamliner at Black Rock. That was another place trains never stopped at.

Heat came at him like he'd stepped through an oven door. Dust kicked up from the boards of the platform. Calling it a platform was an exaggeration. A raised section of wood and nails with three steps at one end that led into the parking lot. Parking lot was an exaggeration too. The hard-packed sand and gravel might have been a parking lot once upon a time, but nobody parked there nowadays. The ticket office was boarded up and closed. No wonder the conductor had looked nonplussed as he pulled the portable stairs back into the carriage. The door slammed shut. The engine roared. There was a hiss from the brakes, then the huge monster eased forward. It slowly built up speed as it nosed into the desert, and a few minutes later Grant was alone in a landscape so bleak he wondered why anybody wanted to build a town there in the first place.

He took his orange windcheater off, slung it over one shoulder, and walked to the ticket office. The boards creaked underfoot. He felt like he should be wearing spurs. Dust puffed up around his feet. The office was just that, a small square garden shed in the middle of nowhere. There was no waiting room or restroom or any other kind of room apart from enough space for one man to sit inside selling tickets. Back when anyone caught the train from here. Grant guessed that was a long time ago.

He glanced over his shoulder towards the town.

Absolution was just a row of uneven rooftops breaking the smooth lines of the horizon. Not as far away as they seemed, and not close enough to pick out any detail. Just flat, featureless buildings among the scrub and rock. He squinted against the blazing sunlight. Even the blue sky looked bleached and unfriendly. When

5

he looked closer, Grant could see there were more buildings than he first thought. Smaller and lower than what passed for the main street. A couple of water towers in the distance. A few weather vanes beyond them.

Nothing moved. There was no sound apart from the wind coming in off the flatlands. Then Grant heard pounding footsteps from the other side of the ticket office. He stepped to one side so he could see. A cloud of dust broke the stillness. A man was running towards him. He didn't look happy.

"What you think you're doin' here, fella?"

The man was out of breath. His words came out in a rasping voice that sounded like a smoker's but was probably just desert dry from a hard life. He carried a key to the ticket office but didn't offer to open it. Grant was visiting, not leaving. He didn't need a ticket. He held the leather holdall in one hand and nodded his head towards the departing train. Explaining the obvious seemed the way to go.

"Just got off the train."

"I can see that. How come?"

Grant could see this was going to be hard.

"Well, it just kinda stopped. Then I got off."

"No need to be flippant, young man." The man spat on the boards to prove he could spit. "This ain't no place for gettin' shirty."

The parchment face looked like it was shaped from stripped hide. It was lined and cracked and as dry as the voice. There was no twinkle in the eye to soften the harshness. It was impossible to guess his age, but Grant figured somewhere between old and ancient.

Running from town hadn't helped. When he got his breath back, his voice leveled out.

"*Sunset Limited* hasn't stopped here in years."

Grant tried a smile to lighten the atmosphere. "That's a step up from never."

The man looked puzzled. "What?"

"Conductor said it never stopped here."

"Weren't far short. Seems like never."

Grant let out a sigh. This conversation was going nowhere. He glanced along the rails at the disappearing train. The long silver streak was banking to the right as it took the long, slow bend around the distant foothills. He turned back to the man with the ticket office key.

"Looks like never was wrong and the years have rolled by, 'cause it sure as shit stopped today. And here I am."

The eyes turned to flint in the parchment face. "Yes, you are. And that begs the question, don't it?"

Grant waited for the question it begged, but it didn't come. This fella was as inscrutable as Charlie Chan but not as friendly. The black trousers, white shirt, and faded waistcoat suggested an official position, but if his job was to sell tickets he must have been on short time. He was no great shakes as a meeter and greeter either.

"You're not much of a welcoming committee."

The parched skin tightened. "Who said you're welcome?"

Grant nodded. "Nobody, I guess."

The town was only a short walk from the station, but it felt like miles away. The buildings were gray and dull, without any hint of life or color. No smoke from the chimneys. No glints of sunlight from moving vehicles. Place was as barren as a long-shit turd. Dried up and dead and full of crap. The station attendant pressed home his point.

"Nobody asked you to come here."

Grant kept calm but couldn't leave that one unanswered. "How do you know?"

Then he set off walking towards town.

TWO

THE MAIN STREET WAS a long stretch of nothing much. A dozen buildings at most on one side of the road. A couple more across the street. Grant stopped on the dirt track from the station before stepping onto the wider dirt track that was First Street. Swirls of sand blew across the road. He realized it was tarmacked, but the two-lane blacktop was so faded it look like cracked earth. The center line was unbroken yellow stained brown with the passage of time. A smell of mint drifted on the wind, and Grant noticed the first piece of greenery since getting off the train. A straggly plant behind a low picket fence surrounding a low-slung bungalow. Like a gatekeeper's house guarding the track to the station.

Grant stepped onto the sidewalk. Nobody was out walking. A handful of people were dotted about across the street. Some sitting on chairs outside the only two-story building, leaning the chairs back on two legs against the wall. A couple more standing in shop doorways farther along the street. Two or three staring out through plate-glass windows coated in dust. Nobody moved. Nobody shouted a greeting.

The building he wanted was obvious. He ticked off the others anyway—standard practice when entering hostile territory. There was a pharmacy, a grocery store, the ever-present hardware store, and some kind of eatery called the Famous Burro. Grant wondered if that should have been burrito, then remembered a burro was a donkey. He didn't fancy eating donkey. A bit farther down the street there was a post office and a clean-looking shop marked Front Street Books. There wasn't anything that looked like a bank. He turned the other way. More of the same, not amounting to much. The town petered out with a few dried-up houses and a gas station and railroad-car diner beyond them.

He turned back to the two-story building. The Gage Hotel. The place with the two fellas leaning back in their chairs. Cowboy boots and faded blue jeans. One had a cowboy hat pulled low to shade his eyes. The only thing missing was a piece of straw hanging out the corner of his mouth, or maybe chewing a matchstick. Neither man spoke. They just stared.

Accommodation was a priority. Looked like the Gage Hotel had the monopoly. Grant left the smell of mint behind and crossed the street. Time to see if the booking clerk was any friendlier than the ticket seller.

THE HOTEL LOBBY SMELLED of cracked leather and coffee. It was dark and dingy and should have been filled with smoke. The overall impression was of a gentlemen's club. Half a dozen leather chairs were grouped in pairs on either side of three glass-topped coffee tables. Two leather sofas against the wall complemented the chairs. A cigarette machine sat at the bottom of a carved wooden staircase. The stairs started beside the reception counter, which had a heavy bound ledger and a manual bell that you pressed for attention—the kind that dinged once when the internal hammer struck.

Reception was unmanned.

A smoke-stained wooden fan spun slowly from the ceiling. The gentle *thwup, thwup, thwup* of the rotor blades reminded Grant of something bigger, but he pushed the thought aside and focused on the reception counter. Patchwork shelving divided into pigeonholes covered the wall against the staircase. Each pigeonhole had a hook out front, and each hook held a key. Room numbers went from 1 to 25. None of the keys were missing. All the rooms were vacant.

Grant crossed the lobby and dropped the holdall on the floor. He spun the register on its rotating stand and looked for a pen. The squiggly writing looked faded and old. Proper fountain pen ink, not biro. He tried to make out the date of the last guest, but it was smudged and indistinct. Didn't look like yesterday though. An old-fashioned quill pen jutted from an inkwell on the counter. He picked it up and studied the ink-crusted nib.

"You is about to deface a historical document there, son."

The voice came from the office door behind the counter. The face that went with the voice was drier and more parchment-like than the ticket seller at the station. The desk clerk limped into the room and spun the register back around. He indicated a desktop computer that Grant hadn't seen below the level of the counter.

"We've gone all newfangled for checkin' in." The desk clerk scrutinized Grant's face. "You must be the fella got off the *Sunset*."

"That obvious, is it?"

"Sure is. First time the *Sunset's* stopped here in over a year. First new face in town for almost the same."

"I guess I've got a choice of rooms, then."

"Ain't got no rooms."

Grant let that sink in. This fella was no more welcoming than the welcoming committee at the station. The only difference was where the ticket seller had nobody to sell tickets to, the desk clerk had a customer right in front of him but wasn't about to rent him a room. Grant figured that made him even less of a welcoming committee. The elephants in the room were the keys hanging from each pigeonhole. Grant nodded at them.

"Got a lot of keys, though."

"That I do. But each one's taken."

Grant felt like he should fold one arm up his sleeve. This was playing like an homage to Spencer Tracy in *Bad Day at Black Rock*. He wondered briefly if the clerk was having him on—a little gentle humor—then dismissed the thought. The lines etched into the clerk's face were more from grimaces and frowns than smiles and laughter. His voice was gravel dry.

"Block bookings."

Grant smiled just to show the clerk how to do it. "Let me guess. Cattlemen from the local ranch. For when they come to town after driving the herd."

"Ain't no cattle ranches in Absolution."

"Oil men, then. For a break from the rigs."

"No oil neither."

Grant kept his voice conversational. "Place hasn't got a lot going for it, then, has it?"

"It's got enough. We like it the way it is. Don't need strangers comin' in and tellin' us our business."

Grant leaned forward and rested his elbows on the counter. "And what business is that?"

"None of yours, that's what."

"Tourism, maybe? You've got Big Bend National Park just south of you."

The man tensed. Grant had touched a nerve. Maybe the lack of tourists was part of the reason the town looked so dry and lifeless. The clerk didn't expand on the theory.

"We get by."

Grant shifted his weight to one elbow and reached over the counter with the other hand. He slipped the nearest key from its hook and tossed it in his palm.

"Well, you just got by with one extra guest. I'll take this one."

The clerk looked indignant. "That room's taken."

"I know. By me. If the fella who's block-booked it drifts into town, I'll change rooms. Name's Grant. Jim Grant."

Grant picked up the holdall, grabbed a town map from the display stand on the counter, and turned for the stairs. The fan continued to *thwup, thwup, thwup*. Grant continued to ignore the memory. There was a thump outside as one of the chair-leaners on the porch stood up. Grant was on the second step before the front door opened, but he didn't look back. He already knew who it was. The one in the boots and cowboy hat.

The clerk finally found his voice. "I need more than that—for the register."

Grant leaned over the banister rail. "Thought you'd gone all newfangled."

"Same applies. Name won't do. Where you from?"

Grant set off up the stairs again and spoke over his shoulder. "Out of town."

The stairs creaked all the way up.

13

CHECKING THE MAP IN his room explained why tourists didn't stop here on their way to Big Bend. The founding fathers had pinned their hopes on the Southern Pacific and built the town on either side of the railroad tracks. Road traffic used the 90 just north. The 385 ran north to south all the way down into Big Bend National Park. The crossing of those two roads was at Marathon, west of Absolution. The road through Absolution went nowhere.

Grant picked all that up from the inset map of the area in the corner. A small square indicated the desert town's position, and the rest of the page was taken up by the Absolution street plan. It didn't really need a full page, but there were more streets than Grant had first noticed. Traditional US grid pattern: streets running east to west and avenues north to south. The main road was First Street, with North Second to North Eighth spreading one way and South Second to South Fifth the other. The main crossroad was Avenue D, the rest being Avenues A to K. If there were any more shops, they'd be on Avenue D.

The Los Pecos Bank and Trust was on Avenue D.

Grant left the map on the bed and unpacked his bag. The hold-all had traveled the world with him, and he knew how to fold his clothes to best effect. Partly military training and partly the boarding school his father had dumped him at as soon as he was old enough. The British Army and Moor Grange School for Boys had a lot to answer for. He hung the orange windcheater on the back of the door and put the T-shirts and jeans in the drawers. He slid the long velvet box from the bag between the T-shirts. His fingers played gently over the scarred fabric. Living in the present was Grant's preferred modus operandi, but sometimes the past wouldn't stay buried. An ironic thought, considering why he was here.

With his normal preparations complete, if not necessarily in the usual order, it was time for a shower. First thing was always to get a map. Second was scout the location. Third was check for enemy personnel. That was from his army days. As a cop, the third option was more wide reaching. As a tourist, all but number one were moot points. He just couldn't turn them off. Getting laid wasn't an option this time. Not in his current mindset.

The en suite shower was hot and roomy. He could stand tall and not bump into the showerhead. That was pretty tall. His shoulders didn't bang the sides. As hotel showers went, this was built for size. He guessed what he'd heard about Texas was right. It was a big country for big men. He toweled dry and walked naked back into his room.

He stopped in the doorway. The muscles of his thighs turned to knotted ropes and his shoulders tensed. He wasn't alone. The man in the cowboy hat was sitting in the bedside chair, leaning the chair back on two legs against the wall.

THREE

"THAT'S A NEAT TRICK, that balancing thing. You should be in the circus."

Grant pulled on a clean pair of jeans and draped the towel over the foot of the bed. He gauged the angle of the chair and the tipping point. The chair legs were a long way from the wall, the angle too steep. The cowboy was trying to look threatening and cool at the same time. It put him in a precarious position. One swift kick and he'd be on the floor with Grant's knee crushing his throat. Grant didn't want that. He decided to play this like Spencer Tracy. Show a hint of cool himself.

"Is this where you tell me I'm in your room?"

The cowboy rested one leg on the bedspread. "That's plain to see, isn't it?"

Grant pulled a black T-shirt over his head and smoothed it down across his chest. He put fresh socks on, then slipped his feet into black K-Swiss tennis shoes and laced them up. He didn't like fighting barefoot. It put you at a disadvantage when it came to kicking or having your toes stamped on.

"Block booking for when you happen to be in town?"

"And I am in town. You can see that, can't you?"

Grant finished fastening his laces and stood up straight. He nodded at the foot draped across the bedspread, making the balance even more precarious.

"Do cowboys have funny-shaped feet? I've always wondered because I don't think I could fit my toes into a boot that pointed."

The cowboy lowered his foot to the floor and the chair legs followed. No longer leaning back. All four legs planted firmly on the carpet. He was learning.

"As opposed to them moccasins you're wearing?"

Grant looked at his tennis shoes, built for comfort and speed. Ideal cop shoes if you didn't have to worry about cacti and rattlesnakes. Maybe cowboy boots had a place down here, but they wouldn't be able to outrun a sports shoe.

"I heard that once in *Back to the Future*—the third one, where Michael J. Fox goes back to the Old West. It was kind of funny that time. Doesn't quite work in modern times. Anybody still wear moccasins?"

"What I'll be wearing is your spleen for a hat if you don't get out of my room."

The words were harsh, but the cowboy was still sitting down with Grant standing over him. Not a position of strength. He was obviously used to his presence alone being enough of a threat. Grant expanded his chest and took a deep breath.

"Register says it's my room."

"Block booking says it's mine."

"No. Block booking holds you *a* room. Take your pick. Rest are empty."

"I like this one."

"That's mighty nice of you, but it's taken."

"You're not catching my drift. I want this room."

"And you're not catching mine. You should have took it instead of sitting on your ass on the porch, practicing your balancing act."

The boundaries were set. Confrontation was inevitable. Pissing contests rarely ended in a draw. Grant still held the high ground, a position where he could strike downward instead of having to stand up first. Doubt flickered across the cowboy's face, but he soldiered on.

"That's not the way it works in our town. We don't need strangers comin' in tryin' to change the rules."

Grant relaxed both hands at his sides. His knees were loose and ready to flex. The situation had reached its tipping point; it could go either way from this moment forward. The choice was his. He thought about the velvet box hidden beneath the T-shirts in his drawer and considered the reason he was here. That thought cooled his temperature down from boiling. He dialed back the menace while keeping a hint of threat in his voice.

"I heard that in a movie once too. The stranger bit."

The cowboy looked puzzled. Grant kept it light.

"In *Rango*. Johnny Depp as a lizard in a spaghetti Western. This little rodent kid comes up to the lizard when he rides into town. Gives him a squint and says, 'You're a stranger. Strangers don't last long around here.'"

Grant smiled. "That would make you the rodent. In the film, the rodent was wrong." The smile disappeared. "So are you. I'm staying. And this is my room."

Grant stepped back and indicated the door. The cowboy stood up, his attempt at crowding the stranger a complete washout. He crossed to the door but didn't open it. Instead his face went through a complicated tableau before he threw his parting shot.

"That'd make you a lizard, then."

Grant laughed. "I can't argue with that."

The cowboy opened the door. "Around here, lizards are roadkill."

Grant squared his shoulders. "We're not in the road. Now fuck off out of my room."

The cowboy fucked off, slamming the door behind him. That should have been an end to it, but Grant followed him onto the landing. Just in case. The stairs creaked all the way down to the lobby. Grant listened as the desk clerk came out of the back office. There was a hushed conversation, but the cowboy couldn't keep his voice down.

"That's him all right. Tell Macready."

Grant was thinking about what that meant when he went back into his room. The map was still spread open on the bed. He'd met the enemy personnel. Maybe he should scout the location a bit more.

Despite the heat Grant still wore his lucky orange windcheater when he stepped into the street twenty minutes later. He didn't hand the key in; possession being nine-tenths of the law, he felt safer with it in his pocket. He turned right along First and walked past the front of the Famous Burro restaurant. He still didn't fancy eating donkey. Two storefronts later he reached the intersection with Avenue D.

Despite the road being tarmac and the sidewalk being cracked concrete, Grant's black trainers were dusted white. Heat and sand scorched the earth, and the hard blue sky held no promise of shade.

There were no clouds, and even the gentle breeze was hot. Grant unzipped the windcheater and studied the crossroads.

The left-hand side of Avenue D, heading south, crossed the railroad tracks with a shallow hump in the road. Back in the UK that would have been a level crossing with automatic gates or barriers that closed across the road and warning lights for when a train was coming. It didn't look like Texas wasted time on gates or barriers. The crossing was unguarded apart from an X-shaped cross on a stick with two red lights and a bell. Grant had heard them in movies, a rhythmic chime and flashing lights. Avenue D crossed the tracks and disappeared into a cluster of low-rent housing that looked even sadder than the main street.

It was the right-hand stretch that interested Grant. The northern leg with its handful of shops and the only red brick building in town: the Los Pecos Bank and Trust. Bars on the windows and a heavy wooden door. Patches of whitewashed plaster over the red brick. It looked like a smaller version of the Alamo. The mission that became a fortress. The fortress that became a shrine. Grant remembered that from the John Wayne film. Whoever built the bank must have seen it too because they hadn't included an ATM machine to spoil the façade.

Grant crossed the street on the diagonal and couldn't help changing his walk to those little steps the Duke used. Momentarily. The rolling gait of a big man. No ATM meant Grant would have to go inside. Not a problem, but he hoped the teller was more helpful than the officials he'd met so far. He was running out of walking-around money.

It turned out the bank teller wasn't only more helpful, he was downright chatty once he realized the tall stranger walking into his bank wasn't there to rob it. Grant reckoned the old fella had watched too many Westerns until he saw the bullet holes in the wall and the armed guard inside the door. The teller examined Grant's debit card like it was some precious metal, turning it over in his hands.

"These things were supposed to replace cash money." He stopped turning it over, a look of scorn on his face. "If'n that were the case, wouldn't need no banks then, would we?"

He jerked a thumb back over his shoulder. "Wouldn't need a safe."

Grant let the teller talk himself out.

"Thank god most businesses in Absolution still need cash payment." The teller put the card down and stared at Grant. "How much you want?"

Now Grant could get a word in.

"Depends. How expensive is Absolution?"

"For what?"

"Hotel. Food. Car hire."

"Car hire? Ain't nowhere to go, unless you're planning to leave like everyone else. Not much of a stay, though, since you only just got off the train."

"I'm not leaving yet."

"Then you won't need a car. Everywhere else is walking distance."

Grant wondered if everyone in town made conversation so difficult. Going round in circles without getting to the point. He plucked a figure out of his head and settled for that.

"Couple of hundred should do."

"Two hundred makes you king of the hill. Carry that much and you'd better watch your back."

"I've got broad shoulders. I'll manage."

The teller looked up at the big man in the orange jacket and nodded. "I'm sure you can. Just saying, that's all. If you'd rather take less and come back. Bank'll still be here."

He lowered his eyes and muttered to himself. "Macready needs it to pay his…"

His voice trailed off when he remembered he wasn't alone. He copied the card details onto a withdrawal slip and pushed it under the grill on the counter. Two hundred dollars. Grant signed it and slid it back.

"You'd save yourself the trouble if you had a hole-in-the-wall machine."

"What?"

Grant recognized his slip-up. Not completely Americanized yet.

"Sorry. Back in England ATMs are nicknamed holes-in-the-wall."

The teller paused in mid-count, the twenty-dollar bills fanned out like a hand of cards.

"You did recognize the façade outside. The Alamo."

Grant wondered where this was going. "Yeah, I got that."

"Well, the only holes in the wall at the Alamo was them damn Mexicans trying to get in. You want cash, use the door."

He finished counting, then rechecked the amount. He counted them out again in front of Grant, then slipped them under the grill. Grant thanked him and put them in his wallet.

"Where can you recommend to eat?"

"Apart from the hotel?"

"Don't think they want to serve me."

"Not surprised."

"How come?"

"You're a stranger. Strangers don't last long around there."

Grant almost laughed. Come to think of it, the bank teller had a small rodent face minus the whiskers. The teller waved in an indeterminate direction.

"Gilda's Grill. At Sixto's Gas and Wreckers. Edge of town."

Grant remembered the gas station east of the main street. "Thanks. And a car?"

"Sixto's again. If he's got one ain't been wrecked."

Grant said a final thank you and headed for the door. As he stepped into the sunlight, he heard the teller pick up the phone and the unmistakable burr of an old-fashioned rotary dial.

GRANT TOOK HIS JACKET off and slung it over his shoulder. He continued up Avenue D to Third Street and turned right. From the map he knew that Second only went three blocks, but Third went right to the other end of town. A white stucco church with a powder-blue steeple stood on the intersection next to the most colorful building he'd seen since getting off the train. The blue, red, and orange walls and outside stairs of Eve's Garden Bed and Breakfast and Ecology Center. It said so on the sign. Everything else along Third was scorched earth and rusty metal sidings. A couple of trees and some rotting picket fence.

The walk took fifteen minutes. He didn't see another living soul the entire length of the road. A dog barked. It sounded desperate. With the sun beating down on the back of Grant's head, he could understand why. Third Street petered out to a dead end and a dirt track. The track was fenced off.

Grant called the map to mind. According to that, Third Street continued until it met the main road at an angle, but in reality the tarmac stopped at Avenue J. The track was all that remained of the final stretch. The reason it was fenced off wasn't on the map either. The battered metal sign was rusting and full of bullet holes.

ABSOLUTION
TOWN DUMP
By Local Ordinance

The dump was long, flat, and wide and spread out on either side of the dirt track. Half a dozen mobile homes formed a border around the outer edges. Ex-trailer-park stock in need of a lick of paint. The windows were boarded up. The doors were open. It looked like they were used for storage. Smaller items salvaged from the rubbish. None of them were lived in except for the trailer nearest the gate, where a hanging basket beside the door swayed in the wind. Whatever flowers had been planted in it were long since dead. There was a sun chair and a garden table next to the trailer steps. Dust swirled around a courtyard formed by the only open space between piles of junk and discarded electrical goods.

If there was a system, Grant couldn't see it.

What he could see was a shortcut that followed the track through the dump and a hole in the wire fence where people used it. The dump was as deserted as the rest of Third Street. There was no sign of the custodian. Grant ducked through the gap and kept straight on. The breeze whipped up rotten garbage smells. Silence enveloped him; it was even quieter here than the rest of town. Desert sand that had drifted across the track muffled his footsteps. It was like walking through a cemetery with rusty washing machines instead of tombstones. There was no movement apart from strands of rubbish flapping in the wind.

He was almost halfway through when all that changed.

Something moved in the corner of his vision.

Then a gunshot split the air.

FOUR

THE RAT EXPLODED IN a mist of blood and flesh, not so much shot to death as vaporized. The gunshot echoed five times around the pale blue sky before the dump returned to silence apart from cackling laughter behind the hanging basket.

"Don't like that, d'ya? Yer little fucker."

Grant didn't move. He turned his head slowly towards the trailer.

"You talking to me or the rat?"

The rifle poking out of the open door jerked towards Grant. It settled on his center mass, then moved gently as the shooter came down the steps. A hairy arm came into view, followed by a rolled-up shirtsleeve and a hunched figure wearing stained overalls, the type with a bib front and no sleeves. The face that came out of the shadows was as dry as saddle leather—a theme Grant was beginning to recognize. Heat and dust working its magic on the residents.

The man stepping into the sun looked older than the ticket seller, the hotel clerk, and the bank teller put together. The voice wasn't quite as harsh, but it was a long way from friendly.

"Why would I be talking to you?"

"Because the rat's past answering."

The old-timer cackled a laugh, then wheezed as he got his breath back. "It was rhetorical anyway. Damn rats ain't much on conversation."

Grant nodded but didn't move.

"Keeping the vermin at bay—I can understand that. But I think we can both agree I'm no rat. So could you lower the rifle please?"

The barrel twitched, then lowered. "I could shoot the wings off a fly. No need for you to worry."

"That's good to know."

The old-timer sat in the sun chair and leaned the rifle against the table. He rubbed his chin, the bristles sounding like sandpaper. He waved a surprisingly steady hand across the yard. "Have to draw the little bastards out so I don't hit the propane store."

Grant followed the direction and noticed propane tanks through the open door of the nearest trailer. Blue gas tanks were stacked around the side and the back as well. He wondered what the other trailers held. The old-timer must have read his mind because he indicated the next trailer.

"And the armory. Apart from that, I can shoot 'em anywhere."

Grant walked towards the courtyard, squinting at the rifle. "Small target moving fast. Nice shooting."

The old-timer swelled with pride. His face broke into a smile. "Young 'uns round here think they's the only ones who know how to shoot. Macready's lot. I've got eyes could outstrip 'em all."

"Eyes like a shithouse rat."

"Rat?"

Grant nodded at the bloodstain in the dust. "Not that one."

He stopped in front of the table.

"A saying back home. If you've got good eyesight, they say you've got eyes like a shithouse rat. Since they live in the dark. You—I'd say you've got the eyes of a sniper."

The old-timer smiled again. It seemed like this was the only flattery he'd been given in a long while.

"Two wars and a skirmish. Back aways."

He didn't say which wars, and Grant knew better than to ask. "Sorry for cutting through your land."

The old-timer's eyes held Grant's with a hint of humor. "Cutting through to where?"

Grant jerked a thumb to the far end of the dump. "Sixto's. Need to hire a car."

"That's the place to do it. Got all sorts. From comfort to ex-army. You goin' anywhere particular?"

Grant nodded. "South. I'm looking for Adobe Flats."

SIXTO'S WAS A HUNDRED yards farther on after Grant reached the main road again. He kept turning the old-timer's reaction over in his mind. The humor had vanished out of his eyes in a flash, replaced by a blank look and a sigh that heaved the old man's chest.

"Good luck with that."

He'd dismissed Grant with a wave.

"And don't step on my rat."

It was fairly obvious what had sparked the change of attitude, and it wasn't the mention of heading south. Adobe Flats. How much weight Grant should attach to the reaction of a crazy old man was something to consider as he followed the two-lane blacktop out of town. Sixto's Gas and Wreckers was on the left just before a battered

28

metal sign on a pole that had been shot so full of holes it had turned around.

ABSOLUTION, TEXAS Est. 1882
Pop. 203—Elev. 4040
Welcome/Bienvenidos

A cluster of bullet holes made the population hard to read, and *bienvenidos* was almost completely obliterated. Maybe Mexicans still weren't welcome. Anybody reading the sign was heading out of town, so the greeting was too late anyway. The tarmac gave way to a dusty forecourt, and Grant bypassed a pair of gas pumps into blessed shade. The canopy was high and wide and decorated with Shell's red and yellow signage. The red and yellow had faded in the constant glare of the sun. The Shell name had been painted out but was still a ghostly memory.

The sales kiosk and office was under the canopy, a glass and wood afterthought tagged onto the front of the main workshop building. Mechanic bays showed through the open shutter doors down the side. A big American car and two army jeeps were parked in front of the bays. A fenced-in compound round the back was piled high with scrapped cars and trucks, any usable parts already cannibalized for resale. A dog on a chain patrolled the compound. It saw Grant and charged the fence—not barking but wagging its tail. If it could have smiled, Grant reckoned it would be smiling.

"Don't mind Pedro. He's harmless."

The voice was good-old-boy Texan. The man it came from was standing in the doorway of the sales kiosk. He was about twenty-five and didn't look as if he'd done a day's work in his life. The pointed boots and cowboy hat were clean and new and hadn't seen hard times since they'd come out of the box. Unlike the tough guy at the hotel, this one couldn't even attempt intimidation. The tone was condescending. Grant disliked him immediately.

"Not a lot of point having him guard the cars then, is there?"

The Texan stepped aside to let Grant into the office. "Old Pedro isn't a guard dog. He's just a dumb old Mex living off the town."

Grant noticed an elderly Mexican cringe behind the sales counter. The Texan paid him no mind as he continued. "Anyway. Nobody steals from me."

Grant closed the door to let the air conditioning cool him down. "You must be Sixto then."

"Nope. Macready. Scott Macready."

He didn't offer his hand. Grant let the name sink in but didn't show it.

"Police around here must have it easy. With nobody stealing from you."

Macready glanced out of the window along First Street.

"Town sheriff has his work cut out, just not with thieving. Public disorder mainly. Mexicans who can't hold their liquor. Wife beating and the like."

The Mexican kept quiet. Grant looked at the Texan and saw the kind of man who'd have to beat up women to have a chance at beating anybody.

"Wife beater. Isn't that some kind of vest?"

Macready smiled to humor the foreigner. "More like a tank top with inch-wide straps and a deeper scoop neck."

Grant nodded.

"A poser's shirt. Bodybuilders wear them back home to show off their muscles. Anybody who beats on women, though, they're just like an empty vest. Full of wind and too much arm hole."

The subtle put-down was too subtle for Macready. "If we need muscle around here, we just hire it in."

Grant glanced down the road towards town. "Yeah. I saw that at the hotel."

"They make you welcome?"

"Like a turd in a swimming pool."

"They're just wary of strangers is all."

"*Bienvenidos* works better if you want to attract customers."

The Mexican smiled. Macready slitted his eyes. "Welcome to Absolution. You've read the sign."

"Sign only seems to apply if you're leaving town."

"That why you want to hire a car?"

Grant's ears pricked up. Now he knew who the phone call was to. "Just exploring."

"Exploring where?"

And that told him the old-timer at the dump didn't have a phone.

"Adobe Flats. Just south of here."

The Mexican's shoulders hunched as he tried to look smaller. Macready blinked but kept his face straight. A fly buzzed around the office, then fried itself on the electronic bug catcher above the door. The sparks made everyone jump except Grant. Tension crept into the room. Macready didn't let the silence become awkward.

"What you want to go out there for?"

"See somebody."

31

"Well, you won't find anybody at Adobe Flats. There's nothing there."

"You sure? That's the address I've got."

"For who?"

Grant considered telling Macready it was none of his business, but since he wanted the Texan to rent him a car, he decided to play along.

"Eduardo Cruz."

The Mexican flicked his eyes up, then down again. Macready shook his head.

"Doc Cruz? He left years ago. Like I said, there's nothing there anymore."

"I'd still like to drive down there. Pay my respects."

Macready's response was too quick. "I didn't say he died. He left."

Grant was getting tired of always going round the houses to make any headway. His reasons for being here were private. He reckoned he'd shared enough.

"Family. One of the jeeps'll do. How much for the day?"

Macready ignored the request. "Cruz ain't got no family down there. Place is empty."

"Then it'll be a short visit. How much?"

Macready looked flustered, uncertain what to do next. Not at all like a man nobody ever stole from. Not like a man in charge of things. His face hardened as he made his decision.

"Jeeps aren't for hire."

"The car then."

"That neither. They're in for service."

"All of them?"

"We don't have anything."

The welcome just kept getting better. Parched skin and dried voices. Not a hint of the famous western generosity or pioneering spirit. Grant's mouth was drying out, the dust finally getting to him.

"How about tea?"

"What?"

"I'd like a cup of tea."

"You're in Texas. We don't drink tea."

"Coffee then."

"This is a gas station, not a café. Diner's next door."

Grant followed Macready's nod of the head. To the left out the window. The railroad-car diner was round the other side of the workshop building. The red neon tubing of the Gilda's Grill and Diner sign barely registered in the sunlight.

Grant nodded at the Mexican, ignored Macready, and went out the door to buy a coffee.

FIVE

Steam hissed up from Grant's lap as scalding hot coffee shrivelled his nuts and turned the front of his jeans into molten lava. At least that's what it felt like when his efforts to peel back the lid of his latte tipped the king-size paper cup over his nether regions and threatened to melt his gonads. Hot coffee in his lap and a swirl of white foam down the front of his T-shirt like a question mark.

The waitress looked up from her work behind the cash register. An elderly couple sitting two booths down let out a gasp. Grant smiled and waved and spoke through gritted teeth.

"I'm all right. No worries."

He picked the paper cup out of his lap and stood it on the table. There was an inch of coffee left. The lid floated in a puddle of spillage on the Formica top. He sat back in the booth, but that didn't help so he stood up, tugging the hot, damp cloth away from his skin. He dabbed at the wet patch with a napkin. That didn't work. It was like trying to put out a forest fire with a water pistol. Spilled coffee pooled around his feet.

"It's okay."

Nobody believed him. Scalding coffee on your private parts was never okay. The elderly couple smiled their embarrassment but didn't get involved. He was a stranger around here. Strangers didn't last long. Right now Grant couldn't argue with that.

The counter flap banged open. The sound snapped Grant's head towards the cash register. The waitress who had served him the coffee five minutes earlier came out with a damp cloth and a roll of paper towels. The sad little smile she gave warmed him more than the coffee. It was the first friendly act he'd received since arriving in the dusty Texas town. Friendlier than the greeting those Mexicans got who visited the Alamo.

"IF THEY DON'T USE lids in England, why don't you spill your coffee back home?"

Her voice was rich and throaty and dripped irony. She was soaking up the spillage with pads of folded paper towels. On the table, not his lap. Grant dabbed at that using the damp cloth she'd given him. The question mark of cream had gone, and the spilled coffee was already cold. After the extreme heat his knackers felt like they were bathed in ice. He pulled the cloth away from his skin again.

"The lid was the problem. Drinking through that little hole in the top."

He stepped out of the booth while the waitress spread paper towels on the floor.

"That's what it's for."

"I know. But I prefer to drink it like a man. Not some kind of pensioner who can't look after himself."

She stopped wiping the floor and looked up at him. "You clearly can't look after yourself."

Grant shrugged. "You think I should've used a straw?"

"Straws are for cold drinks."

He indicated his wet crotch. "It's cold now."

The waitress stood up and leveled steady eyes on his. The throaty voice made her response even more suggestive. "You want me to suck you through a straw?"

She looked shocked when she realized what she'd said. Grant laughed.

"There's no answer to that."

He held out a hand.

"Jim Grant."

She shook it.

"Sarah Hellstrom. Pleased to meet you."

"Not Gilda?"

"What?"

"Gilda's Grill and Diner."

"Oh, that? Place is mine. Name goes back aways."

"Is anywhere in this town named after who owns it?"

"What do you mean?"

"Like Sixto's, owned by Macready."

"Everything's owned by Macready. Can't have everywhere called Macready's. It would confuse people."

Grant watched for her reaction. "Macready doesn't own the diner?"

Sarah clenched her jaw. "No, he does not. It was my dad's. Granddad's before him."

"His name Gilda?"

"He liked Rita Hayworth."

"As in *The Shawshank Redemption*?"

"Sorry?"

"The Stephen King story they based the film on was *Rita Hayworth and the Shawshank Redemption*."

"So?"

"So why not call it Rita's Grill?"

"He was being obscure. She starred in a movie called *Gilda*."

Sarah indicated the next booth, and Grant followed her instructions. He slid onto the padded seat and felt the cold dampness touch his skin. He handed the cloth back, and she nodded towards the counter.

"I'll get you another latte. Without a lid."

"Thanks."

"Then we'd better do something about your pants."

He watched her walk the length of the railroad-car-turned-diner. She had a lovely walk. If he'd been visiting Adobe Flats for any other reason, he thought there might have been possibilities there. He surveyed the parking lot through the diner's windows. Big, wide windows that ran all down one side. He could just make out the first jeep poking round the side of the mechanics bay. It still had the unit markings and combat pattern that should have been painted out when decommissioned. That was something to think about. Then his second coffee arrived with a wiggle and a smile, and his thoughts turned elsewhere.

GRANT WASHED HIS CLOTHES in the utility room at the far end of the diner. Or rather Sarah Hellstrom put his jeans and T-shirt through the washing machine while Grant stood wrapped in a towel like a man in a skirt. He picked up the peg bag from the shelf and dangled it in front of his privates.

"All I need is a sporran."

"A what?"

"Man purse on a string."

She realized what he meant. "Oh, a kilt. You from Scotland?"

"Yorkshire."

"I have no idea where that is. They wear kilts there?"

"No. It was just the towel thing. Never mind."

Jokes weren't funny when you had to explain the punchline. He put the peg bag back on the shelf next to a Welcome to Big Bend calendar and looked around the office and utility room. There was a cluttered desk with two chairs, a filing cabinet that leaned to one side, and the washing machine and tumble dryer combo. The room smelled of washing powder and fabric conditioner. Grant's jeans and T-shirt went into the rinse cycle.

"Thanks for doing this."

Sarah finished folding the tea towels she'd taken out of the dryer. "You're welcome."

Grant moved to the small window near the back door. "Now there's a word been in short supply since I got into town."

"On the train, right?"

"You can see the station from here?"

"Don't need to. The *Sunset* never stops at Absolution. The fact that it did and a stranger walks into my diner—doesn't take a genius."

"Yes. On the train."

"There you go then. Folks around here aren't too keen on the Southern Pacific since they took Absolution off the scheduled stop."

"Judging by the ticket office, that must have been a while ago."

"Thirty years."

"Wow. They really know how to hold a grudge here, don't they?"

"Most blame it for letting business dry up. Folks leaving."

Grant leaned his back against the wall. "And the rest blame Macready."

Sarah stopped what she was doing and leveled a steady gaze at Grant. "Who told you that?"

"Just an observation. Macready's bought up most of the town. Has the heavy mob watching the hotel. Won't hire cars to strangers. Doesn't take a genius."

Sarah put the folded towels on top of the filing cabinet. "Scott wouldn't hire you a car?"

"You on first-name terms?"

"Used to be."

"No car. Don't think he wants me going down to Adobe Flats."

The washing machine began its final spin. Vibration hummed through the floor. Sarah waited a beat, glanced through the window into the diner to make sure there were no customers, then rested her backside against the desk.

"What you want to go out there for?"

"That's what he said."

"And what did you say?"

"Looking for Eduardo Cruz."

She let out a sigh. "Doc's gone. Nobody lives at Adobe Flats anymore."

"Business dried up, huh?"

Her hand came up to touch her cheek, then dropped again. "He's a doctor. Business never dries up. He just moved away."

"But Macready stayed."

"When you own as much as Macready, you don't just walk away."

The machine clicked off, and the spinning drum slowed down to nothing. She opened the front and took the jeans out. They were almost dry. The T-shirt too. She flapped them to stretch out the creases. Grant pushed off from the wall.

"He didn't strike me as somebody with a firm grip on things."

She looked up from draping the jeans over one arm. "Scott? He couldn't grip his wiener. His father. Tripp Macready."

"Not a man to be messed with, I'll bet."

"No."

"Is that why you're going to lend me your car?"

Their eyes met and locked. There was no denial. No discussion. She simply opened the desk drawer and took out a set of car keys. She held them in her hand briefly, then put them on the scarred wooden desktop. Then she nodded over Grant's shoulder at the ironing board and handed him the damp clothes.

"You know how to iron, don't you?"

SIX

ABSOLUTION DROPPED AWAY BEHIND him as he headed south. It didn't take long before the town had all but disappeared. South along Avenue D, across the hump of the railroad crossing, and through rundown residential streets that became more rundown the farther south he went. By the time he reached the outskirts of town, the houses were more like wooden shacks. Cracked tarmac gave way to hard-packed dirt, and that was the best you could say about the road to Adobe Flats. Hard and flat but still wide enough to drive a bus down. American roads always seemed to be wide enough to drive a bus down.

Sarah Hellstrom's car wasn't as wide as a bus. It was small and foreign, not a big American automobile. The waitress might well own the diner, but there was no money to spare on luxuries. A big, comfortable car was a luxury. This one bounced and swayed like a bucking bronco, but it was faster than walking. The directions she'd given were simple: turn left on Avenue D and follow your nose. The only place it went was Adobe Flats.

Grant turned on the air conditioning. In Sarah's car that meant winding down the windows. The breeze moved the air around but didn't cool it. The interior became less stuffy but was still warm. Dust swirled in through the windows, forcing him to choose between choking or sweating. He compromised, winding the windows halfway up to keep most of the dust out. Adjustments made, he concentrated on the road ahead.

Whereas the streets in Absolution were tarmacked and straight, the road south was anything but. After the railroad tracks and the first three cross streets, the dirt road followed the contours of the land instead of cutting through it. Rocky outcrops and low hills soon shaped what had initially seemed like hard, flat desert plain. Corroded buttes and mesas broke the skyline, and Grant felt like he'd wandered into a John Wayne movie—a smaller version of Monument Valley, where he'd made so many classic Westerns. The road sometimes followed dry gulches and arroyos that could have been creeks and riverbeds if there'd been any water. He didn't know if there was such a thing as a rainy season, but if there was, then this road would become part river.

There was no grass to speak of. The only greenery came from occasional plants that looked like they came from another planet. Grant couldn't say if they were cacti or flowering triffids, but they were the only things alive out here—the only things visible anyway. Apart from the cloud of dust following him about a mile back and the glint of sunlight on glass. Not hiding but keeping its distance.

Large hills began to loom on the horizon up ahead. The rugged hills of Big Bend National Park. He knew the road stopped short but wasn't sure how far it was to Adobe Flats. It wasn't on the map, he knew that. The inset square on the street plan positioned Absolution in West Texas but wasn't detailed enough to include Adobe Flats.

"Follow your nose."

His voice sounded dry and harsh in his ears. He'd only been in Absolution a few hours, and he was already beginning to sound like a local. Apart from the Yorkshire accent. He wondered how long he'd have to stay before his face turned to parchment. The car followed a gentle slope out of the arroyo, then the road crested between two crumbling buttes.

He stopped the car. The road continued down a gentle slope into an expanse of open flatland. The final stretch before the foothills that marked the beginning of Big Bend National Park. The open ground wasn't empty. A small group of buildings told him he'd arrived at Adobe Flats.

GRANT KNEW THEY'D BEEN telling the truth before he even got out of the car. Doc Cruz wasn't here. Nobody lived here anymore. He parked in the turnaround out front of the three buildings that formed a partial square. A ranch-style hacienda, a bunkhouse, and a barn. A stone-clad well stood in the middle of the turnaround, with the remains of the wooden tower and windmill that helped pump the water. It disappeared briefly until the cloud of dust settled. The blades of the wheel squeaked as the breeze kept it turning. It was the only sound once Grant turned the engine off and stood beside the car.

Nobody lived here anymore because there was nowhere here to live. The barn was the worst, burned to the ground apart from the splintered wooden frame and two sections of wall. The roof was gone completely, and the barn doors had collapsed inward. The bunkhouse was nearly as bad because that was a wooden structure too. Lower and wider with smaller doors and windows, but just as much a burned-out shell.

It was the hacienda that forced Grant to catch his breath.

He could picture it in its heyday because it had been described to him so many times. Its heyday was a long time past. The adobe structure had stood up best against the fire, but the roof was missing and part of the walls had collapsed. The front porch was still intact. The glassless window frames were still there. The main entrance too, a heavy studded door that could have kept the Mexicans out if it had been on a different building. A mission that became a fortress. A fortress that became a shrine. The similarities were uncanny. Even in destruction it seemed that Texans couldn't resist copying the Alamo.

He closed the car door and crossed to the porch. It was solidly built and paved with slabs of stone. Heat reflected off the bleached walls. The sun was high in the hard blue sky. The windmill creaked, the blades casting uneven shadows across the porch. The rhythmic squeaking grew deeper in tone. *Thwup, thwup, thwup.* Like the ceiling fan at the hotel. Deeper still. More of a *thud, thud, thud.* A throbbing beat that Grant hadn't heard for years.

The hacienda might resemble the Alamo, but the buildings it brought to mind were harder and drier and infinitely more deadly. The thudding rotor blades completed the memory. Another hot country. A harsher life.

THE PAST

There are no friendlies.

—Jim Grant

SEVEN

THE RHYTHMIC *thud, thud, thud* shook the darkened room. Bare white walls and cracked plaster picked out by a single bedside lamp knocked over on the stone floor. The big wooden ceiling fan didn't cool the room, it just moved warm air around. The thudding grew louder and faster. In sync with the helicopters coming in to land at the desert airbase but closer and more urgent. The headboard banging against the wall as Grant made love in the predawn heat.

The woman gritted her teeth and thrust back at him with equal vigor. Her naked body was bathed in sweat. Dark, smooth skin and nipples like bullets. Lying on her back and urging her pelvic thrusts for even greater penetration. Her breasts jiggled with each thrust. Full and tight even on her back. Hard, flat stomach. Fierce eyes. She reached behind her with both hands and grasped the spindles of the headboard.

"Yes."

Grant ignored her urging and slowed down instead. He almost withdrew before leaning forward in a long, deliberate move. The woman closed her eyes and bit her lip to keep quiet. He repeated the move. Withdraw, then penetrate. Her stomach quivered. Her thighs gripped tight. She jerked her hips upwards to chase the withdrawal, unwilling to let him pull out. Grant supported his weight on one arm and looked down at the most beautiful woman he had ever seen. His shoulder muscles screamed. He used the other hand to hold her stomach down from following his withdrawal. Completely disconnected now.

Her eyes flew open and she shook her head.

Grant nodded.

He eased forward. The woman snarled. Then the rhythm started up again, harder than before. The helicopters were touching down, and their thudding rotors tore up the night. Grant tried to hold back. The woman let go of the headboard and grabbed his forearms. She snatched them from under him and twisted her hips. In one swift movement she was on top, breasts swaying above his face and pelvis riding him like a bucking bronco.

She growled. Grant roared. The explosion of ecstasy shook their bodies until they lay quivering in each other's arms. Sweat dripped. The ceiling fan finally helped cool the dampness on their skin. The stethoscope hanging from the headboard stopped swaying.

After a few minutes the engines outside cut off. The heavy rotors *thwup, thwup, thwupped* down to nothing. Grant opened his eyes and glanced at the watch hanging next to the stethoscope.

"Time to suit up."

Cruz smiled at him. She nodded towards the shower curtain in the corner of the makeshift barrack room.

"You first."

By the time Grant's six-man team filed up the cargo ramp of the twin engine, tandem rotor helicopter, the equipment had been checked and the briefing completed. Mack and Cooper stayed together as always, friends since the first day they had joined the Allied Expeditionary Force. A throwback name for several countries banding together to deploy where needed. Like the United Nations, only with a more proactive role. Aggressive, not passive.

The other four were junior in service and age but not experience: Wheeler, Carlino, Adams, and Bond. Mack and Cooper took them under their wings, two each. Grant took the entire unit under his. Three Americans, two Brits, and an Italian. They all kept to the left-hand side of the ramp. Aid parcels strapped to big square wooden pallets were being loaded on the right.

The Chinook's rotors began to turn, the slow whine becoming harder and deeper as they built up speed. The chopper's camouflage pattern was still intact, but the unit markings on both sides had been painted over with a huge red cross in a white circle. This was a famine relief drop into the heart of the township. Three miles from the safe zone airbase on the outskirts of town.

Grant stuck three fingers up, then pointed to a row of makeshift seats on the left. Mack peeled off with Wheeler and Carlino. Grant did the finger thing again, pointing to the seats on the right. Cooper took Adams and Bond. All sat in unison. That left one seat on either side. Grant stood between the two squads. He had to shout over the sound of the engines.

"Final check."

Six heads turned towards him.

"Touchdown in twenty minutes. Predawn."

Nobody nodded. They'd heard this before but listened as if they hadn't.

"Mack. Secure the perimeter. Quiet and deadly force."

Mack looked square and solid in the shadows. Wheeler and Carlino were big but paled in comparison. Grant didn't think Wheeler had started shaving yet.

"Coop. Snatch team with me. Cover all doors. Put down anyone that moves until we reach the target package. Once he's secured, withdraw in reverse, folding in on ourselves until we're back outside."

The engines were getting louder. The cargo was stowed.

"There are no friendlies. We'll be in the heart of the township. Aid drop should draw some attention away but expect the main force to hold firm. Once we've got the package, fall back to the market square for extraction. Same transport on its return trip. Time on the ground: fifteen minutes. Any questions?"

There were none. Grant threw a glance towards the ramp and everyone followed his eyes. The most important member of the team came on board: an army medic in full combat gear. Grant raised his voice one last time.

"Don't forget. The target will be dead weight once the medic's given him his shot. Snatch squad, form into stretcher-bearers. Perimeter team, run interference. That's going to be the danger time."

Nobody disagreed. Grant raised one finger to the medic, then pointed at the seat next to Mack. Cruz tucked the ends of the stethoscope into her webbing straps and sat down. Grant looked her in the eyes and sat opposite. Even with her face blacked up and in baggy combats she looked beautiful. They didn't smile at each other.

The cargo ramp closed with a thump. The engine noise became deafening inside the cabin, and the floor shifted under them. The straps holding the pallets in place creaked. Then they were in the air and leaving the safe zone behind.

EVERYONE HAS THEIR OWN way of coping with pre-action stress. Grant and Cruz had taken care of theirs in the bedroom. Mack chewed gum as if it were going out of fashion. Most relaxed against the bulkheads. Wheeler and Bond argued.

"Just 'cause you share the same name doesn't make you right. Best James Bond is hands-down Sean Connery."

Bond threw a withering look at Wheeler. "Come *on*. Fella wore a duck on his head, for Chrissakes. How realistic is that?"

Wheeler nodded. "In *Goldfinger*. Yes. Best Bond in the best Bond film. Set the template."

"Set the tone, you mean. Downhill from there on."

Wheeler saw an opening. "Exactly. Fucks your argument then. Downhill after Connery."

Bond wasn't fazed. "The Bonds that came after *him*—yes. Up to a point. I mean, Roger Moore. For fuck's sake…"

Everyone knew what was coming next. They all spoke in unison. "PINK PANTHER FILMS."

Nobody laughed but everyone was smiling. Bond raised a finger to emphasize the point.

"Goddamn comedies. Dalton and Brosnan weren't bad, but—"

Wheeler interrupted. "Connery was better."

"I agree. Until Daniel Craig."

The chopper changed course. First leg complete. Now it was the long, low run straight down the main road into the township. Mack stopped chewing. Grant took slow, deep breaths. The argument became more heated. Wheeler's eyes bulged.

"Short and blond, with a nose like a punch bag. Where's the comma of black hair curled over the forehead? Or the slim features?"

"That's Fleming's description. Connery was a truck driver, according to him."

"But Fleming gave Bond a Scottish heritage after that—because of Connery. Can hardly see him giving him a boxer's nose halfway through."

Bond shook his head.

"Short and tough, and a bloody good actor. Tom Cruise is no Jack Reacher physically. But I'll bet he'll make a good fist of it."

Wheeler wagged a finger.

"Don't change the subject. Just because of *Collateral*."

A dull thud hit the side of the helicopter. Then two more. The Chinook swerved, kinking left and then right before settling back on course. Carlino glanced towards the cockpit.

"Are they shooting at us?"

Adams roused from dozing against the fuselage.

"Ungrateful fuckers. Don't they want their rice and Mars bars?"

Carlino lowered his voice to a stage whisper that was still loud enough to be heard over the rotors.

"Maybe we disturbed morning prayers."

Grant waved a hand for them to be quiet.

"Too early. That's why we chose this time. No. This is something else."

A red light went on in the middle of the roof and the ramp motors began to whir. The copilot's voice shouted through the tannoy.

"One minute. We're taking small arms fire."

Almost immediately a staccato beat stitched holes along the right-hand side. High—just visible above the cargo nets. The Chinook veered left, then back on course. The ramp opened like a gaping mouth at the rear of the cargo bay. The night sky outside had become dark blue heading towards dawn. Mack started chewing again. Adams stated the obvious.

"That's not small arms fire. Thought they only had machetes and toothpicks."

The ramp fully deployed. Adobe rooftops flashed by either side of the opening. The chopper was preparing for dust off. Grant pumped a fist then held the hand up, fingers straight. He rested the other hand across the top to form a T. Time. He whirled a finger three times for everyone to get ready. Harness buckles unsnapped in unison. The chatter stopped.

Dust swirled around the open ramp, towed in the slipstream. The flat rooftops rode higher in the field of vision. The chopper was closer to the ground. Slow and even. Approaching the drop zone. Then the floor suddenly tilted to the right and the tannoy blared a single word: "RPG."

The whoosh and explosion were almost simultaneous. High up at the rear of the cabin a gaping hole opened in the roof above the cargo nets. Sparks and flames filled the gap and rending metal twisted off into the night. Grant was on his feet and lurching towards the ramp.

"Everybody out. Now."

Height wasn't an issue. Speed wasn't important. Getting out of the helicopter before it slewed sideways into the passing buildings was. There was no time to see who was moving and who was too slow. First rule of combat: survive. Then regroup and counterattack. Surviving meant getting out of there. Fast.

The Chinook lost all control and direction. The front rotor was softening the sudden descent, but without the rear blades it was sliding sideways towards the buildings. The chopper took more bullet hits. There was another whoosh as a second rocket-propelled grenade missed high and wide.

Grant reached the ramp first. They were only six feet off the ground but moving dangerously fast. Others joined him but he couldn't tell who. They all moved down the ramp at the crouch, using the grillwork for handholds. The dust was a choking cloud, a blizzard of sand kicked up by the thudding rotor blades.

Survive. Then worry about who survived with you.

He saw the adobe wall coming towards him but could do nothing about it. The edge of the ramp slashed into the brickwork and tore from its hinges. Grant could barely hold on. He was knocked off his feet but strong fingers held tight. The sound of tearing metal filled the night. The fuselage crumpled and twisted. The forward rotor blades sheared off and spun into the darkness. The entire front section of the cargo helicopter tilted onto its side and smashed through the next building down the street. Shards of metal became shrapnel.

Grant ducked and held on.

The ramp hit the ground at the slide and skidded on the dusty surface. It bounced twice but stayed flat like a pebble skimming across a pond. Something sharp cut a groove along Grant's cheek.

He kept his head down and clung on for dear life. He was vaguely aware of other figures staying low on either side of him. Peripheral vision told him the ramp was keeping on course down the middle of the street. Sand and grit was slowing it down.

A loud crumpling bang sounded to the right. The helicopter wreckage coming to rest in a destroyed building. There was no explosion. There was only the noise of tearing metal and falling masonry. Sparks filled the sky but didn't ignite the fuel pods. A small miracle amid the greater disaster.

The ramp lost momentum and with it, direction. It veered off to the left and began to spin. The left-hand side of the street was already derelict, the buildings either bombed out or simply old and crumbling. The cargo ramp ricocheted off a low wall, then slid into an open yard. The cacophony of noise subsided but still rang in Grant's ears. His first priority was self-assessment—a physical check for injuries. There was pain and the warm flush of blood down one cheek but nothing else. His muscles ached, but that was a good sign. It meant he still had the limbs the muscles were attached to.

He wiped dirt out of his eyes and looked around. At first he couldn't see anything. The cloud of dust hung like a fog around him. A couple of minutes later, the dust settled. That was the first time he saw how many he'd lost and how many had survived to fight the rest of the day.

THE PRESENT

*Macready senior's too big a
prick to even be a prick.*
                    —Hunter Athey

EIGHT

THE SWIRL OF DUST was back in Grant's rear-view mirror but not as far away as before. The sun was low, and a string of clouds had crawled across the horizon. The hard blue sky was tinged with red that seeped through the clouds, turning them into bloody rags. It was going to be a beautiful sunset.

Apart from the dust cloud in the rear-view mirror.

Grant kept half an eye on that while contemplating his afternoon at Adobe Flats. There was truth and lies amid the derelict buildings, some told by those he'd spoken to and others enshrined in legend. Grant used the word legend loosely. The map he'd studied before setting off to Adobe Flats was compiled from decades of information. Once things were written down, they became fact. Print those facts for long enough, and they became history. It was a short leap from history to legend. The legend said the road ended at Adobe Flats. The map was wrong.

That was the lie.

Eduardo Cruz didn't live there anymore.

That was the truth.

Grant used soft hands on the steering wheel to navigate the dry riverbed, keeping in low gear as he guided the car up the opposite bank. The track didn't become a road again until it was back on level ground, but the route was made clear by deep-rutted tire marks that scarred the hardpan. Years of traffic tattooed on dry earth. Travelling from nowhere to next-to-nowhere. Adobe Flats to Absolution and vice versa. That was understandable. The hacienda and its outbuildings looked like they'd been there a long time. People had to drive to town. Only natural they'd follow the line of least resistance. The same route Grant was taking.

The other tire tracks were harder to explain.

The road ended at Adobe Flats. The map said so. Heavy tracks beyond the turnaround said otherwise. Deep tread patterns, wide wheelbase. Trucks. Heading on past the hacienda towards the foothills of Big Bend National Park. Or coming from there. Not as deeply rutted as the regular trail. Not as many years in the making but long enough to be semipermanent.

Blood-red light glinted in the rear-view mirror. Grant focused on the shape forming in the dust cloud. Hard and fast and closing the gap. Whoever it was had decided not to wait any longer. Following was becoming pursuing. Decision time. Try and outrun them or let them catch up and find out what they wanted. Grant was unarmed. Texas was a land of guns. If this became a face-off, he'd have to tread carefully. Itchy trigger fingers could make the wrong move after a long, drawn-out chase. He'd seen it before. Better to calm things down. That was a good idea in any confrontation. He eased his foot off the gas.

The red glint came again. Closer this time. Followed immediately by a flash of blue light. Then red again. Then blue. The shape in the dust cloud solidified. Red and blue lights flashed their warning. Stop in the name of the law. Grant slipped his Boston PD badge wallet out of his jeans and hid it under the seat. This visit was off the books. He didn't want to involve his boss in Boston. He stopped the car and turned off the engine.

"GET OUT OF THE car with your hands in the air."

Not very original. Not very professional either. From all the way back where the cop car had skidded to a halt amid a swirl of dust. The dust settled. The rooftop light bar continued to flash. The cop stood beside the open door of his unit, too far away to see if Grant had a weapon and not close enough to ensure that Grant didn't restart the engine and speed off. The cop needed to move closer and wider to get a view of the keys in the ignition and order Grant to place his hands on top of the steering wheel until control was established.

Silence engulfed the plain after the roar of the engines.

A gentle breeze whistled through Grant's open windows.

"I said, get out of the goddamn car."

A distinctive click broke the silence. The hammer being cocked. Grant nodded at the rear-view mirror, opened the door, and swung his legs out. The ugly black pistol followed his movement. The cop got that part right. Grant leaned forward and stood up. He didn't close the door. Unnecessary movement was bad for itchy trigger fingers. A cocked weapon only needed a moment's lapse for mistakes to be made. He didn't want to be at the wrong end of that mistake.

"Hands up."

Grant turned to face the man striding towards him and raised his hands.

"Shouldn't that be reach for the sky?"

The cop looked nonplussed.

Grant shrugged as best he could with his arms in the air. "Bad joke. I surrender."

The cop kept his gun trained on Grant as he closed the distance, then stopped six feet from his prisoner. He was big and young and most definitely not local. In plainclothes, not uniform. Neatly pressed khaki pants and a beige shirt. No hat. The dying sun glinted off the silver star pinned to his shirt. The accent wasn't Texan and the face wasn't parched leather. That last bit could be youth, maybe twenty-five. Not what Grant expected of the Absolution sheriff.

"You think this is a joke?"

Grant shook his head. "No. I think there's been a mistake."

"You bet. And you're the one that made it."

Grant waited to be told what mistake he'd made. Procedure was breaking down all over the place. The young cop didn't hold himself like a law enforcement officer. He hadn't approached the situation like a cop either. More like a fan of the Westerns Grant used to watch on Saturday afternoon TV. The broad shoulders and upright gait told Grant something, though. Ex-military if ever he'd seen one. Grant was ex-army. He could spot one a mile away. Not unusual in the police field, but this one needed to learn the rules. Maybe good old country boys did things different.

"Turn around and put your hands behind your back."

Grant turned to face the car and lowered his arms. Footsteps closed the distance behind him, and he felt the cold steel of the handcuffs being snapped on one wrist. The other bracelet dangled there while the cop tried to work one-handed. Another bad move. Grant could use the swinging cuff as a weapon. He didn't. He let his other wrist get cuffed, then relaxed his shoulders. The itchy trigger finger was still a concern. He waited until he heard the cop holster his weapon before he turned around.

This is where Grant should have protested his innocence, but experience told him that would be a waste of time. It had never worked on him when he'd arrested people in Yorkshire, so why should it work in Texas? He'd be told the score. All in good time. Right now Grant didn't want to piss off the young cop. He'd already shown a total disregard for procedure. No search. No reading of his rights. He didn't want to add police brutality to the list.

"Ain't you gonna ask what this is about?"

Grant had never asked a prisoner that either. This boy was working completely off the manual. It was only the police cruiser and the tin star that marked him as a cop at all.

"It's about a mistake. I figure you'll tell me when you read me my rights."

The cop flexed his shoulders, and Grant thought he'd said too much.

"You had the right to stay on the train. You shoulda took it."

Police brutality didn't look imminent. Maybe Grant could engage in a little conversation. He kept his voice nonconfrontational.

"I know things work different here in the states. I've seen the salads—size of a small field. But last I heard, it wasn't illegal to get off a train."

"Maybe not. But you picked the wrong place to get off at."

"Considering how friendly everyone's been, I'm inclined to agree with you."

The cop seemed confident he'd got the measure of his prisoner. This wasn't some criminal mastermind he was dealing with here. He proceeded like he was talking to an idiot.

"That's your rights out of the way."

He jerked a thumb towards Sarah Hellstrom's car.

"What you don't got the right to do is take this here car without the owner's permission. That's what we call theft in these parts."

Grant stayed calm. "Grand theft auto?"

"That's right."

"I always thought that was just a video game. Didn't know you actually called it that when someone stole a car."

The cop squinted against the sunset. "Is that a confession?"

Grant shook his head. "Wouldn't matter if it was, since you didn't Miranda me."

"Oh, I did. You musta forgot. And you just confessed."

"No. I made an observation about if someone stole this car. But I didn't. Because I got Sarah's permission to borrow it."

The cop's face went blank. Grant gave him a few seconds to respond. When he didn't speak, Grant thought he'd better explain further.

"Assuming the definition of theft is the same here as in England. You know—taking property belonging to another with the intent to permanently deprive that person of it, without permission or other lawful authority. I'm sure you've got something similar. Well, I'm returning the car now. So there goes the intent to permanently deprive. And Sarah lent me her car, so that's the permission or other lawful authority."

The cop still didn't speak.

Grant raised his eyebrows.

"No theft. No crime. See where I'm going with this?"

A faint smile feathered the young cop's lips. In the dying light of day it gave him the look of a devil. Twisted red features and a glint in his eyes. When he spoke he sounded more confident than he'd done the last few minutes.

"Where you're goin' is the town jail."

Grant let out a sigh. "I just explained. I have Sarah's permission."

The smile almost turned into a grin. "That don't mean shit. She don't own the car."

The wind went out of Grant's argument. The clouds on the horizon dripped blood, and the evening sky began to darken. The cop took Grant's arm and led him towards the cruiser.

"And that means you stole it. Welcome to my world."

NINE

GRANT SAT ON THE lumpy mattress with his back against the wall and stared at the night sky through a barred window high on the opposite wall. The jailhouse was about what you'd expect for a town with no prospects. Small and functional and bare as a streaker on match day. The front office was just that: an office. There was an old wooden desk in one corner and a couple of filing cabinets in the other. A wall-mounted firearms rack with two rifles and a handgun clipped into the frame. A solid-looking chain was threaded through the trigger guards and padlocked at one end.

There was no charge desk or booking-in counter. Grant had emptied his pockets on the sheriff's desk before being searched and documented. Documented meant giving his name and date of birth and being thrown in a cell. The cellblock wasn't a block. It was two adjoining cells off a short corridor at the rear of the building. Just like every Western he'd ever seen, from *Bandolero!* to *Rio Bravo*. He half expected Walter Brennan to come limping in with a tin cup and a plate of beans. It was a step up from *Bad Day at Black Rock* though. At least there was no alcoholic sheriff sleeping it off in the cell.

Nobody told him whose car he'd stolen, and Grant didn't ask. It was obviously a trumped-up charge to get him off the streets. The question was, how long were they going to play this game and why? What didn't they want him to see? If it was the burnt-out buildings at Adobe Flats, why bother? Fires happened all the time. People moved on. Without any evidence to the contrary, there was nothing to suggest foul play. Until they arrested him for no reason.

There was plenty to ponder but nothing to be gained by it. Insufficient data. So Grant leaned against the wall and looked at the stars. He'd been in worse places in other buildings with bars on the windows and a good view of the night sky. Whoever was behind this would tell him when the time was right or send him packing with no explanation at all. He was guessing it would be the latter. Until that happened, he might as well get a good night's sleep.

BACON AND COFFEE. Two of the best smells in the world. Rattling keys in the corridor stirred him, but it was the smell that woke him up. The old man who came through the door from the office could have rivalled Walter Brennan. Without the limp. He did have a tin cup and a plate of beans, though. Beans and bacon. Two slices of toast. Steam swirled around the top of the coffee cup.

"Stand back from the bars."

A redundant command since Grant was lying on the bed. An order delivered with a hint of apology. The man kept his head down and didn't meet Grant's eyes. It was only the silver star pinned on his chest that gave him any authority at all. SHERIFF was stamped into the metal. Apart from that, everything about this fella said lackey. A man bought and paid for by whoever ran the town.

Grant swung his legs off the bed and sat up. The sheriff opened a drop-down flap in the bars, put the plate and the cup on it, then stood back. The bacon was cut into small pieces. There was a metal spoon sticking out of the beans. No knife and no fork. No cutting tools that could be used as offensive weapons. No crockery that could be broken for sharp edges. The sheriff nodded at the plate but still wouldn't meet Grant's eyes.

"If you don't hurry up, it's gonna get cold."

Grant stood up and took the cup and plate. "And that worries you, does it?"

The sheriff's eyes flicked up to Grant's face, then down to the floor again.

"Just bein' helpful. Suit yourself."

"It'd be helpful to know what I'm doing in here."

"Eating breakfast. For starters."

Grant's stomach rumbled. He hadn't eaten since the train. He sat on the edge of the bed and began to eat. There'd be plenty of time for Q&A after breakfast. The bacon was moist and tasty, not like the cremated hotel bacon he'd been fed in Los Angeles. The beans were beans. A cup of English breakfast tea would have gone down a treat but coffee would have to do. It was strong and black and tasted like shit. This wasn't a latte with two sugars and a squirt of cream.

It only took ten minutes to clean his plate. By the time he looked up again, the sheriff had gone. No clinking of keys or rattling of bars as the flap was closed. Silent as the plague. It looked like Q&A would have to wait until he came back for the empties.

JUDGING FROM THE ANGLE of the sun and the passing of time, it was only an hour before the office door opened again. Grant balanced the cup on the plate and stood back from the bars. The sheriff looked like his confidence had returned because he walked straight down the corridor, unlocked the bars, and swung the door open. The smell of whisky came off him in waves. Dutch courage or whatever passed for that in Texas.

"Come on out and get your gear."

He didn't say that Grant was being released, but that's what it sounded like. The sheriff stood back to let Grant go down the corridor first, then followed him into the office. There was a clear plastic bag on the desk. Grant put the plate down next to it and waited for the sheriff to explain. He didn't. Instead, he sat down, opened the bag, and emptied the contents on the desktop. Grant swept the loose change and his hotel key into one pocket. He folded the banknotes into a worn leather wallet and put it in his back pocket. He clipped the watch on his wrist and signed the release form when it was pushed across the desk.

"That's it?"

"Unless there's anything missing."

"There is. An explanation."

The sheriff leaned back in his chair and looked up at Grant. His eyes were rheumy and wet but focused. He was back in charge, the apologetic figure from earlier a thing of the past. Until he needed another drink to bolster his courage.

"A misunderstanding. You got free room and board. Now you're just free."

Grant didn't move. "A misunderstanding about what?"

"Vehicle ownership. Used to be that rustling cattle was the most heinous offence around here. Now, stealing a man's car can get you shot. You didn't get shot. Consider yourself lucky."

"I didn't steal a man's car either."

The sheriff took the empty bag and put it in the desk drawer. "That's where the confusion arose. About who owned the car."

"Sarah Hellstrom loaned me the car."

"There you go, misunderstanding things again. Wasn't hers to lend. Somebody else owns it."

"Let me guess. Macready."

The sheriff slammed the drawer shut.

"You don't want to go around guessing all the time. Guess wrong and you could be in a world of hurt. Sarah let you take the car. The owner reported it stolen. You got arrested. Simple mistake. Absolution Sheriff's Department won't hold it against you."

Grant nodded and threw a farewell glance around the office. The noticeboard was thumbtacked with pieces of paper. No wanted posters, just official messages and codes of practice. An old recruitment poster was creased and torn where it had been pinned and removed several times.

"You don't recruit locally, do you?"

"Say what?"

Grant looked at the booze-soaked lawman and noted the difference between him and the young deputy who'd arrested him. He doubted the sheriff had any part in hiring and firing. He doubted there was any power at all sitting behind that desk.

"Ex-army, was he?"

"We've all served."

"But some more recently than others."

"What you saying?"

"I'm saying he needs to get his procedures right before his next arrest."

"He didn't shoot you, did he?"

"He did not."

"Count yourself lucky then. If you looked less English and more Mexican, you might have been shot as an illegal. Coming from the way you come. Down there."

Grant considered the map in his head. "Down where?"

The sheriff shook his head in amazement.

"Big Bend. Back door to the border. If you can get over the hills."

TEN

IT WAS ALMOST NOON by the time Grant got back to the hotel. He needed a shower, a shave, and a change of clothes. Breakfast had been taken care of, courtesy of the Absolution Sheriff's Department. Walking into the lobby, the world became dark. His eyes felt like the sun had burned them out. The sudden change was like somebody turning the lights off. He waited for his eyes to adjust.

There was a scurrying noise behind the reception counter. For a second he thought of the rat at the town dump and the old-timer with sniper's eyes. Then the scurrying stopped and the office door clicked shut. If there'd been a woman in the doorway, she'd have snatched her kids off the street and hidden inside. It was that kind of feeling. The ceiling fan *thwup, thwup, thwupped.*

Grant felt the hairs bristle up the back of his neck. He squinted as his eyes quartered the room. The leather chairs and the coffee tables—clear. The reception desk and the pigeonholes—clear. The cigarette machine and the staircase—clear. Whatever the desk clerk had been doing, it didn't seem to involve anyone else. Not down here, anyway.

Something had changed, though. Grant's eyes repeated the cycle. Chairs and tables. Reception and pigeonholes. Cigarette machine and stairs. Twice. By the third pass he'd figured out what it was. The key hooks in front of the pigeonholes were empty. All the keys had gone.

He crossed to the foot of the stairs and looked up at the landing. The bedroom doors were closed, but that didn't mean anything. If there'd been a sudden influx of customers for the block bookings, they'd be in their rooms anyway. He listened for the sound of voices or creaking floorboards. There weren't any. He didn't believe there was anybody up there any more than he believed the rooms were being held for block bookings. The missing keys were to prove a point. He already knew what that point was. Grant was a stranger. Strangers don't last long around here.

The room key felt solid in his trouser pocket. He took it out and hefted it in one hand, then started up towards his room. The stairs creaked all the way up.

THE ROOM WAS EMPTY, the door still locked. That surprised him. Grant had expected a welcoming committee to rescind what little welcome had been offered him. The bed hadn't been slept in. The chair was still there. Nobody was leaning a chair against the wall on two legs.

Grant locked the door behind him and quickly checked the drawers. Nothing was missing. His clothes were untouched. The velvet case was still hidden under his T-shirts. He walked over to the window and looked down at the street. Dry and dusty and bleached by the sun. There was nobody out there keeping an eye on his room. There was no foot traffic. There was no traffic of any kind.

Absolution was dead in the midday sun.

He thought about that and smiled. Only mad dogs and Englishmen went out in the midday sun. That's what the song said. Except in the Saturday afternoon Westerns he used to watch at Moor Grange School for Boys. High noon was the time for showdowns in the street. Even in that lizard Western *Rango*.

The shower was piping hot. Grant soaped himself down and cleaned the jailhouse smell off his body. He shaved in the washbasin, wiping steam from the mirror. Peppermint flooded his mouth when he brushed his teeth. Body spray and aftershave completed the turnaround. He stepped back into the bedroom naked, toned, and clean as a whistle.

The chair was still empty. The bed was still neat and tidy. But Grant wasn't alone. The chair leaner was standing in the open doorway with the room key dangling from one hand. Stetson pulled down over his eyes. Cowboy boots crossed in a vain attempt at being cool. He raised his head so he could peer from beneath the brim.

"You should get some clothes on. You'll catch a chill in the draught."

Grant stood in the middle of the floor.

"There wouldn't be a draught if you'd get your own room."

"All the keys are gone."

"Yes. I noticed. And yet you've got one there."

The cowboy looked surprised at the key fob in his hand. "This? This ain't no room key. It's an official key. Opens 'em all."

"You work for the hotel now?"

The cowboy paused for effect.

"I work for the sheriff's department." He opened the leather waistcoat to reveal a tin star on his chest. "And you're in violation."

Grant showed what he thought of the Absolution Sheriff's Department by grabbing his wedding tackle in the towel and giving it a vigorous rub. When he was satisfied it was dry, he threw the towel over the chair and pulled on a clean pair of jeans. Socks and trainers followed in case this became a fight. Then he took a T-shirt out of the drawer, careful not to uncover the stethoscope case, and pulled it over his head.

"In violation of what?"

"The Absolution Mercantile Association Act. Hotel has strict rules about ex-cons staying in its rooms. And you spent last night in the town jail."

"It was a mistake."

"Yeah. And you keep making 'em. Pack your bags. You're moving out."

Grant could feel the heat burning his cheeks. Anger was beginning to bubble somewhere way down inside him. He took a deep breath in through the nose and out through the mouth to calm himself down. These people kept trying to needle him. Normally he'd be happy to oblige, but this trip was personal. He didn't want to tarnish the memory he was here to honor by getting into a fight over a hotel room.

He put the holdall on the bed and began to pack in reverse order to the way he'd unpacked the day before. He made sure everything was neatly folded. Jeans, T-shirts, socks. Spare trainers. And the velvet stethoscope case. His toiletry bag went in last. He laid the orange windcheater across the top, between the handles, then stepped back from the bed.

"I saw the recruitment poster in the jailhouse."

The deputy pushed off from the doorframe.

"Oh yeah? You thinking of applying?"

Grant stabbed his finger several times as if poking holes.

"It had pinpricks all over the corners. You know. From being put up and taken down so often. I guess that's why there's so many pricks in the sheriff's department."

He tossed his key across the room and the deputy caught it. Grant picked up the holdall and walked through the door so fast the deputy had to back off or get shouldered out of the way. He went down the stairs and straight out the front door without paying. He hadn't used the room anyway.

GRANT KNEW EXACTLY WHERE he was going. He remembered it from the map. Not the only other accommodation in Absolution but the nearest. He turned right out of the door and headed west along First Street. The sun had moved across the sky but lost none of its power. The heat was exhausting. The two-lane blacktop shimmered in the haze. A bird cawed in the distance, but Grant couldn't see what it was. Did they have crows in Texas? He wasn't sure.

He passed the post office and Front Street Books. The bookstore looked out of place in the frontier town, even if Absolution wasn't exactly on the frontier. It wasn't a million miles from the Mexican border, though. That was something he hadn't thought about when he'd decided to come and visit Eduardo Cruz. Or the fact that Mexicans still weren't welcome in the Alamo state. He supposed it was like being a Muslim in New York—not exactly flavor of the month.

The motel was just where Grant expected it to be. Half a mile out of town amid the scrub and cactus of the roadside landscape. The metal sign had less bullet holes than the *WELCOME TO ABSO-LUTION* sign at the other end of town.

ABSOLUTION MOTEL & RV PARK
Come On In and Take a Load Off
(Town Mortuary Around Back)
Hunter Athey, Proprietor

It wasn't one of those highway motels with rooms lined up on two floors across the back of the parking lot. The kind with wafer-thin walls and a walkway veranda that ran the length of the building. Absolution Motel & RV Park was more of your desert motel, with separate cabins arranged haphazardly around sprawling grounds. Cactus abounded. Grant corrected himself—cacti in the plural since there were so many of the prickly little fuckers. The cabins were ranch-style stucco with wooden porches and shiny tin roofs. The office building was another Alamo clone standing guard on the drive-in turnaround just off the main road.

Absolution shimmered in the afternoon heat beyond the stucco walls. A tall, slim windmill with a weather vane sucked water up from the depths—a newer version of the well at Adobe Flats. The similarities weren't lost on Grant. At least the cabins didn't look like the Alamo or the burned-out hacienda.

Grant crossed the turnaround and walked under a dirty brown archway with a carved wooden sign dangling on rusty chains. The letters cut into the wood were primitive and less expansive than the metal sign on the highway.

ABSOLUTION MOTEL

There were no bullet holes this time. He went up a short path, avoiding being snagged by the encroaching cacti on either side, and pushed open the office door. The interior was cool and welcoming. No ceiling fan; air conditioning instead. It was clean and bright and empty. The windows let in plenty of sunlight. The open-plan office had plenty of space. There was no private door to a secret inner sanctum, but there was nobody manning the reception desk either, an ordinary desk instead of a counter. The place was deserted.

Grant looked out of the window towards a wide expanse of cleared land. Stubby monoliths jutted out of the ground at regular intervals, three feet high with connections for water and power. The RV park. For tourists traveling the west in their gas-guzzling mobile homes. The RV park was empty too. Judging by the lack of tire marks, it had been empty a long time.

A toilet flushed, and Grant noticed the restroom door for the first time. Way off to the right in the corner of the room. The door opened and a hunched figure shuffled out, drying his hands on his trousers. He stopped in mid-stride, a comical look of surprise on his face.

"You sure you're in the right place, fella?"

The man wasn't as leathery as the others, but he was no spring chicken either. His eyes burned with intelligence, but his shoulders looked weighed down with unachieved promise. His voice was strong but tinged with worry, as if he was striving to be commanding but unsure if he could pull it off.

Grant dropped the holdall at his feet. "If you've got more vacancies than the Gage, I am."

The man's shoulders drew back, and he raised his head. "They give you that block-booking bullshit?"

"They did."

The man nodded, and a smile played across his lips. "Then you must be the fella off the train. Spent the night at the taxpayer's expense."

"At the sheriff's. Yes. That's me."

The man shrugged. "Al ain't a bad man."

"The sheriff?"

"Sheriff Al Purwin. He just got sidetracked. Like the rest of us."

"If you mean from the straight and narrow, I'd agree with you."

The man waved the comment aside. "The Gage kick you out?"

"They did."

The man perked up. He finished rubbing his hands on his pants and came over. "Any man kicked out of the Gage is welcome here."

He stuck a hand out, and Grant shook it.

"I don't suppose you have any tea, do you?"

THE ABSOLUTION MOTEL DID have tea. Hunter Athey prided himself on it. Little yellow sachets of Lipton's English Breakfast Tea—the ones with a single teabag on a string. He also had coffee and drinking chocolate and all sorts of other foreign beverages, back from when Absolution got its fair share of overseas visitors wanting to explore the rugged landscape of Big Bend National Park. The proprietor brewed a mug of tea while Grant filled in the register and pocketed the keys for cabin number 5. Not because numbers 1 to 4 were occupied but because number 5 was the farthest from the main road. Judging by the lack of traffic, Grant reckoned that was being optimistic, making Hunter Athey the only optimist Grant had met since arriving in Absolution.

Grant tapped his pocket. The keys rattled.

"Just one thing."

He stirred sugar into the mug of tea.

"Number five being round the back, I'm not sharing with the recently departed, am I?"

79

Athey laughed—something else in short supply.

"The sign outside? No. The mortuary's out back of the office. Took my doctor's shingle down years ago, but I'm still the nearest thing this town's got to a mortician."

Grant tapped his mug with one finger.

"If I'd known that, I wouldn't have let you squeeze my teabag."

Athey laughed again. "From what I hear, I'm not the only person who wants to squeeze your teabag."

Grant puzzled over that one.

"How's that?"

Athey tilted his head and looked sideways at Grant. "You don't think Sarah lends her car to just anybody, do you?"

"Gilda's Grill. Yes. That was nice of her."

"Nice is Sarah's middle name. Too nice for that prick Macready."

"Junior."

"Right. Macready senior's too big a prick to even be a prick."

"Unless you're Big John Holmes."

"Unless you're him. Point is, if Sarah gets caught in the middle of this, she could get hurt again. And she's about the only person in Absolution who doesn't deserve to get hurt."

"In the middle of what? I only borrowed her car."

"And ended up in jail on the back of it."

"That as well."

Grant thought of something else. A trace memory that had barely registered when he'd seen it. Sarah Hellstrom touching her cheek when she'd said about Doc Cruz, "He's a doctor. Business never dries up." He decided to test his theory.

"So, when you were doctoring, did you attend to her bruising?"

"Sometimes. Mainly that was Doc Cruz."

"You knew Eduardo Cruz?"

Grant felt a shiver run down his spine. The fact that he was already talking about Cruz in the past tense. He hoped that wasn't a Freudian slip. Hunter Athey shook him even more.

"Sure. We shared the shingle. He was my partner."

Grant thought carefully about his next question. "What happened to him?"

Athey lowered his eyes. The bonhomie dropped out of his voice. "Who said anything happened?"

"He isn't here anymore."

"Didn't live here. Had a house out at Adobe Flats."

"He isn't there anymore either."

A light went on in Athey's head. "Ah. That's why you borrowed the car."

"So? What happened?"

The light went off again. Athey became as reticent as everybody else he'd met, apart from Sarah Hellstrom.

"Business dried up."

Not what Sarah Hellstrom had said. One thing a small town always needs is a doctor. With Cruz gone and Athey no longer practicing, Grant wondered where that left the rest of the people of Absolution.

"And now you just run the RV park and the mortuary."

Athey shrugged his shoulders. They looked as if they were carrying the weight of the world. The effort of shrugging them appeared to tire him out.

"RV park's on its last legs. And people don't even hang around here to die. Not much call for a mortician these days. Town's dying on its feet. Don't need to smell formaldehyde to know that."

"Macready seems to be doing all right."

Athey's face hardened. "Yeah, well. Some businesses thrive on hard times."

"What business is that?"

Athey fixed Grant with a stare that drilled right through him. "The kind I don't want Sarah getting in the middle of."

Standoff. Both men stood in the middle of the room, and neither spoke for a good thirty seconds. The silence highlighted the sounds outside. A car pulling into the turnaround and stopping out front. The engine being turned off and the car door slamming. Footsteps echoing on the porch.

Anger flared briefly in Athey's eyes as the man came through the door. Flared and died. Then he was back to staring at the floor, shoulders stooped. A broken man. Grant turned to see who'd come in. At first he thought it was the chair-leaner from the hotel, but it was another cowboy wearing the same outfit. Pointed boots and a cowboy hat. No spurs and no tin star. He ignored Hunter Athey and directed his words to Grant.

"I'm here to give you a ride. Mr. Macready wants to see you."

ELEVEN

THE CAR TRAILED A cloud of dust as it bounced along the uneven track. Straight north up the side of the RV park, then a dogleg right past the town landfill where all the rubbish was buried. To look at the square patch of land, you'd never guess how much was hidden beneath the surface. A bit like the town itself.

Grant sat in the front passenger seat, wary of being driven out into the desert even after the right turn. The cowboy chewed a matchstick as he drove with one hand on the wheel and the other resting out of the open window. Flat, featureless landscape drifted by outside. Grant kept half an eye on the driver while scouting ahead. He was wrong. They weren't driving into the desert. The car was heading back into Absolution along the outskirts. Low roofs and scattered fences picked out the edge of town. An abandoned athletics track marked their return to civilization. The car turned right again, and Grant noted the street sign. Avenue D. They were coming back into town from the north.

The car slowed at the end of the athletics track and pulled off the road. Whichever school had used the sports ground was long since gone, demolished and replaced by a walled compound solid enough to repel Santa Anna's army. There were two wooden barrels and a water trough next to the entrance, more for effect than necessity. They didn't water horses here anymore. A heavy wooden gate swung open, and the car drove into the courtyard. There were outbuildings and bunkhouses and work sheds, but the main building was yet another replica of the mission that became a fortress. The hacienda looked more like a fortress than a church, and the man standing on the patio to greet him didn't look like a priest.

Tripp Macready was a squat powerhouse of a man dressed all in black. Trousers, shirt, fancy jacket, and casual loafers. Not cowboy boots. That was for his employees. Grant didn't need to be told who he was. The man's authority emanated like the throbbing of a power station. He practically crackled with energy.

The car pulled up at the foot of the stairs, but the driver didn't get out. He sat there chewing his matchstick with an air of dumb insolence. Grant got the message. Dust puffed around his trainers as he got out of the car. Maybe black K-Swiss wasn't the best choice for desert climes. Not if you wanted to keep clean. He reckoned keeping clean would be a problem if you hung around Tripp Macready.

The car door slammed shut. The driver pulled across the yard to one of the outbuildings that housed a triple garage with accommodation across the top. Several men were busy in the shadowy interior. Two more came out of the garage and walked to the building next door, a bunkhouse structure that looked more like a barracks. The men were tall and straight and disciplined. Not slouching. Not making small talk. Not hanging around gawping at the stranger in their midst. A scrawny cat sauntered across the yard, then flopped on its side in the shade of the patio steps.

The man in black gestured for Grant to join him, scrutinizing everything about Grant as he climbed the steps. He paid particular attention to the lack of luggage. His voice was pure Texan, deep and hard.

"You travel light."

"Travel light, travel far."

"Judging by your accent, you sure have traveled."

"Not today."

"No. Today it's just the jailhouse to the Gage to the motel. Where d'you keep your toothbrush in that outfit? Your back pocket?"

Grant shook his head.

"You must be thinking of that other fella. I like my creature comforts. Left my bag at the motel when your driver showed up."

"Hunter Athey. He'll look after it for you."

The man considered Grant for a moment, then stuck out his hand.

"My name's Macready."

Grant watched Macready, gauging if this was going to be one of those knuckle-crushing handshakes intended to mark his territory. He decided to risk it and shook the proffered hand.

"Like Spencer Tracy in *Bad Day at Black Rock*."

Macready smiled. "Except with two arms."

To prove it he waved towards a wooden table near the barbecue pit with his other hand. Solid chairs with plain cushions circled the table. They walked across the patio together. Macready gestured to the nearest chair but Grant chose the one opposite with its back to the sun. Macready sat next to him. Both facing the courtyard. Neither with the sun in his eyes. Macready nodded his approval.

"I understand you're not an easy man to push."

"Depends who's doing the pushing."

Macready clicked his fingers and a jug of freshly squeezed lemonade with two glasses was brought to the table. Ice clinked in the jug.

"In what way?"

"The tree that doesn't bend will break in strong winds."

"So you're flexible."

"I haven't broken yet."

"Maybe you've not been pushed hard enough."

Grant shrugged and changed the subject.

"I see you're an equal opportunity employer."

Macready maintained a level gaze while he poured two glasses of lemonade.

"How do you mean?"

"Local boys at the hotel. Ex-military here."

Macready took a swig of lemonade.

"I believe in putting back into the community. Create jobs. Keep businesses running. But I like the discipline that comes with hiring military types. At a guess, I'd say you know what I'm talkin' about."

Grant clinked the ice in his glass but didn't drink.

"I've seen *The Longest Day*."

"And *The Alamo* too, I'll bet. But we're not talking John Wayne movies here. I'm guessing you're ex-army. Am I right?"

Grant took a swig of lemonade instead of answering. Macready took that as answer enough.

"So the question is, what's a British ex-soldier doing in Absolution, Texas?"

"And I'm guessing you know the answer to that."

Macready put his glass on the table.

"I know what you've been saying around town."

"There you go then."

"But I don't see an Englishman coming all this way to see a Mex."

"A Yorkshireman."

"What's the difference?"

Grant locked eyes with Macready. "Do you consider yourself a Texan or an American?"

"Point taken. Same applies, though."

The sun beat down on the bleached stone around the table. It baked the floor and sucked any moisture out of the dirt in the compound. The ice in Grant's drink had already melted to half its original size. Shards of sunlight reflected off the glass. The mercenaries kept busy. The cat curled up in the shade. Grant tinkled the ice in his glass, then took a deep, cooling drink. He kept his face blank when he spoke.

"That reminds me of a joke going the rounds when I was a kid."

He put the empty glass on the table.

"An Englishman, a Frenchman, and an American are on a plane. Engines cut out and the pilot says there's not enough parachutes for everyone. Wants three volunteers. So the Englishman goes to the open door, shouts 'God save the Queen,' and jumps out. Then the Frenchman goes to the door and shouts 'Viva la France' and jumps out. The American—he gets up and shouts 'Remember the Alamo' and throws a Mexican out."

Macready snorted a laugh. "That might be true around here, but it don't explain why a Yorkshireman's so far from home."

"Visiting."

Macready was still dancing around the subject. "But visiting who?"

Grant kept it brief. "Eduardo Cruz."

He watched Macready, waiting for a more direct question. For some reason the Texan was sounding Grant out. Checking to see if he was who he thought Grant was. The cowboy at the hotel had passed the message that he was. Macready didn't seem so sure. Something was worrying the head honcho. Grant wasn't in the mood to ease that worry. His reasons for being here were private. Whatever troubles Macready had weren't Grant's problem.

Macready drummed his fingers on the table. The cat raised its head, then pushed up onto its feet. The drumming grew faster and the cat followed the sound. Some kind of Pavlov's dog thing going on. Macready watched the cat come towards him but spoke to Grant.

"We've got a rodent problem in Absolution."

The cat jumped into Macready's lap. He began to stroke it.

"A good mouser is worth its weight in gold."

Two mercenaries crossed the courtyard and came up the steps. They bypassed the table and went into the hacienda. Big, solid men who didn't look like they'd back down to anyone. Macready stopped stroking the cat.

"I think you would make a good mouser. What do you say?"

Grant checked over his shoulder to make sure the two heavies hadn't come back out, then focused on the cat.

"I'm more of a save a mouse, eat a pussy kind of fella."

"The job pays well."

Grant nodded towards the bunkhouse. "Thanks. But I think you've got it covered."

The bonhomie dropped out of Macready's voice. His hand tightened in the cat's neck fur. His other hand came slowly under its throat, tickling the Adam's apple. The cat began to purr. Loud and throaty.

"Some of my mousers aren't up to the task. Too many rats are getting past. I don't like that."

His hand gripped the cat's throat and he suddenly grabbed its head with the other. He jerked it sideways in a vicious twist. The neck snapped with a loud crack. The head faced backwards, then lolled to one side. He started stroking the dead cat as if soothing it.

"I could have it cooked and brought to your motel if you really want to eat pussy. But saving rats is a dangerous business in Absolution."

Grant pushed back his chair and stood up. "Good job I'm only passing through, then."

Macready didn't stand. He waved at the garage with a fur-encrusted hand. "I'll get one of my boys to drive you back."

Grant shook his head. "That's okay. I think I'll walk. Thanks for the drink."

He went down the steps and crossed the courtyard. His trainers were coated in dust. The sun was hot on his back but the lemonade was already leaving a bad taste in his mouth. Despite the heat, he felt like a coffee, or maybe just a friendly face. The big wooden gate swung open and he left the compound. The dusty expanse of Avenue D had never felt so empty.

TWELVE

Grant walked back down the street towards the bank. It felt good to be on familiar ground after the claustrophobic atmosphere of Macready's compound. He wondered where the local kids went to school since Macready had turned the old one into his own personal Alamo. He wondered where the locals did anything since the Texan seemed to own the entire town. Almost the entire town.

He took the same route as before to the only place Macready didn't own. Along North Third to the town dump and beyond. The old-timer was still shooting rats and still avoiding hitting the propane store. Grant waited for a lull in hostilities, then waved at the ancient sniper before cutting through the dump. He doubted Macready had been talking about the same kind of rodent problem, but one thing was certain. Tripp Macready was a bigger prick than his son. And a more dangerous one.

By the time Grant crossed in front of Sixto's to Gilda's Grill and Diner, he was ready for a coffee. What he wasn't expecting was the reception he'd receive once he got inside.

"I CAN'T GIVE YOU any coffee."

"I don't want it given. I'm buying."

"Can't sell you any either."

Grant was standing at the counter. Sarah Hellstrom busied herself polishing the chrome boiler like a true barista. There were only two customers—the same elderly couple as before. He couldn't tell if they were drinking coffee or not.

"How come?"

Sarah busied herself with the boiler. The strong and confident woman he'd met yesterday was nowhere to be seen, replaced by this pale imitation who was avoiding meeting his eyes.

"Machine's broken."

"Tea then?"

"We don't serve tea."

"Something cold?"

"Don't have nothing cold either."

Grant lowered his voice and spoke in slow, friendly tones. "Well, something's turned cold in here. I hope you don't hold it against me."

Sarah shuddered as she cleaned the spout, then stopped what she was doing. She braced her shoulders and appeared to make a decision. She turned sad eyes towards him.

"I can't help you."

The old couple sensed the atmosphere and finished their drinks. They pushed back from the table, left money on the tray, and shuffled out the door. Sarah's eyes followed them all the way out. Grant waited until she turned them back on him.

"Sarah. I'm sorry if I got you in trouble."

All the resistance drained out of her.

"You didn't. I got into it all by myself."

"The car?"

"Scott."

Grant took a moment to digest that. He paid close attention to Sarah's face. The cheek she had briefly touched yesterday. It was clean and bruise free. There was no sign of makeup covering any injury. The eye wasn't swollen or bloodshot. That put his mind at ease. Partly.

"I know he wasn't keen on me going to Adobe Flats. Must have told his old man. That's why he had me arrested."

Sarah looked surprised and shook her head. "They don't care about you going to Adobe Flats. Scott just doesn't like me talking to strange men."

"Am I that strange?"

A faint smile crept over her face. "You're off-the-map strange."

Grant smiled back. "You don't know the half of it."

"You're some kind of soldier. I know that much."

"Used to be."

"Ever kill anyone?"

"I was a typist."

"Now that is strange."

Grant changed the subject. "So Scott's the jealous type, is he?"

Sarah put the polishing cloth down on the counter. She kept a straight face but couldn't hide the wince as she straightened her right arm. Her shirtsleeves had been rolled up to the elbow the first time he'd met her. They were only folded down to the forearm now.

"I told you. We're history. He doesn't see it that way, though. Gets kind of possessive."

Grant leaned over the counter and gently reached for her arm. She tried to draw it back but he made soothing noises and she let him slide the sleeve up her arm. Her skin was smooth and tanned with fine blond hairs covering the forearm. The bruise was on her bicep. Dark and vicious. Merging from five smaller bruises. Four fingers and a thumb. Grabbed and shaken but not hit in the face. An old technique to make sure you keep the bruising out of sight. Grant's jaw clenched.

"That's why he had his dad call the police?"

Again the look of surprise. "He didn't need to call his father. He knows the deputy."

Grant carefully rolled her sleeve back down, his hand lingering on the skin of her forearm. The hairs were so soft they barely registered. Sarah laid a hand on top of his.

"It was his father who got you released."

TEN MINUTES LATER THEY were sitting in the farthest booth from the window, the coffee machine miraculously working again. Grant had a latte. Two sugars. No lid. Sarah had her coffee strong and black.

"Macready gave Scott a helluva roasting for getting in the way."

"In the way of what?"

"I don't know. But I get the feeling they want you treated with kid gloves."

"That's not the way he treated you."

Sarah smoothed the sleeve down on her arm. "I'm no threat."

"And they think I am?"

She stopped stroking her sleeve. "You're a stranger. They don't know what to think."

Grant's voice became a low growl.

"I'll tell you one thing he'd better be thinking if he touches you again. He'd better be thinking, 'I really like hospital food.'"

The old Sarah resurfaced. Clenched jaw and fiery eyes. "I can take care of myself."

Grant pointed at her arm. "Looks like it."

Sarah waved his concerns away.

"That's nothing. I took care of myself before you got here. I'll take care of myself after you've gone. You getting involved will only make things worse. You're passing through. I've got to live here."

"No, you don't."

"Huh?"

"America's a big place. I know. I got lost three times trying to find the toilet."

"My roots are here."

"Then uproot. Ground's not so fertile that it's worth sticking around."

She took a sip of her coffee. "That's all right for you to say, globe-trotting all over the place."

Grant took a drink of his. "A rolling stone gathers no moss."

"We don't have moss in Texas. Too dry."

"Well, we've plenty in Yorkshire. You're not missing much."

Sarah nodded out the front window towards town. "I hear you're on your third room in two days."

"News travels fast."

"The Gage to the jail to the motel. Hard to miss."

"I'll start worrying if they move me into the mortuary."

Sarah's face turned to stone. "Don't even joke about that. Around here, that's not much of a stretch."

Grant waved a hand to placate her. "Kid gloves, remember? Don't think that involves putting me in the ground."

"Until they change their minds."

"I'll look out for that. The old feller at the motel seems a decent type."

"Hunter. Yes, he is."

She didn't reach up to her cheek but Grant sensed that's what she was thinking. Steam rose from her coffee and mingled with his. The strands of smoke intertwined, then evaporated. There was a lot of history hiding behind her eyes, not much of it filled with smiles and laughter. Grant tested the water.

"Used to work with Doc Cruz. I didn't know that."

Sarah focused on her coffee. "Yes, he did. They looked after most of the town back in the day."

"When they were together?"

"Yes. Before…"

Grant drummed his fingers up the side of his mug. "Before what?"

Sarah gulped down another mouthful of coffee and ignored the question.

"Hunter pulled his ticket after. Only stuck with the mortician job because it came with free transport."

"Company car?"

"Company hearse. He can get all sorts of supplies in the back of that thing."

"For his liquor cabinet?"

"It helps him forget."

"Forgetting's not all it's cracked up to be."

Sarah let out a sigh. "Oh yes it is. There must be things you'd like to forget."

That made Grant think. He wasn't much for living in the past, but sometimes the past kept creeping up on you. After all, that's what brought him here. He didn't dwell on it, but he hadn't forgotten it either. The past was history. You didn't need to drag it around with you all the time. He reckoned for some people that wasn't an option. That's when they turned to drink. The great assuager.

The door from the street banged open and they both looked towards the sound. Sarah over her shoulder, Grant straight forward. A dust devil swirled around the floor as the door closed.

Grant nodded. "Well, talk of the devil and he will appear."

HUNTER ATHEY NURSED HIS coffee like it was the last drink he'd ever have. He sat next to Sarah, opposite Grant. Three in a booth. The sun had moved around and was now blazing through the windows, making the vinyl seats hot.

Athey looked up from his coffee. "It's hot as be-damn in here, girl. When you gonna invest in air conditioning?"

"When I get enough customers to pay for it."

He noticed the awkward movement of her arm but didn't reach out for it. Their eyes locked.

Sarah put added warmth into her voice. "He knows."

Athey jerked his eyes to Grant, then back to Sarah. A brief moment of panic.

Sarah patted his hand on the table. "About the arm."

Athey's other hand covered hers. "Then he knows the best way to keep you safe is to get out of town."

Grant pushed his empty cup across the table. "The best way to stay safe is to remove the danger."

Athey turned to Grant, his eyes steadier than they had a right to be. "You are the danger."

"I'm not the one did that to her arm."

He paused for effect.

"Or her face."

"You're the one that caused it though. This time."

Grant lowered his voice. "Man like that—there'll always be a this time. The effect is another black eye or a bruised arm or worse."

He leaned forward on his elbows.

"That's the thing about cause and effect. You can't have one without the other. Tripp Macready is a cause unto himself. Remove him."

He leaned back in the booth. "Then no more midnight doctors."

Athey leaned back too. He took a deep breath that puffed his chest out.

"You remove one Macready and you're left with the other. Mean as a rattlesnake and twice as deadly. Won't be a doctor you'll need then. It'll be a mortician."

Grant wasn't fazed. "Remove him too."

Athey barked a laugh. "As simple as that."

Grant shook his head. "Nothing worth having is simple."

"Not achievable either."

"Everything's achievable."

The air went out of Athey and he collapsed like a pricked balloon.

"Not in Absolution it ain't."

Grant glanced at Sarah and blinked once, then looked back at Hunter Athey.

"Then leave Absolution."

Sarah sat up straight. "We've already had this conversation."

Grant softened his eyes. "No moss in Texas. I remember."

The trio fell silent. Steam rose from Athey's cup. The other two coffees were dead. Sunshine blazed through the windows and glinted off the chrome boiler behind the counter. The diner was heating up. The atmosphere was cooling down. Coffee smells and hot vinyl made for a cozy feeling. The silence cut through it like a serrated blade, turning it cold and hard and dangerous.

Athey broke the stalemate.

"You came down here to see Doc Cruz. Yeah?"

Grant nodded. "That's right."

"He ain't here."

"That's what everybody keeps telling me."

"So there's no reason for you to stay."

Grant turned his gaze on Sarah. Under different circumstances… He shook that thought aside. This wasn't the time or the place. He was in Absolution for a reason. Now it seemed that reason was dead. He felt it in his bones. Question was, did he want to do anything about it? The answer was a no-brainer. Considering why he'd come all this way to see him.

Athey leaned forward, strength returning to his voice.

"I know where Eduardo is. And how to get there."

THIRTEEN

How to get there proved to be novel in the extreme. The hearse was big and heavy and a much softer ride than Sarah's little foreign car. It hugged the road and smoothed out the bumps. Terlingua wasn't on the map he'd read at the Gage Hotel. Grant had to check the larger map at the Absolution Motel when he picked up the hearse. It didn't seem that far. Until he'd been driving for an hour.

A hundred miles as the crow flies. A lot more on the winding roads of West Texas. Across to Marathon, then south on the 385. The road was straight enough to begin with but quickly deteriorated into just another desert highway. It rose and fell with the gentle undulations of the landscape, then slowly began to rise more often than it fell. Into the foothills of Big Bend National Park before swinging west between towering buttes and mesas.

Grant thought about what Hunter Athey had told him. He wondered about a world where a man had to hide under a false name just to survive. Hiding in plain sight, true. Working at a half-assed medical center a hundred and twenty miles away but hiding all the same.

Texas. Not the best place to be a Mexican. Unless you were close to the Mexican border. Big Bend National Park ran right along the Mexican border. Terlingua wasn't far from it either.

The 385 became the 170. The blacktop remained the same. Faded and dusty and as winding as Snake Pass back in Yorkshire. Grant kept his eyes on the road, but his peripheral vision couldn't hide from the desert landscape sliding by on either side. He drove past Kathy's Kosmic Kowgirl Kafe on the left, a florid pink barbecue shack and reconstituted schoolbus. The American equivalent of a roadside burger van. The road cut through Study Butte, then dropped down out of the foothills towards Terlingua. A blink-and-you'd-miss-it town so small it made Absolution look like New York.

Grant didn't blink and he still nearly missed it. There was no bullet-riddled WELCOME TO TERLINGUA sign at the town limits. There was no sign at all. It was only the El Dorado Hotel where the road branched right that marked the beginning of anything. It was the first building he'd seen in twenty minutes. He pulled over and stopped amid a cloud of dust. Terlingua Ghost Town Road was a single-lane excuse for a road that didn't look like it went anywhere. The only other building was a speck on the horizon. If Eduardo Cruz was hiding in plain sight, he couldn't have picked a better place. The entire town was hiding in plain sight and Grant hadn't found it yet.

He urged the hearse forward, taking the right-hand fork. The El Dorado drifted by. The dust cloud followed him like a cape. The place was so barren there weren't even any cacti. The sun baked down from a hard blue sky. Sweat trickled from Grant's hairline and down the back of his ears. His T-shirt was sticking to his back as the leather seat grew unbearably hot even with the windows open.

He kept his pace slow. This wasn't a place you rushed through. Not if you were looking for something. Not if you took the right-hand fork.

There should have been vultures circling overhead. If this had been a movie, there'd be tumbleweeds blowing across the road. Neither was true. Terlingua was dry and empty and silent as the grave.

Grant reached over and touched the scarred velvet case on the passenger seat. Long and narrow. Solid. He could almost feel the stethoscope inside even though he couldn't touch it. Hadn't touched it for many years. The hard land sucked all the color out of the day. No greenery. No shade. As Sean Connery had said in *The Wind and the Lion*, "Where there is no shade from the sun, there is only desert. The desert I know very well." Or something like that. In a Scottish accent. The main point was the bit about knowing the desert. Grant knew desert country. The landscape here was similar but different. The difference was people weren't shooting at him or trying to carve him up. Those were his overriding memories of the desert. Where his mind took him now.

THE PAST

What the fuck? You aren't gonna outrun 'em.
—Cooper

FOURTEEN

THE STETHOSCOPE LASTED HALF an hour before common sense prevailed. Half an hour after sunrise. Half an hour after Grant checked the downed Chinook to confirm the obvious. Wheeler, Carlino, and Adams hadn't made it out of the chopper. The pilots were dead too. Grant didn't say any words over the deceased. He didn't waste time trying to recover the bodies. Two of them were half buried under the wreckage. The others were in pieces. While there was a certain amount of honor in the old maxim "Leave no man behind," it made no sense to sacrifice the rest so that families would have body parts at the funeral. Grant's duty now was to the survivors.

He darted back across the dusty street, keeping low and light on his feet. He moved fast and silent and barely scuffed the dirt to raise a dust cloud behind him. Voices sounded in the distance. The mob was gathering. The sun broke the skyline of damaged rooftops and crumbling boundary walls. A crackle of small arms fire joined the shouts of indignation from down the road. Gunshots fired into the sky like a call for celebration. They'd downed a helicopter after all.

Grant threw himself against the wall in the yard across the road from the crash site. Mack was nursing a bloodied leg. Cooper kept his assault rifle aimed along the street. Both glanced over at Grant. He shook his head and raised three fingers before folding them down with his other hand. Then he held up one finger and shrugged his shoulders.

"No sign of Bond. Any ideas?"

Mack pressed a bloody rag into the leg wound. "He made it to the ramp. Didn't see him after that."

Cooper turned his attention back to the street. "He lost his grip after the second bounce. Could have landed anywhere."

Cruz kept quiet. She wasn't part of the team. The bond they shared wasn't her bond. Instead, she busied herself applying a field dressing to Mack's leg. This wasn't the time or place to make a full assessment. They all realized that. First order of business was to put distance between them and the wreckage. Buy some time before planning a strategy.

Grant knew what the priority was.

"Weapons check."

Mack and Cooper followed his lead. They both checked their weapons and ammunition. An M16 each. An ugly black .45 automatic holstered in their webbing. They counted the spare magazines strapped to their belts. Mack had lost his commando knife. It had been torn from his leg scabbard along with a chunk of flesh and muscle. Grant had a .45 and a sniper's rifle. He pulled his knife but only an inch of broken blade came out. The impact had snapped it in half. His leg felt bruised and sore but at least it was mobile.

Cruz tightened the dressing around Mack's leg. Mack gritted his teeth but made no sound. Cruz was unarmed. She was the medic, supposed to be surrounded by armed men while she tranquilized the target package for easy transport. She focused on the job at hand: stopping the bleeding and getting Mack ready to move. There would be time for a more thorough examination once they'd found a safe location. In the desert township a safe location meant anywhere they weren't shooting at you. If they didn't move soon, the enclosed yard would become a shooting gallery. Dawn light glinted off the stethoscope swinging from her neck.

Grant spun a finger in her direction.

"Lose the stethoscope."

Cruz turned an angry stare on Grant, then realized he was right. She finished tying off the bandage before slipping the stethoscope from her neck. She held it gently in both hands, her face telling an unspoken tale. The stethoscope was more than a piece of medical equipment. It had value. Memories. She swung the backpack off her shoulder and unsnapped the fastenings. Her hands rummaged inside and took out a long velvet case. She opened it and folded the stethoscope along its length. She snapped it shut and put it in the backpack. Her eyes told Grant not to argue. He didn't.

"Mack. You good to go?"

Mack flexed his leg. It didn't flex very far. He nodded. "I'm good."

"Coop."

Grant forked fingers at his eyes, then to the rear of the yard. Cooper shuffled back from his position covering the street and went in search of an exit strategy. Grant took Cooper's place, scouting the street for the first signs of enemy activity. Enemy activity was coming. The gunshots and triumphant shouts were getting closer. The first wave was surging along the street towards the crash site. The downed Chinook was drawing their attention. That gave Grant a window of opportunity.

Cooper came back through a gap in the wall.

"Back alley. Parallels the street."

Grant checked the crowd one last time, then scrambled to the rear of the yard. The gap in the wall was wide enough to climb through sideways. He stuck his head out and looked both ways. More derelict buildings. Some with washing hanging outside. Most with bars over the windows. Not many with glass left in the frames. No activity. Good. If they moved quickly, they might be able to flank the crowd and head towards the safe zone. A long walk in hostile territory. He drew his head back and hunkered down.

"Doc. You help Mack."

Cruz nodded.

"Coop. Rear guard."

Cooper didn't need to nod. He was already in position to be last man out.

Grant focused on Cruz.

"Follow my lead. If Bond made it, he'll be doing the same."

Cruz kept her recriminations to herself. This wasn't her unit. She'd have to abide by their rules. Under fire, survival was key. In combat, strong leadership made survival more likely. Grant was a strong leader.

"Let's go."

But he wasn't infallible. The moment he squeezed through the gap into the alley, he knew he'd waited too long. The mob wasn't just swarming down the main street, it was filtering through the network of back streets and alleyways like water finding the easiest route. Chanting and gunfire came from the left—the direction Grant wanted to go. Not in sight yet but closing fast. If Grant stayed here, the squad would be overrun. He needed to put some distance between his group and the mob. In the wrong direction.

He turned right and moved fast along the alley. Mack came out next, then Cruz, forming a human crutch. Cooper brought up the rear, eyes peeled for the first signs that they'd been discovered. The alley wasn't straight. Nothing in the township was straight. That played in their favor. The approaching mob could be heard but not seen.

Yet.

Grant led the way. Steady movement, not sprinting. If he went too fast, Mack wouldn't be able to keep up, and if Mack went down, it would delay them all. He didn't. The alley doglegged left, then right. Once they'd rounded the corners, the sightlines were broken, but the noise was getting louder. Fifty yards was all Grant dared risk. Then he found another crumbling building and ducked in through a hole in the wall. Cruz helped Mack through the gap. Cooper waited until they were all through, then backed in, never taking his eyes off the previous corner.

They immediately took up a defensive formation, Cooper covering the back, Mack leaning against a wall but still covering the middle, Grant at the front window focusing on the street. The mob was congregating around the Chinook and the building it had destroyed, but they were ragged and stretched out at the rear and sides. That's where Grant was looking. What he saw through his peripheral vision turned his blood cold.

Bond had made it as far along the street as Grant's team—but on the opposite side. Behind a low wall with a view directly into the house Grant was hiding in. Bond was injured. He was leaning heavily to one side, blood clotting in a mass of red and black down his left sleeve. He glanced towards the crowd, then made his decision. The wrong one. To risk darting across the street while the mob was engaged dragging the bodies out of the chopper.

Grant tried to wave him back.

Bond was already moving. Concussion or pain or shock from the loss of blood affected his movement. It reduced his mental capacity. Trying to cross the street was a mistake. With a crowd of a hundred people, it only took one to be glancing over his shoulder for the movement to be spotted. Half the mob must have been looking along the street because there was an immediate cry and a surge.

Bond realized the danger he'd just brought upon the squad. His eyes locked with Grant's and he knew what he had to do. He ignored Grant and turned right, away from the squad. The shuffling gait hindered his speed. He only managed to get ten yards before the mob was on him. He turned and fired a short burst with his M16 before machetes rained down. Blood spurted. Body parts flew.

Grant turned to the others.

"Out. Across the alley. Not along it."

He ignored Cruz.

"Coop. Lead. While they're busy. Now."

Cruz looked shocked. Grant didn't have time to worry about her feelings. It would only take a few minutes for the mob to wonder where Bond had been heading and come looking. A rear-guard action was better than a standing fight with a raging mob. Keep moving. Keep them off-guard. Mack and Cooper knew that. They would mourn their losses later. If they survived.

Cooper was first through the hole in the wall. Cruz followed, shouldering some of Mack's weight. Grant looked through the window one last time. The crowd was in frenzy. Bloodied machetes flashed and hacked. Grant clenched his teeth, muscles bulging along the sides of his jaw, then he was out through the hole and following the others.

THE DAY WAS LONG and hot and bloody. Moving from house to house as the squad zigzagged through the ruined township. Staying one step ahead of the mob. Just barely. Somehow the crowd had got wind of the survivors' presence, maybe from Bond's ill-judged dash across the street or perhaps from something they saw. Whatever it was, they were on the hunt, tracking Grant across town.

It was a slow chase. A game of cat and mouse. In this game to save the mouse, Grant would have to do more than eat a pussy. He'd have to kill as many cats as he could and keep moving. So far he'd only had to kill three. Lone pursuers who had literally bumped into the squad as they charged round the alleyways. One at a time. Single shot each. Not enough to alert the mob. Nothing louder than the exuberant firing into the sky.

Despite the constant changes of direction, Grant kept his inner compass on true north, the place where they'd set off. The safe zone. The desert airbase on the edge of town. His sense of direction was unerring. His efforts to reach it weren't. As much distance as they covered traveling through the maze of back streets, they didn't seem to be getting any closer to extraction.

By late afternoon the effort was beginning to show. Grant and Cooper still had plenty of gas in the tank, but Mack and Cruz were flagging. It was time to rest up and take stock. Grant found the perfect place on the northeast corner of a plaza facing back the way they'd come. A street café that hadn't served customers for years. Good sightlines along two sides through large windows.

Grant went in first. Dust lay thick on every surface. Nobody had been in here. He signalled the others, and Cruz helped Mack through the door. Cooper brought up the rear, as sharp as ever. Covering their retreat.

The makeshift counter provided good cover. Grant took up position at one end and Cooper the other. Cruz leaned Mack against the back wall and checked his dressing. Blood had turned the bandage black. Thick and tacky. Still bleeding. Mack's face was pale under his tan. The medic hadn't been able to examine the wound, but the fact that Mack had been able to limp across town at least meant the leg wasn't broken. That was the good news. Everything else was bad. It was still bleeding heavily. The pain was sapping Mack's energy. Infection was going to be a problem if Cruz didn't clean and disinfect the wound. She glanced across at Grant. He nodded. They were staying put. She'd have time to change the dressing.

A complicated silver coffee machine stood above the worktop against the back wall. Chrome boiler. Network of tubes and pipes. Coffee grinder and filter system. Grant took the lid off, but it was empty. The boiler had been dry for a long time. He wondered briefly what the barista was doing now. Part of the mob outside perhaps. The boiler might be dry, but the water tap was working. After a couple of dry coughs, dirty water spurted out before it cleaned up and ran freely. He looked through the window. Still nobody in the street. Cooper knew what to do. He collected everyone's water bottles and handed them to Grant. Once they were refilled, he dropped to a crouch. He'd been exposed for too long. He felt safer behind the counter.

Cooper's eyes hardened.

"Movement."

Grant followed his stare. Across the plaza, coming this way. It hadn't taken long for the crowd to catch the scent. Like blood in the water, the sharks were gathering. A mass of bodies poured out of the alleyway on the southwest corner. They spilled into the square, then began to mill around aimlessly. They had lost the trail. Bloodstained faces quested around. Putting out feelers.

Cooper stayed low. There was no avoiding breaking the smooth, flat line of the counter, but at least it was at one end where he could merge with the clutter of discarded cups and saucers. Grant did the same at the opposite end. Two pairs of eyes focused on the threat from outside. Nobody moved in the confines of the coffee shop. The silence became oppressive.

Cruz shuffled across the floor towards Grant, making sure she stayed below the worktop. Careful that her equipment didn't knock anything or make a noise. Her voice was a harsh whisper.

"How long before they send an extraction team?"

Grant didn't take his eyes off the street. He kept his head still. Cooper glanced across from his end of the counter. Mack stretched his leg out across the floor. The lack of an answer prompted Cruz to carry on.

"We're overdue. The chopper went down. How long?"

Grant slowly lowered his face below the counter, then turned to the medic.

"Chopper crash will be floated as mechanical failure during an aid drop."

"But they will be coming. Right?"

Cooper kept his eyes straight ahead. Mack lowered his head. Grant was matter-of-fact about their situation. No point sugaring the pill.

"Secret."

Realization flooded Cruz's face.

"To the outside world, yes. But not to—"

Grant held up a hand to stop her.

"Secret. Doesn't matter what our people know. Can't admit this mission."

His tone softened.

"Mechanical failure. Tragic loss of life."

He wanted to touch her. Reassure her. But he couldn't.

"Nobody's coming for us. We're on our own."

"Shit."

"It is."

Cruz realized something else, and it showed in her face. Grant nodded his agreement without speaking. Mack's leg was getting worse. There'd be no more chasing along the back streets for him. Cruz's Texan heritage played in Grant's mind. This was going to be their last stand. Their Alamo. The street café was going to be their mission that became a fortress. He hoped it wasn't going to be a fortress that became a shrine.

Mack broke the tension.

"So just for the record, Sarge. James Bond: Connery or Craig?"

Grant knew where Mack was going with this. Bringing up Bond's sacrifice in the street near the crash site without having to mention it.

"No question. Connery's the man."

Mack nodded.

"Yeah. I'm with Wheeler on that. Bond didn't know shit."

Cooper caught the vibe but kept his eyes on the crowd. Cruz was beginning to understand. Grant kept quiet, letting Mack play it his way.

"Apart from one thing. He got that right."

Mack leaned his M16 against the wall and unclipped the webbing belt of spare clips. He handed the .45 to Cruz, then pushed himself upright. The leg could barely carry his weight. Cooper looked from Mack to Grant, then jerked a thumb towards the rear of the café.

"Jim. Back door. Can't be seen from the street."

Grant didn't speak. In combat these were the hardest moments. Cooper and Mack had been together since training. Their bond was forged in combat. Their friendship was a thing of legend. Their minds were in agreement now. Mack walked as straight as his bad leg allowed, but he was veering towards his right. Cooper came from around the counter.

"You go left. I'll go right."

Mack slapped his good leg and shook his head. "I'm faster to my right."

"What the fuck? You aren't gonna outrun 'em."

"Who says?"

Agreement was reached. They went through the door side by side, then separated. Mack lunged to his right and kept on lunging. Cooper went left, firing from the hip as they opened a gap. The crowd split, half surging towards Mack while the other half took cover and fired at Cooper. Machetes were raised. Angry voices shouted defiance.

Grant didn't wait to see the inevitable. He guided Cruz towards the back door, and they disappeared into the shadows.

THE PRESENT

*I always thought Mexicans
were short fellas.*
—Jim Grant

FIFTEEN

DIRT AND GRAVEL CRUNCHED under the tires as Grant slowed the hearse to a stop. Ghost Town Road had given up on tarmac half a mile back. Now it was only the width of the road that stopped it becoming a dirt track. Even minor roads in America seemed to be as wide as the M1.

Grant turned the engine off. The hot metal didn't tick as it cooled because it didn't cool. The sun beat down from a cloudless sky and baked everything it touched. The roof of the hearse was as hot as the hood. The leather seat burned into Grant's back. The Terlingua Trading Company forecourt shimmered in the late afternoon heat, a long, low storefront with a covered walkway out front and the Starlight Theatre restaurant and saloon at one side. A bleached square block of a building stood guard across the forecourt, a historical remnant of days gone by. The words TERLINGUA JAIL were carved into the lintel above the door.

The medical center hardly warranted a mention—an unnamed afterthought at the far end of the Trading Company premises. A small green cross was the only sign that it had anything to do with doctors and medicines.

Doc Cruz's hideaway. In plain sight but almost invisible.

Grant studied the storefront but didn't get out. His heart was pounding. Over the years he'd faced angry men, pissed-off women, and armed insurgents, but this was proving to be the hardest thing he'd ever done. One hand stroked the soft velvet of the stethoscope case. He took a deep breath. He'd come a long way to do this. After a few minutes to gather himself, he grabbed the case and got out of the hearse.

"Have a seat. This won't take long."

The gray-haired Mexican looked younger than Grant had expected. Lined and weathered but with a youthful face. Maybe it was the grin lines around his mouth or the crow's feet that crinkled when he smiled. The Mexican didn't wave Grant to a seat because both hands were busy applying a dressing to a woman's arm. On the floor next to her chair a small child clung to her legs, fear and doubt filling his eyes.

Grant moved slow and gentle. He lowered himself onto a faded wooden chair near the door. The boy's eyes followed Grant's every move. Grant had seen it before on the council estates of Bradford. Children who had witnessed domestic abuse were as much victims as their mothers. The doctor used soft hands to fasten the bandage over cooling cream and cling film. A burns dressing. Either from scalding water or being held against a hot stove. Bullies were universal. Apart from the derelict jail across the forecourt, Terlingua didn't look like it had much in the way of law enforcement. In Texas Grant doubted if Mexican women were high on the priority list.

The doctor soothed. The boy relaxed. Words were exchanged in Spanish. The woman took money from her purse, but the doctor pushed it away. The boy cowered until gentle words coaxed him out of his shell—gentle words and a jar of sweets the doctor took from his desk. The woman thanked him profusely. Even without an interpreter, there was no mistaking that. The boy took a sweet. The woman smiled through her pain. Eduardo Cruz walked her to the door and out onto the porch.

Grant waited nervously on the chair. He hadn't felt this uncomfortable since his last visit to the headmaster's office at Moor Grange School for Boys. Just after he'd cracked one bully's skull and broken the other's nose. This felt worse. This felt like shame.

When Eduardo Cruz came back in, his demeanor had changed. He looked at the stranger with careful eyes. Worry creased his brow. The smile had gone.

"I wondered how long it would be before you came for me."

Grant felt as if he were being admonished. He had no excuses. "I'm sorry."

Cruz looked out through the window. "Stealing a hearse is as low as you can get."

Apology turned to confusion.

"What?"

Cruz's shoulders sagged. "Please tell me you left Hunter alone. He has nothing to do with this."

Then Grant understood. He tried to wave Cruz's concerns away. "Hunter Athey told me where to find you. He loaned me the hearse."

Cruz was cautious with his response. "Why would he do that?"

"Because Sarah couldn't lend me her car again."

"Hunter and Sarah know you are here?"

"Yes."

The doctor's façade began to crumble. Being strong in the face of his enemies. His hands were shaking as relief flooded his body. The aftermath of an adrenaline dump that was as much induced by fear as the fight or flight instinct. He waved a hand towards the hearse.

"I thought Macready was being symbolic. Bringing me back in a coffin."

"I'm not here from Macready."

"Then why are you here?"

This was going to be the hard part. Getting started. Grant felt the words stick in his throat. A pulse thumped at the side of his head. He tried to take a deep breath but his nose felt blocked. He picked the velvet case up from the chair next to him and cradled it in his lap. He paused for a moment, then clicked it open and held the stethoscope out to Pilar Cruz's father.

SIXTEEN

"I DON'T UNDERSTAND. IT wasn't an accident?"

Eduardo Cruz left the stethoscope in its case, his fingers tracing the curves as if they could feel his daughter's neck. He looked at the Englishman who had come all this way to return it. Grant forced himself not to lower his eyes.

"That's the story they put out. Mechanical failure during an aid drop."

"But that wasn't true."

"No."

Silence. Both men were lost for words. Grant because he felt ashamed at leaving it so long before fulfilling his lover's dying wish. Doc Cruz because he was overwhelmed by memories of his daughter. Moisture threatened to leak from his eyes, but he held it in check. For Grant, the best way forward was to tell it the way it was, army regulations be damned.

"It was a snatch squad—in and out to grab a tribal leader under cover of the aid drop. Pilar was our medic. Helicopter was brought down in the township. Mission was secret. So they went with mechanical failure."

Cruz continued to stroke the smooth lines of the tubing. "So she died in combat."

It wasn't a question. It was a grieving father coming to terms with a change in circumstance. He had already put this behind him once. Now it was an open wound, the past dredged up by this stranger from across the pond. It was hard to tell from the old man's face whether this was good news or bad. Grant kept quiet. In the end, what difference did it make how a person died? You were still dead. But he'd made a promise.

Grant nodded at the velvet case. "She said you gave her that."

Cruz smiled a sad little smile. "When she graduated medical school. Her ticket out of Absolution."

Grant put added warmth into his voice. "She was the best medic I ever worked with."

Cruz looked up from the stethoscope. "But she was more than that to you."

"Yes."

"Jim Grant. From her letters. I never thought I would meet you."

"I wish you didn't have to."

"Because if she had lived, you would have drifted apart."

"My fault, not hers. She deserved better."

"She chose you."

Grant shrugged and kept quiet.

Doc Cruz nodded. "Nobody could make Pilar's choices for her. She was like her mother in that way. If she chose you, that is good enough for me."

Grant wondered if the doctor would think the same if he knew the whole truth—something Grant would keep to himself. There was no point piling Grant's guilt on top of the doctor's grief. On a need-to-know basis, there were some things a father didn't need to know about his daughter's death. Grant stuck with the safe path. "She should have got a medal and a folded flag."

Cruz indicated a glass display frame on the office wall. "I got the folded flag."

Grant ignored the interruption.

"She showed more courage than I could have. I always felt guilty that the army couldn't tell you that. Medals are only a piece of metal on a ribbon. What's important is what's behind them."

Cruz slowly closed the velvet case. "And you thought giving me this would bring you peace?"

"There is no peace. Only acceptance. Then you move on."

"Absolution, then."

"I'm past being absolved."

Cruz caressed the scarred velvet. "Nobody is beyond Absolution."

Grant sensed a change in the atmosphere—a shift away from the distant past towards more recent history. There were sounds of a commotion outside. Cruz ignored the distraction and stood. He crossed the room and put the stethoscope case on his desk.

"Nobody is beyond Macready either." He looked out of the front window. "And sooner or later we all get to ride in the hearse."

He turned his gaze on Grant. "That's why Macready is afraid of you."

The commotion was getting louder. Grant stared back at Doc Cruz. "I'm here to see you. I'm no threat to Macready."

Heavy footsteps came along the covered walkway. Cruz couldn't help but glance towards the door. When he looked back at Grant, his shoulders slumped. An air of resignation descended over him.

"That's not what he thinks."

The door burst open, and a big man filled the gap. Dirty jeans and a sleeveless shirt. The cowboy hat was stained with sweat around the brim. He took one step into the room and slammed the door behind him. One hand balled into a sledgehammer fist. His voice was hard as nails.

"Me and you gonna have words."

THIS WASN'T SOMETHING GRANT wanted to do. He'd come to Absolution with every intention of keeping out of trouble. He'd accepted Macready's taunts without response. He'd taken a chill pill and not let any of the needling from Macready's men annoy him. This was a mission of mercy in memory of a fallen colleague and lover. It didn't look as if Macready was going to let that rest.

Grant prepared to get up from his chair.

The big man ignored him and crossed the room towards Doc Cruz. "What you doin' touchin' my wife?"

Grant looked through the window. The injured woman was sitting on the steps hugging her son. The boy was crying. So was the woman. Doc Cruz didn't retreat from the advancing husband.

"Treating, not touching. For the burns that you inflicted."

The man stood tall, puffing his chest out. "Ain't inflicted nothin'."

Doc Cruz counted the negatives but kept a smile in his voice. "That's a double negative, amigo. Means you just said you did cause something."

The big man looked confused. Grant prepared to get up if needed, but Cruz seemed to have this under control. The cowboy hat was pulled low over the man's eyes, and he leaned into his words. "Woman burned herself. She's clumsy is all."

Cruz held his hands out and shrugged his shoulders. "And she grabbed her own arms, causing bruising with her fingers."

Cruz looked at Grant but spoke to the big man. "Bruising I am familiar with."

The big man hunched his shoulders. He'd had enough of the word games. "Familiar with my wife."

Both fists squeezed tight. Grant stood up but didn't advance. He took in the man's sleeveless shirt and dark skin, his Mexican heritage. It appeared that not all wife beaters were Texan. This fella was just a dirtier version of Scott Macready, laying hands on his woman simply because he could. Grant kept his voice friendly. Arms relaxed, flexed and ready for action.

"I always thought Mexicans were short fellas."

The big man turned towards Grant. "What?"

Grant gauged angles and distance. "Or maybe they always looked small next to John Wayne."

He moved in front of the window so the sun turned him into a silhouette. "Small, greasy ratfucks. Mexicans. In *The Alamo*."

The husband took one step forward and squinted into the sun. Grant stepped sideways, letting the full glare blast into the Mexican's eyes. "But you're a big ratfuck Mexican, aren't you?"

The words stung the big man into action before he had time to think. Thinking wasn't his strong suit. He lunged forward and swung a roundhouse blow towards the silhouette in front of him. Grant stepped under the swing and flashed a jab upwards into the man's throat. One blow. Full force. And it was all over.

The man doubled forward, clutching his throat. His face went from red to purple as he struggled for breath. Panic filled his eyes. He became a drowning man in the desert. His eyes watered. His mouth opened and shut like a goldfish. Grant guided him towards the chair and sat him down. He made an it's-all-yours gesture towards Doc Cruz. If a man was going to get injured, then a medical center was the best place to be.

The doctor began treating his new patient. Soft hands. Soothing words. It was no wonder his daughter had been such a good army medic. Grant thought about that while Doc Cruz got the Mexican's airway working again. He waited until the urgency diminished before leaning forward.

"Now. What did you mean about Macready?"

SEVENTEEN

EVEN WITH BOTH WINDOWS open and the speed approaching sixty, the hearse was still as hot as an oven on baking day. Wind swirled around the interior without cooling it one iota, but it helped freshen Grant's mind. Decisions had to be made. Whether to stay or go now that he'd done what he'd set out to do. Whether to go see Sarah Hellstrom one last time before leaving now that he'd put the ghost of Pilar Cruz to rest. And what to do about Tripp Macready, given what Eduardo Cruz had just told him.

Grant replayed the conversation in his head as he steered the hearse through Study Butte towards Absolution.

"MACREADY IS POISON."

Doc Cruz rinsed his hands in the washbasin at the rear of his office. He'd waited for the wife beater to leave before answering Grant's question. "He bought everything in town and then killed it."

"Why?"

"It is what he does. He chokes the life out of everything he touches."

"There are still businesses in Absolution."

"Only the ones he subsidizes to keep the town on life support."

Grant relaxed in the chair by the window. "For appearances sake."

"Exactly."

"He doesn't own the diner."

"The exception that proves the rule."

Grant smiled. "I never understood what that meant."

"Me neither. But in truth, the diner is only open because of Scott Macready."

"Him liking Sarah."

"Exactly."

"And the rest of the town just dried up, huh?"

"The last straw was him buying the school. When he knocked that down, it took the last bit of fight out of Absolution. Anyone with kids left—they send them to Marathon or Alpine. Anyone who really cares moved long ago."

"Doesn't say much for those who're left."

"No fight in 'em. Like I said."

"They all with Macready?"

"Not with him, just not strong enough to be against him. Not many are. You either stay and swallow the poison or you move out."

Grant watched the doctor dry his hands. "And you moved out."

"Not exactly."

Grant changed the question. "Why is Macready looking for you?"

"He told you that?"

"He didn't want me talking to you."

Cruz folded the towel and hung it over the rail. "What makes you think that?"

"Kept discouraging me from going to Adobe Flats."

"I'm not at Adobe Flats."

"That's what everybody said. But I got the impression it was more about me not finding you."

Cruz leaned against the desk and shook his head. "You've got the wrong end of the stick there, my friend."

Grant took his time while he got that straight in his head. "This isn't about you?"

"No."

"It's about Adobe Flats."

Cruz nodded his approval. "If you could check the land registry, what do you think you would find?"

Grant joined the dots. "Macready bought your place at Adobe Flats?"

Cruz shook his head. "No. He bought everything leading to Adobe Flats. I wouldn't sell."

Grant didn't ask why not. He reckoned Cruz was going to tell him.

"My wife would not have wanted me to. It was the happiest time of her life. And she died there giving birth to our daughter."

Despite the heat a chill went down Grant's spine. Pilar had never mentioned that. Their time together had always been focused on the here and now. They hadn't discussed her childhood, and Grant had never mentioned his mother dying giving birth to him or his subsequent isolation—his father sending him to boarding school as soon as he could. Grant hadn't realized just how close he and Pilar Cruz actually were. It made what had happened to her all the worse. He kept quiet and let Doc Cruz continue.

"I could not sell that heritage. I would not."

Grant let out a sigh. "So he burned you out."

"There was a fire. Yes. The sheriff said it started accidentally."

"The sheriff that Macready pays."

"I still own the land. But it was move or die."

"And you chose life."

"It was an easy choice."

Grant considered something Cruz had said earlier. "How does that make Macready afraid of me?"

"You're a stranger."

"Yeah, like in *Rango*. I got that."

"*Rango*?"

"The Johnny Depp lizard Western."

"We don't get much TV down here."

"It was a movie."

"No movie theater either."

Grant shrugged. Some jokes were best left unexplained. "So. I'm a stranger."

Cruz nodded and continued. "I don't know what business Macready is in. But it isn't local, I know that."

"Not legal either, I bet."

"And he is not in it alone. He has partners from out of town. Word is there was some friction there. Macready is wary of strangers."

"Like me."

"A big man. Ex-military."

A light went on behind Grant's eyes.

"He thinks I'm a hit man?"

THE HEARSE FOLLOWED A gentle curve out through Study Butte and began the long, slow descent to the desert floor. That last revelation explained why Grant had been treated with kid gloves. Why Macready had been so annoyed when his son got him arrested coming back from Adobe Flats. It was the rest of the discussion that would shape Grant's decision about how to deal with Macready, though.

His recollection of that was put on hold as he approached Kathy's Kosmic Kowgirl Kafe. The Barbie-doll diner was coming up fast. Then the ugly pink bus pulled out of the parking lot and slammed to a halt across the tarmac, blocking the road. It looked like Macready had decided the kid gloves were off.

EIGHTEEN

THREE THINGS HAPPENED IN quick succession. The bus blocked the road. The hearse closed the distance. And a man with a gun stepped into the road and waved for Grant to pull onto the forecourt. Men with guns always demanded your attention. Grant hated guns. He acted on instinct.

Instead of slowing down, he floored the gas. The hearse sped forward. Grant checked his options in an instant. The road was impassable. A ditch ran along the left-hand side; no room for maneuver there. A dirty pickup was parked next to an ice cream van outside the diner. The Kosmic Kowgirl offered BAR-B-QUE in big letters. The ice cream van offered sno-cones. The pickup offered more men with guns. Two men in cowboy hats, as big and dirty as the first.

The first man realized the hearse wasn't going to stop and whipped his handgun into a hasty firing position. He fired two shots that didn't even hit Texas. Too fast. Too panicky. High and wide. The gunman dived to his right, through the open door of the bus. The other two stepped away from their pickup and turned their guns towards the onrushing hearse. Steadier hands.

Grant swerved onto the dusty forecourt towards the cowboys. More people die on the roads each year than are killed by gunshot wounds. Best way to keep death off the roads was to drive on the sidewalk. Grant pointed the hearse at the gunmen. Steady hands became dithery aim. The three shots they managed to get off were as wild as their compadre's. General direction. Wide of the target. Then they were diving for cover, too, behind the flimsy ice cream van.

The hearse was big and heavy. It was built to carry dead weight in comfort and solidity. At sixty-plus miles an hour it was a hurtling missile. The wheels sideslipped on the hardpan, then steadied, throwing up a cloud of dust. Grant aimed for the ice cream van, and the cowboys dove for cover again, away from the van. The ice cream van disintegrated. Ice cream and chocolate sprinkles shot into the air. The roof of the van, with its giant fake swirl of ice cream, landed on the pickup's cab. The rear axle bounced across the forecourt.

The impact sent the hearse into a skid. It slewed sideways, the rear wheels losing traction, and ended up pointing back the way it had come. Grant feathered the brakes and clutch and got the heavy vehicle moving again, back towards Study Butte and the ghost town he'd just left. The man on the bus recovered first. He stuck his head up above the windows and pushed the cowboy hat back from where it had fallen over his eyes.

Grant saw him and realized his mistake. This wasn't a Macready ambush. It was the wife beater from Terlingua. The big greasy ratfuck of a Mexican trying to prove he was as tough as John Wayne with men as well as women. He smashed the bus window with his gun and fired three shots as the hearse struggled to pick up speed on the dusty forecourt. The wife beater's friends took heart from the reversal of fortune and started blasting away at the hearse.

Two shots thumped into the bodywork.

One shattered the long side window.

Another punched a starred hole in the windshield.

The rear wheels bit and the hearse steadied on its course. In the wrong direction. Grant steered towards the bus, then swerved left, targeting the pickup. If he managed to get out of this, he didn't want them all piling into their truck and giving chase. The pickup wasn't an ice cream van though. Not flimsy bodywork on a split frame chassis. It was a solid-built working vehicle. None of that mattered. Even a pickup couldn't drive without its engine.

Grant handbrake turned, skidding the rear wheels across the dirt. The hearse clipped the front of the pickup with its rear end and demolished the radiator and engine housing. Steam hissed from the twisted hood. Water poured lifeblood onto the ground. The skid threw up more dust. The cloud was almost impenetrable. More gunshots sounded behind him.

One more hit the bodywork.

Another starred hole appeared in the windshield.

The other shots missed the hearse but weren't entirely wasted. There was a ping of metal as a bullet ricocheted off something solid. A spark and a whoosh showed what it had hit: the propane tank supplying the Bar-B-Que. The tank exploded in a ball of flame that took out the front of Kathy's Kosmic Kowgirl Kafe and melted two fluorescent-green aliens sitting at a table outside.

The hearse steadied and drove past the diner. Grant turned away from the main road and swung around the back of the flaming building. A large overspill parking lot for when custom got brisk. Just as dry and dusty as the forecourt. The cloud grew and spread behind him. A second propane tank exploded, ripping the back out of the storage shed. One of the aliens drifted in the wind, its big-brained, bug-eyed head burning at the edges.

There were no more gunshots. The Mexicans were trying to beat off the attentions of a big waitress in a pink smock and a cowboy hat. She looked angry and not to be messed with. The wife beater was no match for her brute strength and extra weight. Unless he planned on shooting her, he'd have to retreat.

The hearse circled the diner and came out the other side. The wheels skidded one more time, then found solid ground on the two-lane blacktop. The pickup reversed out of the forecourt and went in the opposite direction. Steam and smoke chugged from the engine.

Grant threw them one last glance in his rear-view mirror, then focused on what lay ahead. Doc Cruz's parting shot pointed the way.

"Macready ain't sure if you're a hit man or not. That's why he wants to keep you close—until he can figure that out."

"By offering me a job?"

"Can you think of a better way?"

"Wouldn't that get me too close to whatever he's doing?"

Cruz raised his eyebrows and smiled.

"Asked and answered. Maybe you should have accepted."

NINETEEN

GRANT DIDN'T THINK HE could simply walk up to Macready and tell him he'd reconsidered. He reckoned he'd have to take a different route. Luckily for him the different route presented itself almost as soon as he got back to Absolution.

The town hadn't changed while he'd been away. There was no reason that it should. But something was different. He tried to put his finger on it as the hearse bounced over the railroad crossing and approached the intersection with First Street. He stopped at the junction. Avenue D straight ahead. Left towards the Absolution Motel or right towards Gilda's Grill at Sixto's. Nothing strange about that. No obvious signs that the world had moved on or that Absolution had changed its pattern of heat and misery.

Grant surveyed the skyline. The houses were the same as when he'd left. There was no gaping hole where burned-out buildings used to stand. There was no smoke cloud or wreckage or any other sign of violence on the outside. But violence had come to town, and it had come in the shape of Jim Grant. Let off the leash by a wife-beating Mexican and his friends.

The restraint Grant had shown since coming to Absolution was gone.

The engine ticked over in neutral. The needle showed that the gas tank was barely a quarter full. Grant was working up to telling Hunter Athey about the damaged rear fender, but there was no need to give the hearse back running on empty. If he turned left, he could pack his bag and leave Absolution behind. He didn't. Grant turned right towards Sixto's, and the future was set.

"You need to drive more careful once you're off the main roads."

The man working the pump wasn't the old Mexican from before and he wasn't Scott Macready. He could have been Macready's distant cousin though. Same slant of the cowboy hat. Same insolent body language. Same Texan drawl. He uncapped the gas tank and slid the nozzle home. He clicked the trigger on auto and left it to fill up while he examined the broken window and dented bodywork.

Grant made a that's-the-way-it-goes gesture.

"Loose chippings and potholes. It's dangerous out there."

"This is Texas, mister. It's dangerous everywhere."

"Can't argue with that."

The dog was still guarding the compound. Wrecked cars were still piled high beyond the wire fence. The pair of army jeeps was still parked in front of the workshop doors. The dog barked as if it remembered Grant. Its stumpy tail wagged hard enough to bring up dust. Foam dripped from its jaws, and Grant vowed to keep his distance no matter how friendly old Pedro looked.

The pump jockey poked a finger into one of the bullet holes in the bodywork. "Looks like you hit more than potholes."

Grant nodded.

"A statistical anomaly."

"A what?"

"More people die on the roads than are killed by gunshot. The anomaly is that I nearly got two in one."

The pump jockey didn't look any the wiser. Grant gave up.

"Target practice. Too near the road."

The cowboy nodded his understanding.

"Yeah. Them road signs are mighty tempting."

Grant indicated the WELCOME TO ABSOLUTION sign across the road.

"Seems like it."

The gas pump continued to hum, the display clocking up the quantity and price with a little ding for every cycle. Fumes shimmered around the filler cap in the heat. The most dangerous time when filling up. Ninety percent of gas station fires were started by fume ignition, not the petrol itself. Not like Rambo dropping his Zippo in a spreading pool of gasoline. Grant backed away from the smell and glanced towards the diner.

Sarah Hellstrom was looking out of the window.

That was the other decision Grant had been mulling over. He supposed there had never been any doubt which way that one would go. Filling up the hearse might have been the polite thing to do, but the gas station being next to the diner was the real motive.

Grant nodded at Sarah.

Sarah didn't nod back.

A finger of doubt stroked the back of Grant's neck. He watched her turn away from the window and disappear into the shadows. The pump continued to *ding, ding, ding*, the cycle slowing as the tank reached capacity. The trigger clicked off and the pump stopped.

The cowboy followed Grant's gaze and his eyes slitted into a sly little smile. A secret smile that Grant wasn't supposed to see. Grant ignored the implication. In a town this small there would always be gossip and innuendo. Let them think what they wanted.

The pump jockey wiped his hands on a greasy cloth. "You paying cash?"

"Yes."

Grant took the money wallet out of his back pocket and followed the cowboy to the office. He noted the amount on the pump display and began to count banknotes from the wallet. The office door creaked as he went through. Another fly zapped itself on the electronic bug catcher above the door. The old Mexican was sitting behind the counter. He rang in the amount and the till drawer opened. He wouldn't meet Grant's eyes. The first sign that things weren't right. The second, Grant corrected himself. The first was Sarah turning away without acknowledging him.

The pump jockey stood with his back against the door. The Mexican moved to the back of the office. The fly died a slow and painful death. Grant's eyes flicked around the hot interior. Front door—blocked. Door in the rear—partly open. Two men in the room—the Mexican and the cowboy. Grant discounted the Mexican. He was an employee but not hired muscle. The pump jockey was no hard man either. That left the partly open door at the rear.

The pump jockey stuffed the rag in his back pocket. "I hear you're all kinds of accident prone."

Grant looked at the cowboy but half turned towards the rear door. Peripheral vision gave him good sightlines to both.

"You reckon?"

The cowboy moved away from the front door. The Mexican sat behind the counter and almost disappeared. The rear door moved slightly, and a gentle breeze wafted dust across the floor. The view through the opening was sand and scrub and the parched landscape behind the service station.

Grant relaxed his hands. Took half a step towards the pump jockey. The nearest threat. "How d'you work that out?"

The desert wind picked up and slammed the back door shut. The noise was loud in the confined space of Sixto's. Grant tensed, ready for action. Nobody came through the door. Nobody yanked it open to come charging in.

The cowboy smirked.

"Potholes and target practice. And spilled coffee lids."

Now Grant understood what the sly little smile had been all about. Towards the window of Gilda's Grill. The threat wasn't coming from the rear door to the office. Before he finished the thought, Grant was out of the front door and crossing the forecourt.

TWENTY

THE DINER WAS HOT even though the sun was almost down. The full-length windows meant the sun had been blazing across the vinyl booths for most of the day. The smell of coffee and hot plastic filled the room. Hunter Athey was right. Sarah Hellstrom should invest in air conditioning.

Grant came through the door at a measured pace. Years as a cop and a soldier told him never to go barging through a door in a conflict situation, especially if you don't know the enemy's strength or position. Grant didn't know either of them, so he entered the diner with hooded eyes and flexed muscles.

Sarah was alone behind the counter.

The rest of the diner was empty.

Grant felt relieved but didn't relax. He'd learned over the years to trust his instincts, and his instincts told him something was wrong. His first priority was to check on Sarah. She turned to face him as he crossed towards the counter. The espresso machine was gleaming, its chrome boiler shiny enough to see your face in. Sarah folded the tea towel she'd been using and glanced through the window.

"I see you're still having trouble with other people's cars."

The words were light but there was tension in her voice.

Grant went with the flow. "Back roads and hillbillies. Dangerous combination."

"We don't have hillbillies in Texas."

"And you don't have moss either."

Sarah nodded but didn't smile. "Too dry for moss. No hills for hillbillies."

"I didn't want to sound racist."

"Saying it like it is isn't racist."

"Okay, then. Couple of Mexicans took exception to me stepping in on a friend of theirs."

"What did he do?"

"Burned his wife on a stove. Bruised her arms."

Sarah shuddered. She resisted touching the bruises under her sleeve. "That just makes him a man, then. Not a Mexican."

There was bite in her tone. A complete change to when she'd loaned him the car. He didn't have her down as a man hater even though she had plenty of reason to be judgmental. Grant changed the subject.

"Coffee machine working today?"

Meaning was she going to serve him or make an excuse? She didn't make an excuse. Without asking what he wanted, she began to make a latte. Expert hands worked the steam pipes and the coffee grounds. The milk frothed and the coffee poured, leaving a brown swirl across the top of his cream. She didn't put a lid on his paper cup.

Grant sat on a stool at the counter and slid the money across.

Sarah didn't argue, ringing it into the cash register.

An uneasy silence developed. Grant looked at the woman who'd mopped his spillage but didn't press her to speak. This town had a way of crushing people's spirits. He just didn't think Sarah Hellstrom was the crushable type. That was easy for Grant to think. He was a stranger in town. Whatever happened, he would be moving on like a rolling stone gathering no moss. Sarah would have to live here after he'd gone. She'd already rejected his suggestion that America had plenty of room for her elsewhere.

His eyes watched Sarah but they saw a lot more. The gleaming chrome boiler behind her reflected everything. A convex mirror on the rest of the diner. He sensed movement even before he saw it. The utility room door opened to his right. The front door opened to his left. Two men, one through each door. They walked tall and moved slow. Measured steps on either side of Grant.

THE COWBOY FROM THE hotel sat on the stool to Grant's right. The man who'd been sitting out front of the hotel with him stood behind him, arms folded across his chest, standing guard. Grant sipped his coffee and put the cup back on the counter. Steam drifted like smoke from a burning cigarette.

Nobody spoke.

Sarah held her breath.

Grant let his out in a long, steady exhale.

The cowboy swung his stool to face Grant. "You're in my seat."

Grant looked at the cowboy while keeping half an eye on the other fella. "Is this like me being in your room at the hotel?"

"Just like that."

"You block booked this seat as well?"

"It's my favorite."

The different route to getting a job with Macready. Opportunity knocked. Grant wasn't ready to take it yet. He moved to the next stool and slid his coffee along the counter. The cowboy moved onto the vacant stool and shuffled his backside to get comfortable. It didn't work. He looked at Grant's stool instead.

"This ain't comfy anymore. I think I like that one."

Grant could see the pattern developing. The bullies' rulebook on playground intimidation. He let his shoulders sag as if deflated but used the chrome boiler to keep an eye on the big fella behind him. Grant stood and picked up his coffee. Followed the playbook he'd seen in numerous movies.

"Why don't you tell me where to sit?"

The cowboy switched seats again but didn't speak. After a suitable pause, Grant sat on his original stool. He took a sip of his coffee and put the cup down on the counter, tempting the cowboy to make the next move. The bully couldn't resist. As obvious as the movie this scene came from.

"You forgot your sugar."

He picked up the sugar dispenser and turned it upside down. The nozzle poured a steady stream into Grant's cup and just kept pouring. When the coffee had turned to hot, runny sludge, he put the sugar back on the counter. The cowboy smirked. The backup man nodded his approval. Grant looked at his latte, then pushed it across the counter.

"Was that your favorite film growing up?"

The question caught the cowboy by surprise.

"Huh?"

"*Bad Day at Black Rock*."

"Never heard of it."

"Spencer Tracy as a one-armed man coming to town. Lee Marvin as a cowboy trying to goad him."

The cowboy thought he'd try being smart.

"The one-armed man that killed Harrison Ford's wife?"

Grant shook his head.

"Different movie. No. Lee Marvin does all that 'you're in my room' stuff at the hotel. And Ernest Borgnine does the pushing at the diner."

He turned towards the cowboy.

"Only with ketchup instead of sugar. Same thing, though—messing with Tracy's food. Chili, not coffee. But much the same. You must have seen it on TV because you're playing it word for word."

The cowboy let a faint smile play across his lips. "Oh yeah. I think I might have seen it now."

Grant didn't need the boiler to see. He could watch both men from his position swivelled around on the stool. The bodyguard still had both arms folded across his chest. Good for intimidation but not very clever if you needed to move fast. The part-time deputy was leaning on the counter, aiming for threatening but just proving his lack of knowledge about angles and levers. Like leaning back in his chair at the hotel. Looks cool. Completely impractical.

Grant kept his voice friendly but his eyes turned hard. "You remember how that turned out?"

The smile went from the cowboy's face. In the split second before it happened he obviously did remember how Spencer Tracy had beaten Ernest Borgnine senseless using one arm and leverage. He tried to stand up too late. Grant snatched his cup and threw the sludge into the cowboy's face. Still hot enough to sting, but it was the shock factor Grant was looking for.

The cowboy brought both hands up to his face.

The bodyguard tried to unfold his arms.

Grant leaned back on his stool and used the leverage to swing one leg upwards, aiming the kick between the big fella's legs. The wind left him in a gush and he doubled over, grabbing his balls. Grant sidestepped from his stool and used the big man's forward momentum to grab his head and slam it down onto the stool. Blood and snot exploded from his nose, and he went down hard.

The cowboy's eyes were gummed shut. Grant bent one arm so that the elbow protruded, then slammed the pointed end into the cowboy's face. He went backwards over his stool and landed upside down. It was only loose-limbed shock that saved him from breaking his neck. Grant stamped on his balls for good measure, giving both men the same thing to worry about.

Thirty seconds. Two men down. Both disabled for as long as it would take for their wedding tackle to stop aching. They lay moaning on the floor. Grant leaned down and grabbed the cowboy by the hair.

"And you know the funny thing? Tracy's character was called Macready."

He let the head go. It banged on the stool's footrest. "So. Take me to your leader."

It couldn't have gone better. Apart from the look of surprise and disgust on Sarah Hellstrom's face. That wasn't something Grant had planned for. He tried to ignore her as he began reviving the fallen cowboy.

TWENTY-ONE

A BLAZING SUNSET COLORED the end of Grant's second day in Absolution. Scattered clouds along the horizon became torn shreds of golden fire. The sky turned from powder blue to burnt umber, and stars began to blink on the edge of night high up in the darkening stratosphere. The bleached white walls of Macready's compound were painted red by the dying sun as Grant pulled the hearse up to the gates.

The cowboy looked shamefaced in the passenger seat. The other fella had been left at Sixto's. Grant didn't need both of them to prove his point. He sounded the horn, then waited. Thirty seconds later, the gates swung open and Grant drove into the courtyard. The hacienda looked even more like the Alamo in the evening light. Flickering torches burned from brackets on the walls. More for effect than for light, Grant reckoned. Macready seemed to like playing with the Western image.

There was a lot of activity in front of the garages and barrack block. Men packing equipment into canvas bags and strip-cleaning their weapons on blankets spread across the porch. Mercenaries.

The ex-military types he'd seen on his last visit. Grant parked the hearse on the opposite side of the courtyard.

Smoke drifted across the patio. At first Grant thought the torches were burning oil, but then he caught a whiff of cooked meat. The barbecue pit was going full tilt. Three men in cooks' whites were turning steaks on the grill and working a rotisserie loaded with skewered birds. Hot fat flared and spat. Portable heaters battled the cool night air, and patio lights illuminated the table where Grant had sat with Macready. Several more tables had been set up around the barbecue pit. Waiters brought out beer coolers and bottles of wine. Heavy candles flickered on the tables. Again, more for effect than illumination.

Macready stood in the doorway to the hacienda.

Grant nudged the cowboy to get out of the hearse, then he did the same. They walked side by side up the patio steps. Macready barked an instruction to one the waiters, then turned his attention to Grant. The cowboy was limping slightly to avoid crushing his swollen balls. Macready threw him a hard glance and jerked his head in dismissal. The cowboy went inside, leaving the two men to talk. Macready leaned against the doorframe and folded his arms.

"I guess you're not passing through after all."

Grant stood in front of him. "I found a reason to stick around."

Macready smiled. "And it's a good reason. She's a beauty, ain't she?"

"When she's not marked up."

"That is a regret of mine. Scott don't know much about restraint."

"Just so you know. He touches her again, it'll be me not showing restraint."

"That's between you and him. Me? I'm only interested in business."

Grant stepped aside to let a waitress pass. "Party planning? That your business, is it?"

Macready unfolded his arms and pushed off from the doorframe. He walked across to the table and surveyed the preparations. The barbecue pit was spitting fire. The extra tables were set. The only things missing were the guests and the food. Grant followed Macready. The cooked meat made his mouth water. He couldn't help licking his lips. Macready noticed.

"No. I just like to treat my men right. Before going into action. You'd be welcome to join us. If you were one of my men."

Grant wondered what action he was sending his men into. The mercenaries who were busy preparing for battle. He'd worked with soldiers of fortune before during his army days. He didn't like them. A professional soldier had pride in his regiment and unit. Mercenaries only respected the money. Still, beggars couldn't be choosers when trying to find out what Macready was up to.

"As opposed to being one of your cats."

"Cats or employees. If they do their job, they've nothing to fear."

"And what job's that?"

Macready scrutinized Grant as if sizing him up, gauging his strengths and weaknesses. The man in black looking to hire a new hand. Veiled eyes noticing everything. Instead of answering, he asked a question of his own. "I understand you ran into a little trouble near the border."

"Down that way. Yeah."

"But not with the border guards."

"It was a long way from the border."

"Involving Mexicans though. Right?"

Grant didn't answer, waiting to see where Macready was going with this.

"Friends of Eduardo Cruz?"

Grant noticed a change in tone. Harder. He shrugged as he answered.

"Acquaintances of a patient."

"Husband of a battered wife is what I heard."

The head cook stepped back from the barbecue and held up a metal triangle and a stick. He rattled the stick around the frame, signalling that dinner was served. The men across the yard finished what they were doing and began to drift towards the tables. Grant was aware of the approaching menace, but the men seemed more interested in the food than in Grant. He turned back to Macready.

"I can't abide a wife beater. A man or a sleeveless vest."

Macready ignored Grant's answer.

"Three men with guns. You were unarmed."

Grant almost said that he used to patrol West Yorkshire with nothing but a stab vest and a baton but stopped himself just in time. Admitting to being a cop didn't seem like the way to go here.

"Just me and the hearse."

"You acquitted yourself well. You and the hearse. Caused a fair bit of damage though. No burgers and ice cream on the 170 for a while."

"Maybe they can come here."

Macready waved a hand towards the barbecue pit. "We don't flip burgers here. We eat real meat."

Then he pointed at the hearse parked in the shadows. "I don't think Hunter Athey will be too happy with you."

Torch flames reflected off the windows, highlighting the one that was missing and the bullet holes punched in the bodywork. Grant looked at the damage, then turned back towards Macready. "I filled it up, though."

Macready's smile didn't reach his eyes. "I heard about that too. Petrol fumes and coffee stains just follow you around."

That wasn't a question so Grant didn't answer. Macready stopped smiling. "You and other people's vehicles don't mix either."

"It's not me. Other folk seem to have a problem with that."

Macready stuck his hands in his pockets and studied Grant. He let out a sigh and appeared to make a decision. The smile was back on his face.

"That's as maybe, but it relates directly to what I propose. If I was to offer you a seat at my table. And gainful employment."

Grant waited for the proposal.

Macready let the moment stretch a beat before continuing.

"You ain't too good with foreign cars and hearses, that's a fact. What are you like driving a truck?"

TEXAS CLAIMED ITS STEAKS were the best in the world. Grant had heard that claim before. In Adelaide they considered Australian beef to be the best. He'd had a steak in Denver once, and they reckoned Colorado beef was the best. Whatever the truth, one thing was for certain: Texas steaks were the biggest he'd ever eaten. Thick and wide and melt-in-your-mouth gorgeous. Throw in a few fries and a side of coleslaw and this could almost be the perfect meal.

Apart from the company.

There wasn't much small talk, and nobody got too friendly. There was none of that laughing and joking associated with most dinner parties, and nobody drank too much. The beer cooler was there for everyone, or wine if that was their choice. The men surrounding Grant drank one or the other but only one drink each. Nobody was going to get drunk on the eve of combat. These guys might be mercenaries, but they were observing military discipline. Polite in the presence of strangers. Not too friendly with the new man. He remembered that from his army days. Replacements died early. Nobody wanted to get too friendly with them. Grant wondered who he was replacing. Not the cat, he hoped.

Music played in the background, some middle-of-the-road, easy listening stuff. Knives and forks clattered on plates. Ice clinked in glasses of water, served as a side order with the beer and the food. People talked in small groups. There was some backslapping and a few raised voices but nothing too energetic. It was a scene Grant had seen many times during his military career and not too infrequently in the Westerns he'd watched growing up. If this were a spaghetti Western, Clint Eastwood would be sitting quietly while the Italians roared with laughter and badly lip-synced dialogue. The head villain would bring out a suit of armor and use it for target practice while the Man with No Name pretended to get drunk.

Macready didn't bring out a suit of armor. Grant didn't pretend to get drunk. Nobody was getting drunk tonight. There was work to be done. Trouble was, apart from knowing he was going to be driving a truck, Grant didn't know what that work would be. It involved heavily armed men and big lorries and the cover of darkness. That was all he knew.

Melted wax ran down the sides of the candles like blood and pooled across the table. The flames flickered in the still night air. The wall-mounted torches did the same. One by one the soldiers finished their last supper and pushed empty plates away. They drained their beers and swilled it down with iced water. Even the music became quieter. Preparations were almost over.

Macready waved a hand.

Waitresses cleared the tables.

Grant took a drink of water and slid his glass across the table. Light reflected off the flat, calm surface like a puddle in a footprint. A low, dull noise began to compete with the music, as if the bass was turned up too loud. The smooth, calm surface in Grant's glass broke up as vibration shook the ground. Concentric circles in the confines of the glass. The noise grew louder. A noise that seemed to be coming from everywhere and yet from no direction in particular. It changed from an aimless muttering into something more solid. The sound of big, throaty engines coming from outside the compound walls.

Macready stood and everyone fell silent.

"Grab your gear, boys. Time to saddle up."

The mercenaries collected their equipment and moved towards a dried-out wooden door in the compound's side wall. Grant followed, awaiting instructions. The door led to the outside near the abandoned athletics track. There were no streetlamps. The Christmas Mountains in the distance were picked out by moonlight and starshine. The trucks parked in line along the finishing straight were thrown into silhouette. Big desert-camouflaged military trucks, their unit insignia standing out in the cold blue light. They weren't army surplus. They were still in service. This was an army-approved operation.

TWENTY-TWO

THE TRUCKS RUMBLED THROUGH Absolution in the dead of night. Column of five. A big noisy military convoy plus the two army jeeps from Sixto's, one up ahead and one bringing up the rear. The town was dark and silent. Nobody turned their lights on to see what was happening. Nobody wanted to see who was passing through in the middle of the night. Absolution turned a blind eye to what it didn't want to know.

Grant was driving the third truck. Middle of the convoy. The navigator in the passenger seat was largely redundant since all Grant had to do was follow the truck in front. There was no small talk in the cab. The truck bounced over uneven ground as it left the two-lane blacktop and headed south on the same road Grant had taken in Sarah Hellstrom's little foreign car. Dust formed a cloud trail in the darkness that a blind man could have followed. In Absolution even the blind men weren't looking.

Headlights scythed through the dark, a string of lights picking out the winding road and dry creek bed on the way to Adobe Flats. Absolution fell away in the distance, and pretty soon the last few outlying dwellings disappeared too. The properties Macready had bought so that he owned everything along the route towards Big Bend National Park. All except the hacienda at Adobe Flats that he'd burned out to clear his path. Where the path led was still in question since nobody had told Grant where they were going.

The truck churned up sand as it bounced out of the creek bed and back onto the road. It followed the winding contours of the landscape up from the arroyo, then crested the ridge between two crumbling buttes. The road continued down the final stretch before the foothills that marked the beginning of Big Bend. The small group of buildings at the bottom stood out in the moonlight. The burned-out hacienda and bunkhouse that used to be Eduardo Cruz's home.

"How far we going?"

Grant focused on the taillights of the truck in front. There was no dust trail now that they were driving on rock and gravel. The convoy had driven straight past the turnaround for Cruz's Alamo and followed the deep-rutted track into the foothills. The trucks were way beyond the foothills now, following a winding trail among the rocky outcrops and ledges of alien terrain. The right-hand wheels were close to the edge of a sheer drop, but there was no room to move left. The other drivers must have followed this route before because they drove faster than Grant felt comfortable with. He used soft hands and full concentration to keep the wheels on course and away from the edge.

Grant kept his eyes on the road, using peripheral vision to see the navigator. "Just so I know how long I've got to keep us from plunging to our deaths."

The passenger spoke for the first time since they set off.

"You're doing fine. Trust me, I'd let you know if you were gonna get us killed."

Moonlight showed a deep valley to the right. Hard terrain of scrub and rock and a few straggly trees. A cliff wall was the only view to the left, twisting and turning along the hillside path. The convoy was still climbing, making the drop to the right even deeper.

"I wouldn't want the US Army coming after me for denting the fender."

The passenger unwound a touch. "That what the British Army would do?"

"The British Army would come after me if I scuffed a shoe."

"Well, don't worry about dinging this baby. So long as they get 'em back, the mechanics'll spruce 'em up. Drop it off the cliff and we might have a few questions to answer."

"They sound more understanding than Hertz, then."

"They're getting paid more than Hertz."

Grant didn't want to press the point. Who was hiring the vehicles out or how high up the ranks it went. He doubted the US military had a policy of letting mercenaries use their vehicles. That meant somebody in high places was doing a deal on the side. It didn't explain where they were going, though.

"So how much further?"

The passenger turned to Grant. "How's your Spanish?"

Grant nodded that he was impressed. "They let us cross the border?"

The navigator was almost becoming friendly because he laughed. "This is a military exercise. You think we don't know where to cross?"

"A live fire exercise?"

"It's the only kind. Gotta be careful with Mexicans."

"Remember the Alamo. Right."

The navigator nodded.

"Wouldn't want anyone slipping away on the way back."

Grant agreed even if he didn't know what he was agreeing to. "Hell no."

The road began to widen up ahead. It swung to the right, around a jagged outcrop, then curled back into the mountain. As Grant negotiated the curve, he eased off the gas, just in time to avoid the truck in front of him. The driver up ahead slewed to his left and slammed the brakes on. The back wheels skidded towards the sheer drop on the right. Brake lights turned the road bright red. Grant stopped the truck inches from a collision.

Air brakes hissed. Engines idled. Doors slammed up ahead. Some slammed behind Grant's truck. He got out to see what the problem was. The navigator slid across to the driver's seat because the cliff face blocked his door. Grant moved around the stricken truck, watching his footing near the edge. His silhouette went from blood red in the truck's taillights to black in the darkness round the corner.

Three men were standing in the shadows. A fourth stepped from behind the truck's brake lights like a demon in red. The cowboy hat was still pulled down over his eyes. Grant reckoned this was as close to hard work as Scott Macready had ever come. When he snapped his fingers two more men came up behind Grant and cocked their weapons. For effect, so that Grant knew they were serious. The three men in front did the same.

Scott Macready just smiled.

THE TRUCKS SHUDDERED AS their engines were turned off. Silence filled the void. Away from the headlights the world was dark and dangerous, picked out only slightly by a pale blue dusting of moonlight. Grant kept his body loose and his breathing even as he weighed his options. There weren't many to choose from until he knew what Macready's intentions were. So far the omens weren't good.

Scott Macready stepped in front of his men, proving that he was as much a stranger to combat as he was to hard work. He had immediately negated two of the gunmen, and the third had as much chance of shooting the two behind Grant as hitting Grant himself. First rule of catching your enemy in crossfire is to angle your aim away from your colleagues on the opposite flank. That told Grant something about the mercenaries too, but it didn't improve his situation.

The two blocked gunmen stepped to either side of Macready, opening up their angles across the killing zone and protecting the two behind Grant. So much for that idea. Macready wasn't the threat; he was the catalyst. Whatever was going to happen would happen on his command. It would be better if he wasn't calm, clear, and collected when he made that decision.

Grant decided to probe. "Does your dad know you're out this late?"

Macready's smile didn't falter. "My father knows a lot of things. But he ain't here."

Grant took half a step to his right, careful not to get too close to the crumbling edge of the road. "I heard he wasn't too happy when you got me arrested."

Five gun barrels followed Grant's movement.

Macready stayed in the middle. "There were some questions about that."

"He give you a hard time, did he?"

"He gives everybody a hard time."

"But not when you're slapping Sarah around."

Macready's eyes blinked. A nervous tick began to twitch at one side of his mouth. He worked hard to calm the twitch down, but it still trembled at the corner of his lips. He tried for a steely glare and almost achieved it. It was the toughest he was ever going to look.

"Me and Sarah are none of your business."

"It is if you touch her again."

The glare disguised a hint of embarrassment. Macready didn't want his dirty laundry being aired in front of the hired help. Grant didn't want the hired help opening fire from a position of strength. He took another slow half step to his right. Dirt and gravel crumbled off the edge of the road and tumbled into the void. Grant listened to gauge how far it fell. It sounded like a long drop over uneven ground.

Macready slid a hand into his back pocket. "My father was wrong about you."

Grant watched the hand and got ready to move. "How d'you figure that?"

Macready's forearm tensed as the hand gripped something behind him. "He wanted you treated like gelignite on a bumpy road. In case you'd been sent from up north."

"Business partners not happy with him, are they?"

"They're happy with results."

"But they don't trust him, huh?"

"In this business nobody trusts anybody."

"The party organizing business?"

The hand began to move from behind Macready's back. "The business we are partaking in tonight."

Grant only had one place to go. He relaxed, ready to go there. "Armed men and lorries across the border?"

"Lorries?"

"Sorry. Trucks."

Macready shook his head. "Armed men protecting trucks coming back across the border. Wouldn't want any of the cargo wandering off."

"No, you wouldn't, would you?"

Macready brought his hand round. It was holding something small and black. "The old man thought you were a hit man sent to stir things up."

He swung it out in front of him. "He needn't have worried about his partners though, did he? 'Cause you ain't no hit man."

He opened Grant's badge wallet.

"You're a cop."

The badge wasn't going to save him, but the revelation did put a moment's doubt in the mercenaries' aim. Five gun barrels lowered briefly. Decision time. Stay here and die for certain or take the fall and maybe die on the way down. It was no decision. The gun barrels swung up again. Macready closed the wallet. And Grant stepped over the edge and into the abyss.

TWENTY-THREE

PAIN AND GUNFIRE FILLED the night. The drop was steep and uneven. It was dotted with rocks and scrub and dry, twisted trees. The trees and bushes slowed his descent. The rocks broke bones and tore skin. Despite trying to keep his body limp, the pain forced him into reflex actions to protect his head and face. Grant tumbled like a rolling stone gathering no moss. What he did gather was pain and blood.

The side of his head slammed against a boulder. One arm snapped above the wrist. His knees were skinned and his back knocked so hard he felt paralyzed from the waist down. He flipped over, landing on his side before bouncing and rolling some more. He kept his mouth closed to protect his teeth and stop himself biting his tongue, but something mashed his lips and grazed the side of his face. Miraculously his nose avoided any damage.

Dust and rubble tumbled with him. Snapped-off tree branches snagged at his clothes. Pain filled his world. Pain and gunfire. He could hear it despite the sound of breaking bones and jarring concussion. He couldn't see the muzzle flashes because his eyes were closed. Ricochets careened all around him.

And still he kept tumbling. Less than halfway down the rugged hillside. When his eyes flicked open, the moonlight seemed brighter down here, away from the headlights and the gunshots. It was a silver disc in the sky one minute, then a powder blue dusting of light on the landscape another, depending on which way was up at any given moment. Rolling and bouncing. Up was down, then down was up. His world kept turning and pain was added to pain. The slope leveled out towards the bottom, but it was a false hope. It was a dusty ski jump at the bottom of the hill, and it shot Grant out for one final drop into empty space. He flew through the air like a rag doll. The impact of hitting bottom knocked the rest of wind from his lungs and left him dead and broken.

Almost dead.

Torches cut through the night, searching the hillside for the body. The gunfire stopped. The torch beams were off target by twenty feet. To Grant's left. Or was it his right? He was barely conscious. The pain had become all-encompassing, leaving no room for any other feeling. Not heat nor cold nor the warm breath of life.

Raised voices sounded on the road above. Nobody tried to come down and find him. They were running out of time. There was a schedule to keep. A rendezvous at the border. Nobody could survive a fall like that. They were almost right. Grant lay in the shelter of the rocky outcrop that he'd sailed over and listened. The engines started up again. Doors slammed. Then the trucks set off towards their rendezvous, leaving the meddlesome cop for dead.

GRANT SLEPT. OR WAS unconscious. Whichever it was, he was out for so long that the night sky had turned to predawn blue before he woke into a world of pain. He knew he should have stayed awake.

Letting himself slip into the half-life in this condition was danger-ous. That's how people died—when their bodies gave up and told them to rest. Just take a nap. Let your senses shut down for a while. Then, when they tried to wake up again, their systems wouldn't come back online. That's when the doctor would pronounce life extinct and you'd get your toe tagged in the county morgue.

Grant jerked awake. The mortuary out back of the Absolution Motel. That was his destination. Not as a corpse but as the first stop towards recovery. Recovery was a long way off. Surviving at all wasn't a foregone conclusion. First thing Grant had to do was take stock. Judging by the pain pulsing through his body, that stock was going to be low.

He went to sleep again. He couldn't help it. Sleep eased the pain, or at least when he was unconscious he didn't notice it. Even before assessing his injuries Grant's body began the miracle of self-healing. He'd seen it in combat. He'd seen it at road accidents. Mangled bod-ies that had no right to be alive, clinging onto that most precious of gifts until help arrived. Help wasn't going to arrive at the bottom of the rocky escarpment. Grant was going to have to go to the help. But first he needed rest.

THE SECOND TIME GRANT woke up, the pain had eased. Until he tried to move. Then it came back full force. That was good. Pain was an indication of where the damage was. According to the pain, the damage was everywhere. He started at the top down.

His head was throbbing but his eyes worked fine. A bit blurred at first until he blinked the dust out of them. That was essential. He'd need his eyes to help assess the damage. Sight and touch. To exam-ine his head, he raised one hand to check for cuts and fractures.

Pain knifed up his arm.

Wrong hand. The one that was broken just above the wrist. He blinked tears of pain out of his eyes and examined the wrist. He was wrong. The arm wasn't broken above the wrist; the pain just felt like it was coming from there. The wrist jutted at an unnatural angle: dislocated. That was better than a break because it was something he could reset himself. It was worse than a break because it meant there was more pain to come. Imminent pain. Right now.

Grant shuffled into a sitting position. A band of pain set his chest on fire. A couple of ribs were broken, but his spine felt okay. The numbness in his legs receded to pins and needles. He ticked those things off his list, then concentrated on the wrist. Using his good hand he laid the forearm across his lap. The wrist bulged out of its socket on the top of the arm and the hand lay flat, forming a fleshy S-bend. He gritted his teeth and carefully took hold of the hand. The dull ache became hot, sharp fire. The path of the dislocation was clear. The route back into the socket was equally clear. He'd seen it done before, just never done the procedure on himself.

He took the hand in a firm grip. Sweat broke out on his face. He slowly pulled forward. The pain intensified. The joint resisted. He pulled harder. His stomach threatened to lurch up his throat. He roared a primal scream to distract himself. Then a loud pop and a stab of pain signaled success. The wrist ached but the pain eased. He wiggled his fingers. They ached too.

He let out a sigh and focused his mind.

The predawn mist had burned off and the sky was already a dazzling blue. He checked his watch, but that had been on the injured wrist. The band had gouged flesh when it was torn off during the fall. He checked the length of the shadows. They were still long across the canyon floor. It was early morning. The rocky outcrop he was lying behind was still in shade. He had no idea how long the midnight operation had taken, but he guessed it must have been completed before dawn. That meant they'd already driven back along the winding road above him. Either they didn't have time to look for his body or they'd searched and not found him.

That didn't mean they wouldn't come back in daylight.

He quickly finished his injury report.

There was dried blood and pain down one side of his head, but it didn't feel like he'd cracked his skull. His lip was cut and swollen. The wrist he'd already attended to, and his ribs were cracked. That was the upper body sorted. The rest was easier to examine visually and physically. His jeans were torn and both knees skinned but there were no broken bones and no cuts so deep they'd need stitches. His trainers had stayed on his feet. Good. He'd be doing a lot of walking.

A loud squawk made him jump. He squinted into the sky and saw a huge black silhouette circling overhead. He'd seen buzzards in the movies but usually as a matte effect or a composite shot. Back in Yorkshire they had hawks and crows. Whatever this thing was, it was bigger than a Yorkshire bird. Typical America. Even the carrion was super sized.

He checked the sun again. It was beyond the hillside he'd tumbled down. East. His eyes followed an arc across the sky towards the west. He wasn't sure how far they'd come from Absolution but he reckoned not as far south as Terlingua. That would be a long haul west across rough country.

Using the path of the sun as a guide, he turned right. North. The direction that any search party would be coming from. An injured man struggling over harsh terrain would be easy pickings. Even if he reached Adobe Flats, there was no way of getting a message to Hunter Athey. Grant would have to do some creative orienteering, and he'd better get started now.

He pushed himself up onto his feet. The world swayed around him. His vision swam, and he thought he was going to pass out. He took another deep breath. The horizon settled down. Everything ached, but the pain became more manageable. Holding the bad wrist across his chest to help protect the cracked ribs, he headed west. Just like Kirk Douglas and Robert Mitchum and their wagon train in *The Way West*, only slower.

TWENTY-FOUR

"HOLY SHIT ON A stick."

Hunter Athey jerked back in the doorway when the mortuary lights flickered on. Twilight was descending into night after another long, hot day in Absolution. A long, hot day that felt like an eternity for the bedraggled figure peering over the side of the wooden coffin. Grant lowered himself back into the cushioned interior.

"That bad, huh?"

Athey glanced over his shoulder, then stepped into the mortuary and closed the door. The dirt-encrusted blood down the side of Grant's face was cracked and weeping. His knees were tattered shambles of torn skin and bone.

Athey sized up Grant's needs in a few short glances. "They told me you'd gone missing when they dropped the hearse off."

Grant's lips were sore when he spoke. "Sorry about the damage."

Athey waved the apology aside. "What I heard was they've been looking for your body all day."

He went to the stainless-steel washbasin and rolled up his sleeves. "When they didn't find you, they searched here and the diner."

He soaked a towel and brought it over to the coffin. "How on earth did you…"

Athey was lost for words.

Grant tried to move his lips as little as possible. "Evade and destroy. Without the destroy bit."

His eyelids began to flutter, and the room tilted. He coughed up blood as he stared at the ceiling lights. Slipping into unconsciousness, the light grew brighter and hotter and infinitely more deadly.

EVADE AND DESTROY. PART of Grant's military training. Fine when you're fit and healthy. Harder when you're battered and bleeding and lacking proper equipment or supplies. Slow going over harsh terrain when your legs don't want to work and your head is spinning.

By the time the sun had reached its zenith, the rock and scrabble plain was baking hot. Grant had no food or water. There was no shade. He was a slow-moving target on open ground wearing an orange windcheater that stood out like a sore thumb. He took it off and turned it inside out. The beige lining blended with the desert landscape. There still wasn't any shade. Sean Connery's voice played in his head. "Where there is no shade from the sun, there is only desert. The desert I know very well." The Raisuli with a Scottish accent. Connery's Berber pirate might have known the desert well. Grant simply followed his nose.

He gave little consideration to evading his hunters because he wasn't convinced they'd come hunting for him. Not in daylight, when they'd have to explain what Grant was doing out here in the first place. It was a plausible argument, but in the end Grant didn't have much choice. Keep moving. Keep breathing. Anything else was icing on the cake.

Heading west into the wilderness instead of north towards Absolution would help a little bit. This wasn't one of those Saturday afternoon Westerns he'd grown up watching. Macready employed mercenaries and local heavies, not Navajo trackers. Even so, Grant was careful not to leave any obvious signs. He tore strips off his T-shirt to bind his knees. The blood down the side of his face had already congealed into a scabby carapace. The desert floor was threaded with layers of rock. He avoided the sandy bottom and made sure he didn't leave scuff marks on the rock. There was no blood trail to follow.

That was the extent of his evade and destroy technique. After that it was simply a case of keeping going. The heat was brain melting. The sun was so bright it forced his eyes into slits just to avoid going blind. It reflected off the rocks and the sand, turning the desert floor into a giant yellow fire. Even the hard blue sky was bleached to nothing, barely blue at all.

The heat was bad, but the dryness was a killer. Grant used his tongue to help salivate but it wasn't long before moisture was a thing of the past. He tore another section off his T-shirt and tied it around his head. He barked a laugh at the thought of himself on a Scarborough beach with a knotted handkerchief on his head. The seaside postcard image of the Yorkshireman on holiday.

He looked back over his shoulder. Time had become meaningless, but he must have been going for hours because the hillside road had faded into the distance. The world had become bright and dusty and colorless. What little greenery had clung to life on the rocky hillside had long since gone. Out here on the hardpan, there was nothing alive apart from Grant and a few scuttling creatures he didn't recognize. Then he saw a glint of light on the horizon to the east. He dropped to the ground and lay flat on his stomach to disguise his profile. So they were looking for him after all. He focused as best he could. Another glint of light. Then another. Further north of the first position. Towards Absolution. The obvious place for an injured man to be heading.

Grant rested for a few minutes until he was sure the hunters weren't coming his way, then he slid backwards into a gully and began trekking west again. Less concerned about the sandy bottom now. More concerned about the pain and the dizziness and the complete lack of moisture.

The day dragged on. His progress slowed down. The heat muddled his brain and dulled his senses. The sun arced across the desert and pointed the way. At one point he came across a stretch of two-lane blacktop running north to south. The 170 to Terlingua. Too far for him to reach in a single day. Too much heat for him to survive out here for two.

He crossed the road and turned right after a hundred yards. Using the 170 as a guide, he headed north towards Absolution. If he kept moving, he reckoned he'd be there before sunset. He was wrong. Twilight was already biting by the time he crossed the railroad tracks west of town. The office light was on at the motel. What surprised him was the damaged hearse parked out front.

That stopped him short.

If Macready's men had brought the hearse back, they might be waiting to see if Grant turned up as well. He watched from across the road. There was no obvious sign of a welcoming committee. There were no extra vehicles in the turnaround. There was no movement inside the office.

In the end, none of that mattered. Grant was out of options and out of water. He needed urgent medical attention. Careful not to be seen from the motel, he crossed the road at a crouch. He skirted the reception building and headed for the best place for a corpse to hide. The mortuary.

JARRING MOVEMENT WOKE HIM up. The glaring overhead lights had gone. The world had collapsed into a small, dark space that Grant couldn't identify. He wasn't in the mortuary anymore. He was in something that bounced and swayed and had a wooden lid.

Panic flared his eyes. He had a brief Edgar Allen Poe moment, a vision of being buried alive. He pushed at the coffin lid. It lifted easily. It wasn't nailed shut. Using his good hand, he opened a two-inch gap and peered out. Broken glass framed the window, and cool night air drifted across his face. The hearse was moving at more than a funereal pace but wasn't speeding. That would look suspicious in the middle of the night. The hearse driving anywhere after dark would be unusual. Which begged the question, where the hell were they going?

"I'd keep my head down if I was you."

Hunter Athey pulled out of the motel turnaround and headed west, away from town. The moon was up again, silvering the stretch of tarmac Grant could see all the way back to Absolution. There was no telltale glint of red from the taillights. Athey was driving dark.

"Too many prying eyes back that way."

Grant nodded even though Athey couldn't see him. What he was thinking was *eyes like a shithouse rat*. Cracked lips hurt when he smiled. Fifty yards along the road, Athey swung the hearse south onto a dirt track. Grant pictured the street map in his head. The traditional grid pattern with a few outlying streets forming the outskirts of town. South Lee Street looked impressive on the map but was barely even a track in reality. There were no houses and no railroad crossing, just the silver rails with packed earth built up along the sides. The hearse rolled and bounced again. Grant banged his head on the coffin lid.

"Where we going?"

Athey raised his voice over the creaking suspension.

"Told you. I hung up my shingle. Don't keep much in the way of medical supplies anymore. Only one man around here can patch you up and keep quiet about it."

Grant's voice was a croak. "Terlingua?"

"Too obvious. We're going to the Alamo."

TWENTY-FIVE

DAWN BROKE TO A world of pain. Grant clenched his teeth as Doc Cruz cleaned the dried blood from the side of his face before seeing how many stitches would be needed. Not as many as he'd feared. More than he'd like. Hunter Athey handed Cruz towels soaked in warm water. Cruz used them to dab away the ugly mass of dirt and blood.

"You must have one helluva thick skull, my friend."

Grant tried not to smile. "Safest place to hit me."

He swivelled his eyes instead of his head to indicate the room they were in.

"The Alamo?"

Doc Cruz continued cleaning the wound. "Safest place to hide."

"Didn't work out for John Wayne."

"Didn't work out for me and Hunter either."

"I can see why you didn't go into real estate."

The Alamo was Cruz and Athey's nickname for Fort Pena Colorado Park, a tourist campsite with cabins, trees, and a manmade lake. The creek was dammed just after it rounded the bend. The camp was an oasis of trees and lawns in the lee of a huge bluff that shouldered the eastern sky. There was no fort, it wasn't in Colorado, and it was barely a park. Strike three for the medical entrepreneurs who had sunk their money into the white elephant twenty years ago, only to see it dry up with the creek that was supposed to feed the lake. The cabins had long since fallen into disrepair, but the tourist center was built of sterner stuff. Just like the Alamo.

Athey poured more water from the faucet into the kettle.

"I still use it sometimes."

He waved towards the back room.

"Staff quarters. Buys me some peace away from Macready town."

Cruz finished cleaning the side of Grant's face and leaned close to examine the wound. He rinsed it with water from a jug.

"I get all the peace I want in Terlingua."

Grant winced. "Apart from battered wives and angry husbands."

"Apart from that."

Cruz stood back from his assessment.

"Half a dozen stitches should keep your brains in place. Strap up your ribs. Then work on your knees."

He opened a suture kit and selected a needle.

"This is going to hurt you a lot worse than me, I'm happy to say."

Grant braced himself. "Is that your idea of a bedside manner?"

Cruz stared into Grant's eyes. "It is my idea of saying you should not have come to Absolution."

Grant stared back. Neither blinked for a long time. They both knew Grant had no choice but to come visit Absolution. Some things a man just had to do no matter how much he'd rather not. Cruz nodded his understanding, then got to work on the stitches.

"So he's not smuggling illegals across the border, you reckon."

"There is no need for army trucks to bring Mexicans into America. There are hundreds of easier ways to cross the border."

Grant had drifted in and out of consciousness during the hours that Cruz treated his wounds. He was feverish and weak and had to fight bouts of shivering that threatened to spill his mug of tea. Hunter Athey had left to take the hearse back before anyone missed him. Grant's mind was still working, though, and it was working overtime trying to figure out what Macready was bringing across the border. Top of the list was drugs. In America, most crime seemed to boil down to drugs. Cruz didn't think a small town like Absolution would be the choice for a drug baron. Grant thought about the Dominguez cartel and reluctantly agreed. Macready didn't seem like the drug-lord type.

"Guns, then?"

"Señor. You have traveled around America. Do you see a shortage of guns?"

A shiver rattled Grant's teeth. Sweat beaded on his forehead. He'd come to the same conclusion in Boston when he'd been interviewing Freddy Sullivan before he'd been blown up at Jamaica Plain. That brought another possibility.

"What about women?"

"For the whorehouses?"

"I hear that Mexican women are very popular."

He felt ashamed even thinking that, but it was true. The escort industry was full of dark and dusky beauties from south of the border. Pilar Cruz had been one of the most beautiful and courageous women he'd ever known.

Doc Cruz shook his head. "There are plenty of whorehouses in Mexico. Why import them? All you have to do is take a day trip."

Grant was reaching, he knew. He remembered reading something like that in a Jack Reacher novel. A truckload of young women brought in from across the border. Canada, he thought. And that James Lee Burke book *Rain Gods*. Sheriff Hackberry Holland finding nine dead prostitutes buried behind a barn. Life might well imitate art, but fiction was often inspired by life. Grant knew that women were shipped in from overseas to satisfy niche markets.

"It's just what they said about not wanting anyone slipping away."

"They could mean slippage. You know? One of the soldiers getting greedy with whatever they were bringing across."

Grant nodded his agreement and immediately wished he hadn't. The headache had been raging for hours, but it was the dizziness that kept making him feel like vomiting. He closed his eyes and wiped sweat from his brow.

Cruz lowered his voice. "You should rest, my friend. You are too weak to trouble yourself over this."

"It's the *this* that's been troubling me. What is it?"

Cruz rested a hand on Grant's arm. "Whatever it is, you won't find out in this condition."

Grant couldn't argue with that. He felt weak and sick and dizzy. Racking his brains over the problem was just making him feel worse. There wasn't enough information to reach a conclusion, so there was no point pursuing the matter. He decided to change tack.

"Where did he get so many army trucks from?"

"From the army, I should think."

"The army doesn't rent its trucks out. They're not Hertz."

"They don't engage in smuggling either."

Grant drummed his fingers on the table, watching the steam rise from his cup.

"I wouldn't put it past them if it was something they needed. America hasn't exactly been shy about invading foreign countries when it suited them."

Cruz squared his shoulders. "This accusation from the country that colonized half of the world before raping its natural resources."

Grant held his hands up in surrender.

"You're right. But either way, I don't see the army sanctioning a smuggling operation across the Mexican border."

He sat back in his chair and almost fell over. A wave of nausea swept over him, and the room began to spin. Cruz dashed over and helped steady the battered Yorkshireman. He tested Grant's forehead with the back of his hand.

"You are burning up. Let me get you in bed."

Grant waved him off and took a deep breath. He took a drink of tea, the cure for everything according to Yorkshire fishwives. The room stopped spinning. He gave Cruz an old-fashioned look.

"You've seen my tattoo, right?"

Cruz looked nonplussed. "Only when examining your back for injuries."

Grant pointed to the base of his spine, just above his backside. "*NO ENTRY*. My ass is one-way traffic. No way you're getting me into bed."

Cruz finally understood the joke. His face broke into an embarrassed smile. Grant felt the pressure lift. Humor. Every cop's secret weapon. It could diffuse violent situations and alleviate stress. It worked in the military too. Pre-mission nerves were often calmed by ribald talk and inappropriate comments. He thought of Wheeler and Bond arguing over who was the best 007. The memory saddened him, so he changed the image. Phil Silvers barking orders as Sergeant Bilko. Military comedy at its best.

He stopped with his cup halfway to his lips. Sergeant Bilko. The motor pool sergeant at Fort Baxter. A man who was always open to a good deal, whether it was legal or not. Bilko wouldn't think twice about hiring army trucks out for private enterprise. Life imitates art. Every army base had its dodgy dealmaker. He put the cup down.

"Where's the nearest army camp?"

Cruz scratched his head, then rubbed his chin. The overt show of concentration was comical. Humor arising from a serious situation. "There is a unit at Fort Davis, west of Alpine." He shrugged his shoulders. "It is not very big, though."

Grant began drumming his fingers again. He was on the right track. "Any garrison towns? Something big enough to have a motor pool?"

Cruz blew out his cheeks, then took a deep breath. His eyes lost clarity as he turned the focus inwards. Grant could almost see the wheels turning. After a few moments, Cruz blinked and stared at Grant.

"There is a garrison at Fort Stockton. Through the hills north of Absolution, at the junction of Route 67 and the 385."

His eyes widened as he thought of something else. "And the 385 goes right past Macready's factory outside town."

Grant pushed his cup across the table so hard he spilled his tea.

"What factory?"

TWENTY-SIX

GRANT CAREFULLY SLID BACK from the ridge on his stomach, then sat up against a flat rock once he was hidden from the industrial complex on the other side of the hill. Cruz had been close when he'd said Macready's factory was next to the 385. It was actually ten miles north of Absolution on Iron Mountain Road, a straight-as-an-arrow continuation of Avenue K. The desert road went past the factory, then joined the 385 on its way through the hills towards Fort Stockton. Passing traffic used the 385. The army convoy used Iron Mountain Road. That's what had made Doc Cruz nervous driving Grant out there on the same road.

"This is madness. They will see you coming from miles away."

This while Cruz had kept his battered Ford from bouncing off the uneven road and Grant had kept his head down on the back seat.

"I thought you weren't hiding from Macready, just keeping a low profile."

"Driving up to his factory is not keeping a low profile."

"His factory's on the other side of the Iron Mountain. They won't even see your dust unless they're headed back towards town."

181

"Exactly."

"They've just crossed the border heading north. Whoever they've paid to use the trucks will be wanting them back. Once they've dropped the cargo and refuelled, it'll be straight up the 385."

Grant had been right. There had been no vehicles on the road out of town. He sat with his back against a tombstone rock in the dying light of the day and looked down at Cruz's Ford parked in a cutting behind the hill. Cruz looked unhappy. Grant waved to show everything was all right apart from his aching ribs and the stinging knees. He ran through the factory layout in his head.

The industrial complex was situated in a horseshoe indentation in the side of the mountain. The flat piece of land was perfect for keeping the factory private while allowing secluded access from Absolution and good transport routes along the 385. The factory itself was fairly basic. An L-shaped block. Brick-built storage units along one arm and workshops with a chimney along the other. Two antiquated gas pumps bordered the narrow cutting that formed the entrance, the only way in or out. There was no gate and no security fencing. The factory was protected on three sides by the mountain and a guard hut next to the filling station.

There was ample space in the angle of the L between the storage units and the workshops. That's where the trucks had been parked. Even from this distance Grant had been able to see the swirl of tracks where they'd been reversed for unloading before refuelling on the way out. The trucks were gone now. The pair of army jeeps was parked at the gas pumps. Grant wondered how Macready had swung the extended loan, the jeeps having been parked at Sixto's for the last couple of days. He must be paying a king's ransom to get that kind of cooperation.

Loose rocks rattled down the hillside.

Grant snapped his eyes forward.

Cruz was scrambling up the hill, worry etched across his face. Waiting alone at the car had obviously got to him. Despite the heat and glaring sun, the doctor wanted company more than rest. The climb brought sweat patches out under his arms and down his spine. He was out of breath by the time he sat next to Grant.

"This much exercise—it is not good for your condition."

Grant smiled at the doctor's discomfort. "Is that your medical opinion?"

"It is the opinion of a man who has just climbed a mountain. A man who still has two knees and no broken ribs."

Grant couldn't argue with that. His knees were sore but his ribs were the worst. They hurt like hell whenever he moved. Add to that his head felt muzzy and he was running a temperature. Sweat stung his eyes even without the effort of climbing the hill. Sometimes, if he looked down at his feet, the world tilted and spun out of control. Control was something he normally took for granted.

"I'll be fine. I'm only going to take a look inside."

Cruz shook his head.

"You are not fine. And to look inside, you will have to climb down this mountain. I guarantee you will feel worse at the bottom than you do at the top."

Grant didn't shake his head. It was already spinning. He took a deep breath and blinked sweat out of his eyes.

"I'll take it easy."

Cruz didn't look convinced.

"Easy would be to do this after dark. Isn't that what you military types do? Sneak around in the dark?"

The sun was low but still bright. It blazed across the western plains.

Cruz made another point.

"And don't forget, once you have looked inside you will have to climb back up here. That is three climbs too many, my friend."

At last Grant had an opening for his defense.

"I won't be climbing back up here because you're going to pick me up round the corner."

"What? You're just going to walk out? In plain sight?"

This time Grant did shake his head and regretted it.

"This side of the factory there's a dry creek. Runs right past the entrance, all the way to where you're going to pick me up. Nobody's gonna see me."

That's what he kept telling himself, but Cruz was right. Grant should really wait until dark. Trouble was, he didn't think he could last until dark. The fever was taking hold and he felt weak and shivery. If there was any trouble, he doubted he'd have enough strength to defend himself. Back in his army days this mission would be aborted. As it was, Grant was relying on the low sun glaring down the hillside to blind anyone looking this way. After that it would have to be stealth and secrecy.

It was a forlorn hope. He should have listened to his doctor, because things were about to get a whole lot worse.

He was halfway down the hill when the first bout of sickness threatened to empty his already empty stomach. He crouched behind a rock and let the cramps double him over. His eyes were watering. Sweat poured down his face. The cramps eased, but his head was spinning. It was a few minutes before he was able to look around the rock.

The trucks might have gone, but the factory was working full tilt. The noise came up the hill in waves. A dull roar sounded from inside the workshop, and a constant banging and clattering came from everywhere. Smoke puffed around the tall black chimneystack. Voices shouted above the noise. Nobody was trying to be secretive. Everyone felt safe this far out of town.

One of the jeeps started up and crossed the yard to the gas pumps. Grant's eyes followed the movement. A man came out of the guard hut and jerked a thumb towards the fuel gun holstered in the side of the pump. The driver stopped the jeep and began to argue with the guard. Didn't look like he wanted to serve himself, and the guard didn't consider himself to be a gas pump jockey. There was a lot of chest beating and violent movement but no actual violence. Another example of pissing contests coming in all shapes and sizes.

Grant scanned the open space below him. The other jeep was unmanned. There was nobody else around. The only eyes on the ground were too busy arguing about who should work the pump. Holding one arm across his stomach, Grant scurried the rest of the way down the hillside. Easy movements. Careful not to start a rock-slide. He reached the gully at the bottom, then dropped to a crouch. His head was spinning. A sudden cramp doubled him over, but he wasn't sick. Sparks of light jumped around behind his eyes. He took half a dozen shallow breaths to clear his head.

The factory noise was louder down here. That was good. It meant he didn't have to worry about anyone hearing him scramble up the riverbank. He poked his head over the top for a count of five, then ducked below the parapet again.

He was at the end of the long side of the inverted L—the storage wing. Several roller shutter doors faced the courtyard. Only one was open. He couldn't see inside from this angle, but sparks flickered in the dark. An electric motor whined, and more banging noises drifted out of the door. A forklift truck? A motorized trolley?

Approaching from the angle of the L was too dangerous. The guard wouldn't be distracted for long, and the thing about factories was that workers might come out of the door at any time. Grant moved to his left so he could see down the outside of the L—the external walls that were protected by the mountain. The side where they felt safe. Like he'd noticed from the ridge, there was no guard position along the outside, but there were three fire escapes. And they were all open to let air into the work area.

Grant moved left and forwards out of the creek bed. He threw one last glance towards the guard hut, where the discussion had reached a stalemate in the dying shafts of sunlight, then approached the nearest fire escape. It was at the top of a rusting metal staircase about ten feet up the sidewall. The other fire exits were at ground level. Grant preferred to view the inside from an elevated position. He paused at the bottom of the stairs and rested one hand on the bottom step. There was no vibration. No footsteps echoing from the top of the solid metal structure.

Walking softly on the balls of his feet, Grant took the stairs one at a time. This wasn't about speed, it was about stealth. Rushing ahead would be a mistake. The way his head kept spinning, this was probably a mistake anyway.

He went up three steps and paused.

No movement up ahead.

He went up three more.

Still no movement or voices at the top.

Another three steps.

The chaotic noise of a workforce in full swing grew louder. Metal banged on concrete. The electric motor whined, stopped, reversed, then whined again. The dull roar was constant. Grant could smell hot metal and flux, like a soldering iron multiplied by a hundred. A furnace.

The next three steps took him to just below the landing. The noises made sense now. It reminded Grant of the steelworks in Sheffield back home, back when there had been a steel industry in Yorkshire. Knives and forks around the world had been made from Sheffield steel. He doubted Macready was making cutlery.

Grant edged forward at a crouch. He reached the landing and peered through the door. At first all he could see was the elevated walkway around the inside of the factory and the foreman's office at one end. In the distance, to his left, sparks jumped and spat when the furnace door was opened.

That wasn't what caught his eye. Molten metal was just molten metal. There was no way of knowing what kind of metal it was until it cooled and oxidized. The factory floor was the place to look.

He crept to the edge of the walkway, keeping low, and looked over the side. Then a voice shouted a warning to his right.

TWENTY-SEVEN

GRANT JERKED HIS HEAD towards the sound, and the world spun into oblivion. He pushed back from the edge of the walkway and braced himself against the wall. His hands came up, ready to fend off the attack, and his knees screamed as he prepared to push upwards. He turned towards the shouted warning. To his right, the voice shouted again—from the glass and wood office at the end of the walkway.

"I said, watch your back!"

There was a loud bang and a yell from the factory floor. Metal clattered across the concrete, and there was a rending crack as wood splintered. Confusion reigned. There were more shouts—from the factory floor this time—and everybody stopped work as they dashed to help the stricken man.

The forklift truck had reversed away from the jaws of the furnace just as two workers were wheeling a wooden crate across the floor. Their attention had been on the conversation they were having instead of what they were doing. They didn't hear the warning beep as the motor went into reverse.

Crash.

The foreman dashed to the nearest stairs at the far end of the walkway on the other side of the office. Using both hands on the railings he slid down, his feet barely touching the steps on the way. Another man jogged towards the accident carrying a first-aid box. The other workers formed a circle around the crash site, all facing inwards towards the injured man.

Grant's head continued to spin. He felt nauseous but managed to fight off the stomach cramp that threatened to double him over. This was an opportunity too good to miss, but he was almost too ill to take advantage of it. He glanced towards the office—the place where any documentation would be kept. Invoices, transport orders, and cargo manifests; the place to look for evidence of Macready's activities. That's if Grant was looking for evidence. For now, all he wanted to know was what the Texan was bringing in from Mexico. This wasn't going to court.

Manifests and transport orders were the sort of things a legitimate enterprise would require. The army convoy across the border wasn't a legitimate enterprise. Any paperwork filed for tax purposes would be false and misleading. The real evidence was on the factory floor in the crates being emptied into the furnace. Grant ignored the office and went in the opposite direction.

The walkway tracked the back wall around the factory. Metal handrails gave some cover but not much. Grant stayed low despite his screaming knees and kept his back to the wall. His head was just above the angle of the walkway's edge, giving him a view down into the gathered workforce. He passed the nearest set of stairs and continued to the end nearest the furnace. From the outside, the inverted L shape looked like two separate wings, the storage units and the factory. Inside, it was all one big workspace: the smelting works at one end and the factory floor at the other. The roller shutter doors were simply delivery bays with loading docks for the trucks. Most of the wooden crates were stacked at the loading docks.

Most but not all.

Grant paused at the top of the stairs. Down on the factory floor, the circle had widened so the injured man could be treated. The first aider was examining the man's extremities while talking to keep him calm. Grant wondered how Doc Cruz would have handled the situation. He remembered how he'd dealt with the frightened boy at the Terlingua medical center. He doubted the foreman would be giving out sweets. With the examination over, the first aider opened the box and began to splint the man's leg. Another helper unfurled a folding stretcher. This was going to take a bit of time. Grant took advantage of the distraction.

The steps were metal, like the fire escape. Heavy footsteps would sound the alarm. Grant tiptoed down one step at a time, keeping balanced and light and aware of the group in the middle of the floor. He reached the bottom without incident and quickly sidled behind the walkway supports. One final glance at the gathered workforce, then he turned his attention to the furnace.

It wasn't Sheffield steelworks, but it was big enough. The door was large and circular. Whatever they were feeding it was poured in through the door. Whatever was coming out ran in a glittering stream of liquid metal. The narrow trough split into rectangular casts about six inches by three. Ingot size. Smaller than the ones Auric Goldfinger had been making out of the metal parts of his Rolls Royce Silver Ghost. Same principal.

Gold ingots. Made in Texas. Stolen from Mexico.

That was obvious the moment Grant saw the molten stream. What wasn't clear was just what kind of gold they were smelting. It wasn't body parts from a Rolls Royce, that was for sure. The broken crate was too far away for Grant to risk taking a look. The spillage was too indistinct to identify: small stuff, certainly, and some bigger pieces, all glittering in the overhead lights.

The furnace door was closed, but the next mouthful was waiting at the side. A sturdy wooden crate with the lid off, ready to be emptied. Grant checked the crowd. They were in the middle of the floor on the other side of the spillage. The forklift truck blocked Grant's view. Good. That meant it blocked theirs as well. The furnace was in a darkened corner of the factory, a rough-hewn alcove of dirt and grime. The shadows highlighted the sparks and molten metal. The sparks didn't light the corner Grant was hiding in or the crate he wanted to check.

One final glance, then Grant walked to the crate. Upright and steady. Not rushing, not crouching; looking for all the world like he belonged there. Nothing to draw attention to himself. He reached the crate in four easy strides, then bent to look inside.

The world spun again. Not because he felt dizzy but because of the brilliance of what he saw before him. Light danced off the contents, and he thought he understood the reason Humphrey Bogart had gone gold crazy in *The Treasure of the Sierra Madre*. He dipped a hand into the crate to make sure it was real. Then a door opened behind him and he heard the flush of a toilet.

THE MAN WAS RUBBING his hands together as he came out of the darkened corner. A stenciled sign above the door read RESTROOMS.

It didn't specify gender. Judging from the workforce, this was an all-male environment. The man wore grease-stained overalls and heavy work boots. He paused mid wipe and performed a comedic double-take.

Grant held an intricate gold medallion in one hand and stood still. He felt like a naughty boy caught with his hands in the cookie jar. For a split second. Then he moved fast. Three strides towards the restrooms as he dropped the medallion into his pocket. He walked right up to the worker and didn't slow down, driving the heel of one hand into the man's throat, then grabbing him under the arms as he collapsed, gasping for breath. He walked the man backwards under the stairs and laid him gently on the ground.

"Sshhh. Take it easy. Breathe slowly."

He remembered that Doc Cruz hadn't done anything apart from reassure the Mexican wife beater until he'd got his breathing regulated, and Grant hadn't hit this fella anywhere near as hard. He was a factory worker, not a wife beater. Not one of the bad guys, just a bad guy's employee. He patted him on the shoulder—"You'll be fine in a couple of minutes"—then walked to the nearest fire exit before the other workers noticed their friend was taking a long time in the restroom. The ground floor fire door was open like the others for fresh air. Grant was through the door and scrambling down the dry creek bed before the strain caught up with him.

Lights blinked in his eyes again.

His head felt like it didn't belong to him.

His stomach most definitely did. It cramped fit to cut him in two. Despite having nothing on his stomach, he doubled over and threw up. Dry heaves brought acid phlegm up his throat. Sweat stung his eyes and ran down his neck. His entire body shivered despite the heat. His face felt like it was burning up.

There was no time for this. He forced himself to keep moving even though he couldn't stand upright. That was a good thing because the gully wasn't deep enough for him to stand up straight and remain hidden. He shuffled and walked past the bottom of the inverted L. Past the enclosed yard where the trucks had parked. He could smell petrol fumes and almost threw up again.

He risked a quick look over the top of the embankment. Both jeeps were still at the pumps, but only one was being refueled. The last patch of sunlight from the hillside lit the filling station and the guard hut. A golden haze to end the day. The rest of the factory was in shade. Nobody came running out. Not yet.

Grant kept low and crabbed his way along the gully. The first driver was still arguing with the security guard while he struggled with the filler cap. Fumes drifted around him like a heat haze on the highway. The second driver ignored the discussion and simply worked the pump. The soft *ding, ding, ding* came down the embankment. Grant was level with the filling station. He kept going. Fifty yards ahead, the gully swung to the right around the bottom of the hill. Not far to go before he could collapse into Doc Cruz's car and listen to his "I told you so."

He didn't get fifty yards, just ten before the factory siren broke the silence. Three men came dashing out of the fire exit and around the side of the storage wing, shouting and screaming. They waved to catch the guard's attention, then pointed along the gully.

Grant tried to move faster but that only made his head spin worse and his eyes go out of focus. Running blind and dizzy on a rock-strewn riverbed was a recipe for disaster. Disaster was coming for him anyway.

The guard saw him first and yelled for him to stop. He didn't draw his gun. In that regard he showed more sense than the two drivers, who were also armed. The first man abandoned the filler cap and stepped into the cloud of vapors. The second left the pump nozzle in the side of his jeep and drew his weapon. Both took a two-handed firing stance like they must have seen Dirty Harry do.

Grant kept going.

The guard waved for the drivers to lower their weapons.

The first driver had had enough of the guard pulling rank. He racked the slide to chamber a round. His partner did the same. Grant wondered if Texas filling stations had warning signs at the pumps—the ones that said not to use your cell phone when filling up or the ones about not smoking. He was pretty sure there weren't any signs about discharging a firearm while standing in a cloud of petrol fumes, it being the fumes that ignited more than the petrol itself.

Grant tried to zigzag to throw off their aim. It didn't matter. The delay between petrol fumes igniting and the petrol catching fire became a moot point. Both drivers fired simultaneously; the muzzle flash was like striking a match. The ball of flame engulfed them, then immediately flashed back to the source: the gas pumps. The nearest pump blasted apart, sending a fireball and shrapnel flying into the air. The second pump took a second longer. A moot point because both drivers were out of action and the security guard was diving for cover.

The fireballs combined. The pumps disintegrated, leaving two holes in the ground gushing flames. The guard hut was a scorched remnant. The guard was afire, patting himself furiously to put out the flames. Nobody was interested in the intruder. Nobody was going to be driving through the only exit from the factory.

Grant slowed to catch his breath. He could barely see the bend in the river. He could hardly walk without falling over. He didn't hear the car come round the corner or see it skid to a stop. His vision was so blurred by the time he got in the car he didn't even know it wasn't Eduardo Cruz picking him up. Five minutes later he didn't know anything at all.

TWENTY-EIGHT

THE WORLD WAS FULL of pain and fire. Again. Everything ached. Some parts felt like hot needles were being shoved into his joints. Fever cranked up the heat until he thought he was being boiled alive. The furnace bubbled and sparked in Grant's mind. His eyes remained glued shut no matter how hard he tried to open them. The fact that he couldn't see made his head spin even more. He was on his back, that much he could tell, but it felt like he was lying on a spinning top that was tilting and swerving so much his stomach felt seasick.

Fight it.

Stay awake.

Do not sleep under any circumstances.

Sleep equals death.

Grant forced his mind to evaluate the situation. Retrace his steps to the point where the movie went blank. He remembered the long drive out on Iron Mountain Road. Doc Cruz warning him to delay his insurgency until after dark. The climb down to the factory and the industrial accident.

For a moment Grant wasn't sure if it was him or the man in overalls rubbing his hands who had been hit by the forklift truck. Was that why his body was racked with pain—because somebody had run him over when they'd caught him in the factory? His hand twitched and tried to reach in his pocket. What was he trying to get? A gun? No. Grant hated guns. That was a deep-rooted memory that no amount of pain could erase. A gold coin. That was it.

The movie restarted. The accident. The opportunity. Grant checking the wooden crate and the glittering reflection in the light from the furnace. Disabling the worker coming out of the restroom and his mad scramble along the riverbed. Even at that point the world was beginning to spin. The gunshots and the fireball were the last things he remembered. That and the vehicle skidding to a stop as its doors flew open and rough hands dragged him inside.

Grant's eyes blinked open.

It wasn't Doc Cruz's car.

His eyelids felt heavy. They had been gummed shut so long it was a force of will to unstick them. He didn't know how long he'd been unconscious. He didn't know where he was. All he knew was that he couldn't see any more with his eyes open than he'd been able to see with them shut. At least the spinning stopped, or most of it.

The room was dark; no light whatsoever. In his experience, lying in a darkened room either meant the curtains were drawn or it was night. Even with blackout curtains there was no way to keep all the daylight out, so he reckoned it must be after dark. He checked the movie in his head. It had been just before sunset when he'd climbed down the hillside. The last shafts of sunlight had illuminated the security guard and the drivers. He didn't feel like he'd been unconscious for days, although he wasn't sure how you could tell, so that would make it the night of the same day.

That still didn't explain where he was or who had brought him here. His eyes grew accustomed to the dark, and he realized it wasn't pitch black after all. There was a sliver of light coming under the door to his right. He focused on that until the light spread into the room. It picked out the doorframe and a wooden chair and something that could have been a desk or a table. Everything else was too far from the light source to be of much help.

The strip of light blinked. No, it didn't blink—a shadow moved across the gap beneath the door, from one side to the other, then disappeared. There was a murmuring of voices in the other room. The shadow crossed the light in the opposite direction, then came back. It was joined by another. The door handle rattled.

Grant held his breath. The world stopped spinning. Light glinted off the handle as it turned and the latch clicked free. The sliver of light across the bottom was joined by a longer slit up the side as the door opened a crack. The voices stopped. The door opened all the way, and light flooded the room.

Then the Mexican wife beater stepped through the door.

"Hey, amigo. You remember me?"

Grant tried to sit up, but his ribs were a band of fire across his chest. He couldn't summon the energy to push up on his elbows. The Mexican was a giant silhouette in the doorway. Behind him, two more shadows stood in the background. His friends from the Kosmic Kowgirl Kafe. The wife beater leaned against the doorframe and crossed one leg, aiming for cool and succeeding. He was in control of the situation.

"You a hard man to find."

Grant tried to reply, but his voice was harsh and silent. His vision drifted in and out of focus. The queasy feeling in his stomach threatened to crawl up his throat. He croaked it back down. His mouth opened and shut like a beached goldfish. The wife beater put his own interpretation on that.

"Agua?" He lifted one hand to his mouth and jiggled it as if holding a glass of water. "Thirsty?"

The interpretation was correct. Grant's throat was dry and painful. He gave a cautious nod. The Mexican seemed unimpressed.

"You should have thought of that before messing in another man's business."

The wife beater didn't move from the door. He clicked his fingers, and one of the other shadows came into the room and disappeared behind Grant. There was a clink of glass. A faucet was turned on. Moments later, a glass of cold water was held to Grant's lips. He drank slowly. Too much too fast wasn't good. The water cooled the fire in his throat and moistened his lips.

"Where am I?"

"Somewhere you don't got no right to be."

Grant remembered the wife beater's use of double negatives at Terlingua. He didn't think this was the time to educate him.

"We're not in Mexico, are we?"

The big man pushed away from the doorframe and flexed his shoulders.

"The place that's full of small greasy ratfuck Mexicans? That's what you called us, isn't it?"

The glass was taken away. Grant finally managed to push himself up onto his elbows.

"I was trying to distract you."

"That so? Well, now it's you who got distracted. All the way here."

The wife beater stepped towards Grant. "And guess what? I'm one angry, distracted muthafucka."

Grant gauged angles and distances. Even though he was leaning up on his elbows, his legs were pointing roughly towards the big man. Three feet off the ground, probably on a table or a bed. His police training back in Yorkshire had included what to do if you were on the ground in a public order situation. Always keep your feet towards the danger. Kicking was the first line of defense. He prepared to swivel on his back and use the leverage to kick out. His personal mantra was to delay offensive action as long as possible. Best way to do that was to keep talking and try to diffuse the situation.

"You know who you sound like?"

The wife beater tilted his head to one side, a default pose to aid his concentration.

Grant took that as permission to carry on.

"Samuel L. Jackson. If he was playing a Mexican."

He smiled to show he wasn't being offensive and continued. "I didn't know Mexicans said mother fucker."

The Mexican got into the swing of things. "After Bruce Willis in *Die Hard,* everybody says muthafucka."

"That right? I thought it'd be more like Sam J in *Pulp Fiction.*"

"That too. Point is, muthafucka crosses all borders."

"Glad we got that cleared up. You still feeling angry?"

The Mexican looked surprised. "No, I'm not."

Grant kept his tone light. His usual tactic. "Point I'm making is, I wasn't racially stereotyping."

"No. You was just stereotyping me."

"As a wife beater. Yes. That wasn't hard. Since your wife was being seen by the doctor for burns and bruises at the time."

The Mexican knotted his eyebrows in a frown. "The same doctor that treated you for cuts and bruises and three broken ribs. Does that mean you were the victim of spousal abuse?"

Grant felt a tickle of gooseflesh run down his spine. He wasn't sure if it was from wondering how the Mexican knew about being seen by Doc Cruz or the surprising use of good English. He prepared for things to get ugly and flexed his sore knees, ready to defend once the Mexican took the bait. An angry lunge was preferable to a considered attack.

"You saying you didn't grab her? Push her against the stove? Is that it?"

The Mexican took a deep breath while he chose his next words.

"Imagine this. A child leans against a hot radiator. Burns himself. A man grabs his arms to pull him away. How you gonna tell if the bruises and the burns are from him being pushed against the fire or pulled off it?"

"Is that what you're saying? You pulled her away from the stove?"

"I'm saying you should be careful who you listen to."

"Your wife?"

"The doctor."

Again that tickle of gooseflesh.

"So why'd you try to run me off the road?"

"This is Texas. You don't choke a guy out in front of his wife and son."

Grant could feel the temperature rising. Same tactic as before. Get the man angry, then defend against the thoughtless lunge.

"Technically they were outside."

The Mexican's voice grew louder. "They were there. Near enough."

Grant turned his legs slightly towards the threat. "Okay, I get that. In Texas. But are you a Texan or a Mexican?"

The big man moved towards the light switch. "I'm a Mexican in Texas. What you got to understand is Mexicans in Texas stick together."

He flicked the switch and the overhead fluorescent flickered into life. The room was lit by harsh yellow light. The same room that Grant had been treated in before. Remember the Alamo. Not the real Alamo but Fort Pena Colorado Park. Staff quarters, not the derelict cabins. The other two shadows stepped aside, and another man came into the room. Grant's eyes blurred as he tried to fight off the fever. The man shrugged his shoulders.

"I told you the climb was not good for your condition."

TWENTY-NINE

GRANT FELT DEFLATED AND betrayed by the father of the woman he'd come to Texas to honor. A shiver that had nothing to do with portent shook his body. The fever was taking hold again. His stomach cramped but there was nothing to bring up. His elbows slipped, and he lay back down. He rested his eyes and heard the rustle of clothes as someone approached the bed. Cool hands checked the temperature of his forehead.

"Relax. Pilar chose you for a reason. I respect her choice."

Grant's eyes flickered open. Eduardo Cruz was leaning over him, making soothing noises. Grant tried to glare at him, but his vision was swimming in and out of focus.

"Then why…"

His voice faded.

Cruz raised Grant's head and tipped the glass of water to his lips. Cool liquid eased his throat and moistened his lips, but his voice didn't return. The room began to spin again.

The doctor spoke quietly.

"Jim Grant. You have nothing to fear here."

The spinning grew faster.

"You are among friends."

Grant's mind couldn't grasp that. The staff quarters of Fort Pena Colorado Park became a dark smudge as his vision dimmed. The doctor deployed his best bedside manner. Soothing voice and gentle words.

"Let me explain."

So he did.

WHAT HAPPENED WAS THIS. Cruz was getting in the car at the bottom of the hill. Iron Mountain Road stretched out in the distance, all the way back to Absolution. The factory had no view of it, but Cruz could see the cloud of dust racing towards him in the evening sun. He checked his watch. Grant had been gone twenty minutes. It was time to get in position for the pickup.

The cloud grew closer. Its shadow was long and low across the desert floor. Cruz couldn't make out the car hidden in the dust. Sun glinted off the windshield. That was all he could see. It couldn't be Macready's men. The trucks had headed north towards Fort Stockton. Grant had said so, and Cruz had no reason to think he was mistaken. So who would be speeding along the desert road at this time of day?

Cruz stood in the open door of his car. He couldn't wait. Grant would be needing him soon, around the mountain where the gully came out. He threw one more glance at the approaching cloud and realized it wasn't one vehicle but two. He thought he recognized one of them, but it was only a glimpse.

Why would Hunter Athey be driving the hearse towards the factory?

Then he saw the second vehicle. A battered pickup with a repaired radiator. Doc Cruz got in the car and slammed the door. He started the engine and reversed out of the cutting. Too late. The cloud engulfed him as both vehicles turned off the road into the cutting and skidded to a halt, blocking him in. Tony Sabata got out of the pickup, his wife beater vest covered by a flapping shirt. Hunter Athey got out of the hearse, waving for Cruz not to panic.

Cruz wasn't convinced. "What you mean, don't panic?"

Sabata spoke for Athey. "He means I hate Tripp Macready more than I want Jim Grant."

Athey approached his friend. "They came looking for Mr. Jim."

Cruz raised his eyebrows. "Why come to you?"

Sabata stepped forward. "Because he's the only one around here who drives a hearse."

The cloud dissipated and the hearse came into view. The bullet holes and broken window were rimmed with dust. Even the pickup's new radiator looked like it had been on the road for years. That's the thing about driving in desert country: everything looks old. Cruz felt old as he sagged against the side of his car.

"And why have you come here?"

Sabata glowered at the doctor. "Because I want to know what Macready is bringing across the border."

He nodded towards the mountain. "Is he inside now?"

Cruz let out a sigh. "He should be coming out the front anytime now."

"Out front?"

"Along the gully."

"Then he'll be able to answer a few questions. Won't he?"

A gentle breeze whistled across the plains, blowing the rest of the dust cloud away. It wasn't as hot now, and the engines ticked as they cooled. The sun was low in the west. The three men stood in silence for a moment, then Sabata jerked a thumb towards the factory.

"Let's give him a—"

The factory siren cut off his words. It echoed around the cutting. Everybody dived into their vehicles and started the engines. The pickup turned around quickest. It was speeding back to join the road before Cruz and Athey got their handbrakes off. It disappeared around the corner just as an enormous blast thumped the air. The second explosion was even bigger.

DAWN FILTERED THROUGH THE curtains, but the fog in Grant's mind didn't clear. The world had stopped spinning, but pain still invaded his body. He felt weak and shivery. He wasn't sure how much of what he'd taken in was Cruz's story and how much was simply fever dreams. It sounded plausible enough. His brain wasn't sharp enough to tell right now.

He ungummed his eyes long enough to see it was daytime, but he couldn't keep them open. The next time he opened them, the light was stronger and higher. Midday? It was hard to tell. The only thing he was certain of was that the Mexicans weren't in the room. Grant was alone. Then everything went dark. In the darkness, visions of his past played like home movies. A specific past that included gunfire and machetes and bloodshed. He had no control over which images he saw. He couldn't help the injured or the dying.

By the time he opened his eyes again, Grant had lost an entire day. The sun was low in the sky, but his world felt more stable. A hand checked his forehead. The touch startled him. Soothing noises and a gentle hand on his shoulder put him at ease. The fever had reduced to mild sweats. The shivering had stopped. He still felt weak, but the pain that held his body prisoner was reduced to a dull ache. The ache was all-pervading but at least it was bearable.

Spicy cooking smells drifted in from the other room. Grant remembered them from a Mexican restaurant he'd once visited. The aromas made his mouth water but triggered his defenses. Mexican food meant Mexicans. Grant could only remember the gist of Doc Cruz's explanation, but he did know that the wife beater disliked Grant only slightly less than he hated Tripp Macready. That wasn't a glowing endorsement. It would behoove him to be careful.

A figure stepped into his field of vision carrying a glass of water. Grant looked up at the doctor and prepared for more bad news. Doc Cruz placated him with gentle hands and soothing words.

"Sshhh. Take it easy. Drink."

Grant sat up on the makeshift cot that had been his bed for the last twenty-four hours. He swung his feet off the mattress and felt solid ground that didn't sway underfoot for the first time since he'd climbed Iron Mountain's hillside. He took the proffered glass and nodded his thanks. This time he gulped down the water. His mouth was as dry as the desert that had almost claimed his life. His throat felt as rough as the riverbed that had tripped him up.

Cruz refilled the glass. Grant drank it all again. He passed it back to the doctor, then surveyed the room. It was the back room of the Fort Pena Colorado Park staff quarters. No doubt the place where Hunter Athey rested his head when taking a break from Macready town. The furnishings were faded but clean. The main office was through the door, where the food smells were coming from. Grant took a deep breath, then looked at the doctor.

"How long?"

Doc Cruz glanced at his watch out of habit. "A day. We brought you here last night."

Grant checked his wrist, then remembered his watch had come off during his tumble from the high road. That dangerous escape felt like a lifetime ago. The same as some other memories that he preferred to keep hidden.

"You were right."

Doc Cruz put the glass on the bedside cabinet. "About what?"

"I should have waited until dark."

"Enemy action is always better after dark. Pilar told me that once."

The mention of her name reminded Grant why he was here in the first place—the promise he had made and the price she had paid. It reminded him that she too had been a soldier, even if her chosen field had been medical, like her father. Grant looked at his feet to avoid Doc Cruz's eyes. He remembered boarding the Chinook in the predawn darkness.

"Doesn't always work out that way."

Doc Cruz reversed the wooden chair from the desk and sat opposite Grant with his arms folded across the top. He stared at Grant until Grant was forced to look up from the floor. Sadness creased the doctor's face.

"You were talking in your sleep."

Grant braced himself but didn't speak.

"You shouted my daughter's name."

Grant blinked instead of nodding. He still didn't speak.

"When you gave me her stethoscope, you told me she was killed in action. Not by mechanical failure."

Doc Cruz paused, plucking up courage to ask what he shouldn't really ask. "How did she die?"

Grant let out a sigh. "Does it matter?"

Grant had never held with the grieving-relatives-needing-closure theory. He didn't understand the urge to leave flowers at the scene of an accident or to go visit where their son or daughter had been killed. As far as he was concerned, you simply grieved and then moved on. The fact that he didn't agree with it didn't make it any less important for some people, Doc Cruz included.

"It matters to me."

He removed his arms from the top of the chair and sat up straight.

"How did Pilar die?"

Grant thought long and hard about how much to tell the grieving father. How much Grant needed to unburden himself. He closed his eyes for a few seconds, took a deep breath, then decided to tell it all. He looked Doc Cruz in the eye.

"I killed her."

THE PAST

Can you take the shot?
—Pilar Cruz

THIRTY

THEY RAN INTO THE man with the machete as the sun was dipping towards the horizon. After a long, hard day playing cat and mouse with the hoards of local militia. Militia in the broadest sense, in that they were armed and dangerous and aligned to a common purpose, supporting the warlord who ruled the township. They wore no uniforms and only a few had automatic weapons, but what they lacked in firepower they made up for in enthusiasm. And machetes.

Grant and Cruz kept alternating the lead and rear guard. They'd been zigzagging across town ever since the street café and were no nearer the safe zone than when they'd started. Every time Grant thought they'd made some headway, they had to divert around the mob that was searching the back streets for them. Grant had shot five so far. Lone searchers who were sweeping the alleyways behind the main force. Three they'd run into around blind corners, and two had come up behind them when Cruz had stopped to catch her breath. If Grant had been taking the lead this time, things might have turned out different, but it was his turn to be rear guard.

Cruz kept her back to the wall as she sidled along the shady side of the street. Shade was easy to come by now that the sun was so low.

The baking heat that had been draining them all day was replaced by the gentle warmth of early evening. Dying embers of sunlight picked out the top of the crumbling buildings across the street, but the ground was gray and colorless without the bright yellow torch.

She paused at the intersection with a battle-scarred alley. Listened to the distant crackle of gunfire as the mob vented their frustrations, shooting at the sky. There was no sound around the corner. This was the tenth junction she had scouted, but it might as well have been the hundredth. Every corner was the same. The sameness bred complacency. Cruz threw a casual glance round the edge of the crumbling building, then looked back at Grant as she stepped into the mouth of the alley.

The shadows were deeper there. Grant was checking behind him as he joined her in the narrow opening. Cruz barely glanced into the shadows. Grant was two steps behind her. Then sudden movement and a gasp of surprise snapped his head forward, and Cruz let out a shout of pain.

The man had been checking the alley when they'd surprised him. Instinct had taken over, and he'd slashed with the machete—a swift downward stroke that missed Cruz's gun hand but sliced flesh on the meaty part of her thigh. The pain forced a spasm through her fingers, and she dropped the gun. She was a medic, not a combat soldier. Reflex action was to put pressure on the wound. Grant's reflex was to fire twice. Center mass. Critical injury. The man was blasted backwards into the alley, his chest a tangled mess of blood and bone.

Cruz dropped to the ground, her leg unable to support her. Blood seeped through her desert fatigues, standing out against the sandy colors and camouflage pattern. It didn't take a doctor to realize it was serious. It didn't take a tactician to know they couldn't stay here while they treated the wound.

Grant picked up her gun and shoved it into his webbing. He scooped her up with one arm around her waist and hurried across the street in the opposite direction. Away from the dead man and the dying echoes of the gunshots. Down one alley, then across to another. A left turn, then a right. Two hundred yards farther on, he found a building that was almost intact apart from the door hanging from its hinges. He helped Cruz through the opening and lowered her to the ground. The door creaked as he wedged it shut.

Cruz leaned back against the wall. "I'm sorry, Jim."

Grant ignored the apology and tore her trouser leg open.

"You're the medic. What do you need?"

Cruz barked a laugh. "A vacation."

Grant smiled, but the smile didn't reach his eyes. "I'd settle for an exit strategy. For now, let's make sure you don't bleed to death. You're the medic. Get it done."

Cruz responded to the steel in Grant's tone. She swung her kitbag onto the ground and unsnapped the fastenings. Grant watched as she sprinkled powder over the six-inch gash in her leg, then laid a field dressing over the cut. He knew what to do next. Using both hands he applied pressure to the wound while Cruz tied it down with a length of bandage. Blood soaked through the dressing, so she applied another one over the top and tied that one down too. Tight. The blood flow slowed but didn't stop. Grant knelt beside her and wiped his bloody hands on his trousers. Camouflage wasn't an issue anymore.

"Give yourself the jab."

Cruz shook her head. "Better save it."

"What for? You don't have any other patients."

"Yet."

This time Grant's smile was ironic.

"Now there's a positive attitude for you. Give yourself the fucking jab. We're gonna have to move fast. Pain slows you down."

Cruz took a morphine ampoule out of the bag and snapped the end off. She stabbed herself in the leg and almost screamed at the pain. Sweat broke out on her brow. Tears leaked from her eyes. She clenched her jaw and nodded. Done.

Footsteps sounded in the alleyway. Half a dozen, running in this direction. Grant noticed the trail of blood across the living room floor. Sometimes all you can do is your best; Grant's best hadn't been good enough. In his haste to get Cruz away from the dead man, he'd forgotten the first rule of evade and destroy: don't leave a trail of breadcrumbs. The bottom feeders had followed the trail. Now the only question was how many of them there were.

The first one burst through the door. Grant snapped his gun up and fired twice. The second and third men charged in blind, machetes raised. Grant shot them before they knew who was in the room. The bodies formed a barricade in the doorway. There were fewer footsteps outside now. Grant reckoned this was a small hunting party thrown out wide of the main body. Five or six. The remaining two or three were reluctant to come barging in. They were gathering outside the door.

Machetes were close-quarter weapons. Effective for a mob that could charge you down before you could shoot enough to stop the rush. The local militia might not be well armed, but they were unlikely to send out a hunting party without at least one gun between them. Maybe two.

Grant couldn't wait for that gun to be brought to bear. He took Cruz's pistol out of his webbing and moved across the room to the shuttered window, away from the door. He could hear the muttering voices outside. Two, he reckoned. At least one of them would be armed. He doubted they would be sharpshooters.

The shutter was as unstable as the door—hanging from one hinge, no glass in the window. Grant braced himself against the wall. He raised Cruz's gun and readied his own for when the shutter was opened. Using the butt, he knocked the slatted wood from the window and leaned through the opening.

He was wrong. There were four men standing in the doorway. Two had machine guns. Neither looked like they knew how to use them. Grant shot the nearest in the back. He went down hard, dropping his machine gun. The second gunman was partly hidden behind another machete man. The machine gun swung towards Grant and opened fire. Bullets kicked holes in the adobe wall, high and wide but near enough to deflect Grant's aim. He fired both guns, blasting the machete men and catching the gunman in the leg and arm.

The machine gun stopped firing as the man dropped to his knees. Grant shot him three times in the chest to make sure. The alley echoed with thunder. The acrid smell filled the air. Grant didn't wait to see how many would follow the sounds of gunfire. He dashed across the room and helped Cruz to her feet. He considered letting her use the rifle slung across his back as a crutch but dismissed the thought. The way this was going, he'd be needing it soon.

"Let's go."

Redundant urging. Cruz knew they'd have to move and move fast. She picked up the kitbag and threw one arm across Grant's shoulder. He walked in a crouch so he wouldn't lift her off the ground. Towards the far corner of the room and the back door.

Another alleyway. Another race across the township. The sounds of outrage were somewhere behind them, polarized around the last burst of gunfire. The house of blood and death. Heading in the opposite direction, Grant guided Cruz along one back street after another. He checked the shafts of sunlight across the few bits of sky he could see to get a sense of direction.

"Come on. You can make it. We're going home."

At the time he said it, he wasn't lying. The setting sun told its story. Grant was finally leading them in the right direction. Towards the desert airbase and the safe zone.

THE SUN HAD SET. The room was dark apart from the moonlight through the gaping hole in the roof. The windows had been blown out years ago, but the metal bars were intact. Grant felt like he was sitting in a jail cell looking at the stars through the bars. He smiled at the matching of words with his thoughts. Stars and bars. An off-kilter description of the American flag that was stitched into the lid of Cruz's stethoscope case.

He glanced to his left and watched her eyelids flutter as she slept. In the pale blue moonlight, her dusky skin looked white. She could be your typical English rose—dark hair, full lips, and pale skin. He doubted if she'd take that as a compliment. Pilar Cruz was defiantly Mexican. Grant gently removed his arm from across her shoulders and stretched his legs out. They were both sitting on the floor with their backs against the wall. Another play of words that mirrored reality. They were up against it. In deep shit. Facing a final dash that was every bit as doomed as the one that awaited Butch and Sundance.

He leaned over and kissed her gently on the lips. That was something Newman never did to Redford. Thank goodness. *Brokeback Mountain* would never have been made in the sixties.

Grant smiled despite the coming tragedy. He'd been surprised that Cruz even knew about *Butch Cassidy and the Sundance Kid*. She hadn't struck him as a movie type until the conversation that eased sunset into night. Just after they'd made it to the last house on the edge of town and collapsed against the kitchen wall.

"What's it look like?"

Cruz fought to keep the pain out of her voice.

Grant was peering into the shadowy no man's land beyond the crumbling wall.

"Like manna from heaven."

"What about the route from here to there?"

"That doesn't look so good."

The sun had gone down over an hour ago but there was still enough blue in the sky to pick out the rubble-strewn expanse beyond the edge of town. Stars twinkled in the darkening sky, but the moon wasn't up yet. In the distance he could just make out the long, straight road that the Chinook had followed two days ago. A road built by military engineers once they'd completed the desert airstrip and army base. The base was in lockdown. Light discipline meant an enforced blackout. There were no choppers in or out. No runway lights or navigation blinkers. The shit had hit the fan after the Chinook went down. Shit was black. No light.

"It looks straight and even and plain for everyone to see."

Cruz sounded calm. "No cover, then?"

"Only the cover of dark."

"That won't help. Not with my leg."

Grant looked at her shadowy figure leaning against the wall beside him.

"You're in a real glass-half-empty mood, aren't you?"

"Leg half empty—as in I've only got half of my full complement of two."

"You'd better rest the one that you've got, then."

He slipped his arms under hers and lowered her to the ground. In better circumstances it would have been a romantic gesture. He would have cupped her breasts and kissed her neck as he lowered her to the bed. In the shattered wreckage of the last house on the left, there was no bed. No furniture at all. Cruz shuffled back against the wall and stretched her legs out. The morphine had dulled the pain but it was still there, waiting in the background.

Grant went back to the window. The killing ground was too open and too long for them to traverse without being seen. The prize, if they made it, was life and freedom. The cost would be great. Because there was no way that Cruz would be able to cover the ground without the waiting hordes cutting her down—cutting them both down. One for all and all for one. What happened to one happened to the other. Just like Butch Cassidy and the Sundance Kid.

The natives had camped for the night. Fires showed their position a hundred yards south of the crumbling house and fifty yards east of the killing ground. They'd been searching the derelict buildings along the edge of town until bad light stopped play. A cricket term. Grant doubted Cruz would understand if he mentioned it. Bottom line was that the mob was too close for Butch and Sundance to make a run for it. They had their backs against the wall, with nowhere to go but out—either in a blaze of glory or a decoyed run.

Cruz tugged at Grant's trouser leg.

"Wait a minute. You didn't see Lefors out there?"

Grant was surprised, not only that Cruz knew the line but also that she'd tapped into his thoughts about the movie. He gave her Redford's line.

"Lefors? No."

"Good. For a minute I thought we were in trouble."

Grant threw one last glance at their version of the Bolivian army, then sat against the wall beside Cruz. He drew his legs up and rested both arms across his knees. The stars twinkled through the barred window. The moon wouldn't rise for another half an hour. It didn't matter. The darkness wasn't dark enough to hide a big man and a cripple dashing across open ground. He turned his eyes on Cruz.

"Lefors was a one-man tracker. Followed Butch and Sundance all across the west. It wasn't him that did for them in Bolivia."

"They didn't know that."

"We do. It's not the tracker we should be worried about."

"It's the local militia."

"Bolivian or not."

Cruz let out a sigh. "We can't sneak past them?"

Grant shook his head. "Nowhere to hide."

Cruz nodded. "And I can't outrun them."

Grant felt the sweat on his back turn cold. Goose pimples sprang up on his forearm. Sometimes he and Cruz felt almost twinned, their thoughts running so close they could be as one. Grant wished he couldn't read her mind now. He looked her in the eye, then turned away. The stars were bright in the darkening sky, a perfectly framed starfield through the jailhouse window. Cruz broached the subject from the side.

"What was the punchline to that airplane joke again?"

Grant played along.

"The American said 'remember the Alamo' and threw a Mexican out."

Cruz stared into Grant's eyes. "I'm the Mexican. Gotta lighten the load."

"No."

"Yes."

She laid a hand on his knee and squeezed. "Did you ever think how things would have been if only Newman had gone out the front door? Drawn their fire while Redford slipped out the back? Whole different ending. Right?"

Grant put his hand on top of hers. "And did you ever think how bad Redford would have felt letting his best friend go out alone?"

"You'd have to be alive to feel bad."

"No."

"Yes. You know it makes sense."

"No."

"I'm gonna die one way or the other. Might as well go out in a blaze of glory."

"Like Butch and Sundance."

"Except only Butch."

Grant knew she was right. If he thought about it in a totally practical sense, it was the obvious choice. Normally Grant could do that—set aside emotion and do what had to be done. This time he couldn't engage his practical side. Emotion kept getting in the way. He held her hand and didn't speak. Cruz respected his silence and closed her eyes. Now that the decision had been made, she relaxed. Amazingly, she even slept. Grant watched her eyelids flicker as she dreamed. He supposed there was a kind of symmetry at work. The rule of threes. Bond had sacrificed himself for the unit. Mack and Coop had sacrificed themselves for the surviving pair. Now Butch was going to sacrifice herself for Sundance. It all made perfect sense.

He let her sleep and waited for dawn.

GRANT LEANED OVER AND kissed Cruz gently on the lips. That was something Newman never did to Redford. Thank goodness. Cruz's eyes flickered open and she smiled. It was still dark but dawn was already turning pitch-black night into shades of blue.

They were out of water. Low on ammunition. One rifle between them, which was just as well because Cruz couldn't shoot for shit. She'd smiled when Grant had told her that. He leaned forward and kissed her dry lips again. She kissed him back, holding his head in both hands as she gave him the last good memories of the love they had shared.

Cruz took the blue velvet case out of her haversack and held it in both hands. They sat in silence as the sky paled in the east. Dawn began to remove the cover that had been hiding the final stretch of ground to the safe zone. Grant should have gone while it was still dark, but darkness would have also hidden the decoy.

She handed Grant the velvet case.

"My father gave me this. Make sure he gets it back."

At first Grant couldn't take it because that would be accepting what was to come next. She held it out to him. After a few short moments, he reached over and took it. His hand brushed her fingers. Her eyes became serious.

"Can you take the shot?"

"Before they lay a finger on you."

"It's not their fingers I'm worried about."

Joking to the end. Cruz sidled up against the half-demolished wall and peered towards the fires that signaled the final battlefield. She took an emergency flare out of her pocket and didn't look back. Dragging her ruined leg behind her, she clambered over the debris and shuffled across the open ground. At first there was no sound from the resting natives. Darkness protected her until she was halfway there.

Grant slipped out of the side door and jogged in a crouch, keeping as low as he could while not sacrificing speed. He covered the distance with an easy loping trot. The rifle hung loosely from one hand. He focused on the rocky ground. This wasn't the time to turn his ankle or trip over the uneven terrain. Cruz was depending on him, and he was depending on Cruz. The ideal partnership.

The sky began to pale. The sun lay hidden below the horizon but was already making its presence felt. Darkness drew back the curtain, and the scope of Grant's vision became wider and longer. He could see rocks and sand farther ahead than just at his feet. He could see the manmade embankment that formed the boundary of the safe zone. He was halfway there. When he glanced over his shoulder he could make out the shambling figure moving across the killing ground, approaching the campfires on the edge of town.

Cruz slowed down. She looked towards Grant, gauging how close he was to his destination. Dull gray light filtered across the landscape. Grant was a darker smudge of gray in the distance.

Grant scrambled behind the only piece of cover, a gentle undulation in the desert floor, and threw himself to the ground. He lay facing the township and the woman he loved. The shadowy figure was growing more distinct by the minute, but she still wasn't clear enough for him to take the shot. She would have to provide more light for him to kill her. A burden of self-discipline Grant wasn't sure he possessed. Cruz had courage in abundance. One day he would have to tell her father that. He shuffled into a prone firing position. Legs apart, one knee cocked. He sighted along the barrel and waited.

Cruz stared across the open ground. Grant had disappeared. For a moment panic fluttered her heart until she caught the glint of light off the rifle barrel. She took the empty canteen from her belt and unscrewed the lid. She raised her arm and dropped the metal container. It echoed and banged on the rocky ground. Voices shouted around the campfires. There was a rush of movement.

Grant took a deep breath and relaxed his aim.

The voices grew louder and more aggressive. The mob smelled blood. Silver blades caught dawn's early light. The crowd surged towards the injured medic. The sight of her bloodstained combat fatigues inflamed them. Machetes flashed in a ritual dance of bloodlust. They closed the distance on the lone soldier in minutes.

Grant eased one finger into the trigger guard.

The surge became a charge.

The shouts became a roar of anger.

Cruz held the flare in front of her and threw one last glance towards her lover.

Grant took a deep breath, then let it out slowly.

Cruz yanked the fuse.

Then everything came together in a blaze of symmetry. The flare went up, a whoosh of brilliant white light. The charging militia were frozen for a split second as if in a photographer's flash. The army medic stood with one hand above her head like the Statue of Liberty. The torch she held spat fire. Her silhouette was sharp and clear and an easy target. The rifle barrel settled as Grant's breath reached empty. Machetes were raised. The crowd reached Cruz.

Grant took the shot.

THE PRESENT

He controls everything.

—Eduardo Cruz

THIRTY-ONE

THE ROOM WAS SILENT. Grant's voice had descended into a whisper by the end. He'd drunk three glasses of water. It had only taken half an hour, but daylight had already turned to dusk. The smell of Mexican food was stronger. Doc Cruz brought Grant a fourth refill and then stood beside the cot. Grant took a sip, then held the glass in both hands on his lap. He looked spent, and not just because of what the fever had taken out of him. This was the first time he'd spoken about the shooting since he'd left the army.

"So now you can bring your friends in. Do what you will."

Doc Cruz swung the chair around and pushed it back under the desk. When he turned to face Grant, the sag in his shoulders had gone and there was a sense of purpose in his stance. He looked taller, his chest full of pride.

"What do you think I want to do?"

Grant looked at the man standing over him. "I killed your daughter."

"And yet she asked you to return her stethoscope."

"Yes."

"Do you think she would have done that if she thought I would do you harm?"

"Probably not."

"Definitely not. She spoke of you often. Always with affection. What you did was…"

Doc Cruz's voice faltered. He let out a sigh.

"…necessary."

Grant put the glass on the bedside cabinet. "What I did was run. And she paid the price for it."

"That was her choice. She was going to die anyway. At least this way one of you survived. Pilar could always make the hard choices."

Grant knew Cruz was right. He knew that Pilar had been right too. Her father appeared to have forgiven him. One of these days he'd have to forgive himself. In the meantime, he was in a house full of Mexicans who had already shown their dislike of him.

"So. Why are we here?"

Cruz leaned against the desk. "We are here because you did not follow doctor's orders."

Grant nodded at the door. "And why are they here?"

Cruz pushed off from the desk and went to open the door. He paused with one hand on the doorknob and turned back to Grant.

"Because Tony Sabata has been smuggling illegals across the border for years. Until Macready started using the same route and shut him down."

SABATA WASN'T ONE FOR explaining. What little he confirmed he did between mouthfuls as they all sat around the dining table. The rest Grant learned from Doc Cruz and the old Mexican that Grant had seen before working behind the counter at Sixto's—one of many illegals Sabata had helped find gainful employment in America. The fact that the old Mexican worked for Sabata's rival was either ironic or intentional. The more Grant heard, the less he believed in irony.

The way it went was this.

Sabata was a coyote: a man who facilitated entry into the United States and escorted his immigrants across the border. He brought them through the mountain passes of Big Bend National Park and north past Adobe Flats. He took payment, but only enough to bribe officials on the border and cover transport costs. Families came across in small groups, not always together. Reunions were emotional affairs and prone to exuberant celebrations. Sabata was never short of food or goodwill donated by the people he had helped. If they prospered, Sabata ate well. If they struggled, he helped tide them over until things picked up.

In recent times, things had not picked up. It became harder to place illegals in work, and the few he did find jobs for struggled to make ends meet. Texans were not known for their love of Mexicans. Sabata had to range far and wide to support his imports. The pressure exaggerated his already short temper. Family reunions became few and far between. He took out his frustration on the only person available.

"So you did push her against the cooker."

Sabata made another tortilla wrap but left it on his plate. The room fell silent. Grant had just breached an unspoken code: interfering with the privacy of marriage. He didn't care. As a cop he'd been to plenty of domestic disputes. There was always a reason for relationships turning sour, but that was never justification for shoving your wife against a hot stove. Sabata stared at the Yorkshireman.

"She fell against the stove. I pulled her away."

"That's not what the bruises say."

The old Mexican sucked in his breath. The other two men were suddenly intent on folding minced beef into soft tortillas. Sabata locked eyes with Grant, preparing to escalate the confrontation. To defend his honor. This could get ugly. Neither man was going to back down. Grant flexed his legs under the table, ready to push up if Sabata lunged forward. He'd dealt with angry husbands at domestics too. The coyote didn't blink. The stare brought water to his eyes. Then he lowered his voice and nodded.

"The bruises were an overreaction."

Grant waited for an explanation. Sabata looked sheepish. Maybe because he was talking in front of his men or maybe because this was something he was embarrassed about.

"I am not proud of my temper. She got burned. I dragged her from the heat. I shook her for being so careless. Too hard. She is the mother of my child. The shock made me forget that. I will never forget it again."

The tension didn't ease. Grant didn't relax. This could still go either way.

Sabata leaned forward. "I hurt my wife. You stood up for her. That is the only reason I allow you to ask about this matter. I will not speak of it again."

Grant nodded. "Fair enough."

He scooped some spicy chicken into a soft wrap and folded it into a parcel.

"What happened with Macready?"

"About what?"

"About your smuggling."

"I don't smuggle. I help people find a better life."

Grant chewed and swallowed. The chicken was delicious.

"Until recently. What changed?"

Sabata banged the table. Everybody's plate jumped.

"What happened was Tripp Macready learned about my route and took it for himself. He paid more. I could not outbid him. The border guards grow fat on the smuggler's money."

Sabata lowered his voice.

"You have upset him more than you upset me. That is the other reason I break bread with you."

Grant held a tortilla in one hand and raised his eyebrows.

Sabata smiled. "Figuratively speaking."

He leaned his elbows on the table.

"What I want to know is what you saw in the factory. What is Macready bringing across that means he can pay so much?"

Grant finished his tortilla and wiped his mouth. "Let me show you."

He reached into his pocket and took out the gold medallion.

THE ROOM FELL SILENT again. Everybody stopped eating. Grant stood the coin on its side and flicked it into a spin. The gold blurred into spinning top. It glided towards the middle of the table until it began to wobble. Before it tumbled to a stop, Sabata slammed his hand down on the coin. He exploded with a string of swearwords in Spanish.

The other Mexicans sat back, startled.

Grant waited for a translation.

Sabata didn't explain. He glared at the medallion with fire in his eyes. Doc Cruz rested a hand on Grant's sleeve and leaned in close.

"Aztec gold. Was it all like this?"

Grant looked at the coin lying flat in the middle of the table. "A lot of it, yes. Some other pieces—ornaments, goblets."

Cruz seemed reluctant to ask the next question. "What was he doing with it?"

"Melting it down into ingots."

Sabata slammed the table again. "That bastard. He is not only raping my country, he is destroying its heritage."

Grant didn't comment.

Sabata was on a roll.

"You should have blown up his entire fucking operation. That would have taught him a lesson."

Grant shrugged. "The factory's only a waypoint. Smelting works on its way up the chain."

Doc Cruz turned in his chair. "There is more?"

Grant glanced at Cruz but spoke to Sabata. "He might be bribing border guards to get his stuff across, but he's paying a lot more farther north."

He rubbed his fingers and thumbs together as if counting money. "Army trucks don't come cheap. That many trucks don't go missing without somebody high up giving the okay. That costs more than a few corrupt crossing guards."

Sabata allowed a touch of admiration to enter his voice. "You have cost him time and money. He will not like you for that."

"I don't think he liked me from the start."

"He will like you even less now. He will be looking harder to find you."

Grant laid both hands flat on the table. The hairs on his forearms bristled. A cold shiver ran down the back of his neck. He looked at Sabata. "You found me."

"I found out where you'd gone."

"How?"

"Like I said, there aren't many people who own a damaged hearse."

Grant turned to Cruz. "Or who are friends with the man everyone in Absolution knows I came here to find. Damn."

Grant wished he'd been more tight-lipped about why he was visiting Adobe Flats instead of telling every man and his dog who he was looking for. The doctor who had hung his shingle with Hunter Athey. Even before he asked the question, he knew it was too late.

"Do you have a phone here?"

THIRTY-TWO

THE ABSOLUTION MOTEL AND RV Park was in darkness by the time they arrived, a two-car convoy in the mouth of South Lee Street, just across the railroad tracks. Doc Cruz's little puddle jumper and Tony Sabata's pickup. They had driven the last half mile without lights, so Grant's eyes were already adjusted to the dark by the time he got out and surveyed the turnaround out front. Down on one knee, low amid the scrub and cactus beside the two-lane blacktop.

Cruz stayed in the car. Sabata crouched next to Grant. The two men who had exchanged blows and gunfire looked at each other. Both men knew this wasn't good. There had been no phone at Fort Pena Colorado Park, and the cell phone coverage south of Absolution was for shit. Grant always reckoned that was a convenient plot device in the movies. He found it extremely inconvenient now. Texas should invest in more cell phone towers.

He turned his attention back to the reception office. The last time he'd done this, he had been close to exhaustion and bleeding everywhere. Tonight he was in better shape, but he thought the outcome was going to be worse. There was no sign of Macready's men hiding in wait. There were no vehicles in the turnaround. There were no fresh tracks in the moonlit dust. None of the tourist cabins were occupied. Even the one that Athey had rented to Grant was empty. The only part of the motel and RV park getting any trade these days was the mortuary. Grant hoped that wasn't going to be true this time.

He checked both ways along the highway, then sprinted across the road doubled at the waist to stay below the height of the windows. He doubted that would make any difference, but he felt less conspicuous that way. Sabata trailed him, and they went through the archway together. Grant dropped to one knee next to a cactus that looked like Mickey Mouse getting acupuncture. Big round leaves or whatever they called them. The carved wooden sign hung above them, still with no bullet holes in it. It swayed gently for no reason Grant could fathom. There was no breeze. The night was still and quiet.

Grant scanned the front of the building for security cameras high up under the eaves. There weren't any. There were no security lights either. Who was going to burgle a desert motel in the middle of nowhere? Satisfied that nobody could be watching on camera, Grant darted forward and flattened against the wall. He dropped to one knee again and peered through the window, his head low and down in one corner so it wouldn't stand out.

There was nobody inside. Grant could tell that because the office had been destroyed, and nobody was tidying it up. There was no movement at all. The table had been tipped over. Catalogs and brochures for Big Bend National Park were scattered across the floor. The chairs were upended. The telephone had been ripped out of the wall. Grant checked the shadows on the floor. If anything had happened to Hunter Athey, that's where his body would be. The only shadows were smashed furniture and ripped cushions.

A red light blinked inside.

Grant tensed. His eyes flicked from the red light to the office space to the door that Athey had come out of drying his hands. There still was no movement inside. The red light blinked again. Grant tried to remember if there was an alarm panel somewhere in the office. No, there wasn't; same reason as the security cameras. Who was going to burgle a desert motel? He didn't feel safe going in just yet. He turned to Sabata and made a walking man symbol with one hand, indicating for Sabata to go one way and Grant the other, round the back of the motel reception, then meet back here.

Sabata nodded and set off at a crouch.

Grant set off anticlockwise.

The stars were bright in the night sky. The moon wasn't up yet. There were no streetlights to pollute the darkness. Pale blue starlight was the only illumination. It turned the journey around the motel into a shadowy ghost train ride on foot. Every crevice in the motel exterior was a black hole threatening to hide an assassin. Every bush and cactus was a possible henchman. Grant avoided the gravel path and the flower border. His footsteps were silent and continuous. He worked his way around the building quick but careful. He crossed paths with Sabata round the back and exchanged a brief nod before continuing all the way to the front again. A double check in case one of them had missed something.

By the time he'd reached Mickey Mouse again, Grant was satisfied there was nobody lying in wait. That only left the red light blinking in the darkness. If it wasn't an alarm sensor, then what was it? He reached for the door handle, then stopped. His mind ran through what he knew about Macready. He was the wealthiest man in Absolution. He had no compunction about killing people. And he employed ex-army and mercenaries.

Grant lowered his hand from the door handle.

Mercenaries were explosive experts. Had Macready set a trap in case Grant came looking for Hunter Athey? Was there a trip wire or an infrared device waiting to blow up the building if Grant stepped inside? He pushed his face to the window and squinted at the red light. It blinked again in the far corner next to a drift of cardboard matchbooks and paper sachets spilled across the floor. Foreign coffee pouches and teabags with the little drawstrings for dangling in your cup.

Grant nodded his understanding.

He reached for the handle and opened the door.

TEN MINUTES LATER, THE office was secured, all the corners searched. There was no sign of Hunter Athey apart from the battered hearse they'd found parked round the back. Grant unplugged the electric kettle, and the red light stopped blinking. Despite the lack of starlight in the darkened office, he had no trouble following the track of the struggle.

The overturned chair and table.

The slew of papers and area maps scuffed with dirty footprints.

The cups and plates broken amid the scattering of teabags.

The kettle on its side on the carpet.

Leading to the phone ripped out of the wall.

The disturbance wasn't wanton destruction or signs of an over-enthusiastic search of the motel reception. It was evidence of a man being caught by surprise who tried to make the warning call before it was too late. Who Athey thought he was going to call, Grant wasn't sure. There was no phone at the Fort Pena Colorado Park, and he must have known that cell phone coverage was bad south of Absolution. Grant righted the chair and sat down. He drummed his fingers on the overturned table leg. Sabata leaned against the wall.

Grant thought about the cat—the one with its neck snapped around backwards. An old saying ran through his head: in the dark, all cats are gray. He didn't know what that had to do with anything here, but the thought persisted. He needed a second opinion, so he turned to Sabata.

"What do you think?"

Sabata pushed off from the wall. "I think it is very bad."

"Where would they take him?"

"That depends what they want him for. To make him talk? That he can do anywhere. Macready is not worried about what people think. He is not afraid of the law. So, the hacienda."

Grant nodded. Macready owned the law in Absolution. If he wanted Athey to disappear, the body would never be found. There would be no evidence that he was killed at Macready's compound.

"What else could he want?"

"He wants you."

Grant was leaning towards a theory but wanted Sabata to confirm his thinking. "So?"

"So, if he wanted to send a message, there is only one place you have shown an interest in."

"Adobe Flats."

"What is left of it."

Grant nodded his agreement.

"That's what I was thinking."

He'd been staring at a fixed spot during all this. Focusing his mind. That odd saying popped into his head again. In the dark, all cats are gray. The spot he'd been staring at was the scattered papers near the telephone. The smudged footprints and crumpled maps. A dark stain on the wall where the phone's wire had been yanked out. Dark gray. All cats are gray. In the dark. He remembered taking witness statements in Yorkshire, especially ones about cars fleeing the scene of a crime in the dark. How many times had the color been disguised by the night or the orange sodium lights?

The stain on the wall was dark gray.

The smudged papers were the same.

In the dark, all cats are gray.

Grant stood up and picked up a book of matches from amid the spilled teabags. He went to the stain and struck a match. Sulphur flared. The light flickered and settled down. The smudge wasn't gray. It was red. The crumpled papers on the floor obscured the trail of blood, but it concluded the struggle that Grant had tracked. It didn't end with the phone being yanked from the wall. It ended with somebody being dragged towards the back door. The one that led to the mortuary.

Grant closed his eyes and extinguished the match. He counted five seconds to allow the burned image to dull, then opened them again. With his eyes readjusted he crossed to the door, barely registering the smell of gas in the background.

STARLIGHT BATHED THE MORTUARY in pale blue light through the skylight that Grant hadn't noticed before. The last time he'd been in here, he had been somewhat the worse for wear. Hiding in a coffin until Hunter Athey had entered and turned on the fluorescent lights.

Neither of them turned the lights on this time. Grant remembered Vince McNulty blowing his gas-filled flat up in Leeds, the ex-detective not being quick enough to stop Donkey Flowers from flicking the switch. Tony Sabata wasn't that stupid. Both men smelled the gas. Both saw the propane bottles standing against the back wall, the taps partly open for a slow feed. Two bottles that hadn't been there the last time. The RV park might use gas bottles for its visitors, but the mortuary was fully electric.

Grant went straight to the gas taps and turned them off. Sabata wedged the back door open to ventilate the room. The gas was heavier than air. It was slow to clear. Grant finished with the second bottle, then turned to face the coffin on the trestle—a different coffin than the one he'd been hiding in. The same layout: heavy wooden box with the lid resting loosely on top, not nailed down, slightly off center. Blood trail on the floor.

Sabata followed Grant's gaze. Both men stood rooted to the spot, one at either end of the coffin. Grant was the first to move. He stepped forward and stood at the shoulder of the coffin. He would have taken a deep breath but the gas was still thick in the atmosphere. He pushed the lid to one side. Six inches. Just enough for the glow through the skylight to pick out the inside.

Hunter Athey stared up at him. The glassy-eyed stare of the long-time dead. One side of his face was swollen and bloodied. The wrinkles had smoothed out, making him look younger than in life. That wasn't the thing that shocked Grant. The body was lying on its stomach in the bottom of the coffin, but the head was turned all the way round, the neck snapped as cleanly as the cat's.

Grant felt anger boiling inside him.

He pushed the lid another six inches.

He wasn't surprised to find what he was looking for.

The sleeves of Athey's shirt were wrinkled just above the elbow. Tight creases where strong hands had held him while Macready had performed his favorite trick. Snapping a man's neck takes more effort than killing a cat. A man is unlikely to sit still while you do it. Grant knew that if he rolled Athey's sleeves up, he would find bruises on both arms. Four fingers and a thumb. Like the shake injuries on Sabata's wife or the bruises on Sarah Hellstrom's arms.

The anger cranked up a notch. He felt like turning it loose on Sabata for beating his wife despite the extenuating circumstances. He felt like taking it out on Scott Macready for beating Sarah because she'd lent Grant her car. Mostly he wanted to tear Tripp Macready's head off and shit down his neck. None of those things were going to happen. Not yet.

A shiver of foreboding ran up Grant's spine. His mind replayed the struggle that had taken place in the front office. The overturned table. The spilled papers. The telephone yanked out of the wall. Who had Athey being trying to warn? Not Eduardo Cruz because there was no phone at Fort Pena Colorado Park. That only left one person.

Sarah Hellstrom.

Chances were that Tripp Macready had come to the same conclusion. The only other person who had helped Grant since he came to Absolution. The only person aside from Doc Cruz who might be hiding him.

"Shit."

He grabbed the coffin lid to slide it shut. Then he saw the red light blinking in the bottom near Athey's feet. Not an overturned kettle but a delayed timer tripped by Grant opening the coffin. The gas had cleared slightly but was still thick enough to be dangerous.

"Double shit."

He turned and pushed Sabata towards the open door. Grant slipped on the smooth floor. He went down hard on one knee. The wound opened again, but he ignored the pain. The red light blinked faster, accompanied by an almost imperceptible *beep, beep, beep*.

Sabata got through the door first.

Grant didn't make it.

The light stopped blinking.

THIRTY-THREE

THE PEACE AND TRANQUILITY of Absolution, Texas, was torn apart by the explosion and fireball half a mile west of town. It ripped the silence and shook the ground like a medium-scale earthquake. Half a mile west and three quarters of a mile southwest of the athletics track and Macready's compound. Everybody in town heard it, including Tripp Macready. The town dictator would have been quicker off the mark if he hadn't already been knee deep in his own preparations.

Jim Grant didn't know that.

If he had, he might have made some different choices.

GRANT'S BACK WAS ON fire. Rubble and debris bounced all around him. Shards of broken glass became deadly blades of shrapnel. Grant curled into a fetal position and protected his head with his arms. Shrapnel sliced his jacket and cut his hands. The flames were hot, but he couldn't risk putting them out until the fallout dissipated. He gritted his teeth and waited until the debris shower stopped. The fireball receded almost immediately, blown out by the force of the explosion and the lack of fuel. The debris took a few moments longer.

Sabata was up and running first. He whipped off his coat and smothered Grant's back. The flames went out but Grant's hair continued to smoke, singed down to patches of ugly stubble. As soon as he realized he had survived, he let out a roar of anger. Once he'd got that out of his system, his thoughts turned to the telephone warning.

"Sarah."

He struggled to his feet but couldn't get his body moving. He tried to get his bearings. Gilda's Grill and Diner was at the other end of town. Sabata grabbed his arm.

"That is the first place they will go."

Grant shook his head clear but didn't struggle. "This is the first place they'll go."

Sabata nodded. "And very soon. Everyone in town will have heard the explosion."

"Then let's go to the diner."

"Straight through town? I don't think so."

Grant wasn't thinking clearly, but he knew where he wanted to go. "Yes. Right now."

His mouth said it, but his body wouldn't respond. His head began to spin again. This was too soon after the fever. He hadn't regained full strength yet. It seemed like he'd spent his entire visit to Absolution being pushed around or treated for injuries and illness. He tried to shake his arm free.

Sabata let go and held up his hands. "Evade and destroy. That's what you told Eduardo."

Grant was confused. Had he really said that? Yes, he had. After struggling across the desert while Macready's men had searched for his body. Well, they could have his body now. Because he was going to find them. And make them pay.

"Destroy. Yes."

Sabata persisted. "Evade first. Instead of standing here waiting for Macready to come get you."

Grant nodded. Sabata was right. He was about to agree with the coyote when headlights sped around the back of the mortuary. Two pairs skidded to a halt and caught Grant in the crossfire. He held a hand to his eyes but couldn't see beyond the glare. Doors slammed shut and footsteps raced towards him.

"Amigo. There is no time to waste."

The concern in Doc Cruz's voice snapped Grant out of his daze. The doctor and the Mexican from Sixto's took Grant by the arm and urged him towards the car. Two other Mexicans shouted for Sabata to do the same. The pickup spun in a tight arc and headed back out of the motel. Cruz's car followed. The convoy crossed the road again and bounced over the railroad tracks. Headlights were turned off. The convoy disappeared into the darkness from whence it had come, heading south at the edge of town.

Grant looked out of the rear window at the smoldering ruin. He'd had enough of running and hiding. It was time to take the fight to Macready. But first he needed to make sure Sarah was safe.

"The diner."

Doc Cruz squinted in the dark to follow the pickup. He indicated the old Mexican sitting in the back seat.

"Sixto's. Use the friends that you've got."

The Mexican was nodding. The pickup took a left. Cruz followed.

"But not yet."

He indicated the Mexican again.

"Javier lives down here. We need to regroup."

Grant settled in his seat. "You hear that from Pilar?"

"I heard many things from Pilar. Enough to know you are a man to be trusted. Form your plan. Decide your tactics. After I have put out the fire in your back and treated your burns at Javier's house."

Javier's house was on South Fifth Street, just off Avenue D. The low-rent houses Grant had seen across the railroad crossing on his way south. The bottom edge of town. In the opposite direction to Macready's and Sixto's. The pickup knew where it was going. Cruz pulled in behind it. In the yard of a ramshackle bungalow with torn curtains and a rusty children's swing.

Ten minutes later Doc Cruz was applying soothing balm to Grant's burns. Just like the first time Grant had seen him with Sabata's wife. The orange windcheater had taken most of the blast and protected his back, but he was still bruised and sore. The coat was scorched and tattered but was still hanging together, a bit like Grant himself. It was time to stop being the target and turn his fury on Macready. Cruz was right, though. Not yet. Not until he'd reconnoitred the enemy positions and not until he'd got Sarah Hellstrom out of the firing line.

That meant using the old Mexican's connections at Sixto's.

Grant hated waiting, but the Mexican had already set off while Grant was being treated. The band of desperados waited in the kitchen for Javier to return. Sabata and his friends. Doc Cruz. Jim Grant. The father and the Yorkshireman who had only come to Absolution to return the daughter's stethoscope. They didn't have to wait long.

The kitchen door creaked as Javier slipped inside. It was the first sound the group had heard. The Mexican might be old, but he moved like a cat. It gave Grant hope that the news would be good. It wasn't.

"Miss Sarah is gone."

No surprise there. Grant clutched at straws.

"She left?"

Javier stood with his back to the door.

"Taken. By the pup."

Nobody asked who the pup was. If Tripp Macready was the top dog in town, then his son was still wet behind the ears. Grant had hoped Hunter Athey had got through with his last phone call, but it had always been a forlorn hope. Sarah was the only other person in Absolution who had helped Grant. Scott Macready was the jealous type. Those two things added up to a world of trouble for the woman who refused to sell out.

"Adobe Flats?"

Javier shook his head.

"The hacienda."

The old Mexican came to the table and pulled up a chair. He sat heavily, with slumped shoulders and a troubled brow. There was more, and it didn't look like good news. Doc Cruz waited patiently. Sabata leaned his elbows on the table. Grant looked from one to the other, than back at Javier.

"What?"

"The boy does not like you, and his father wants you dead. Miss Sarah is the bait. A trade—you for her."

Doc Cruz huffed and stood up from the table. Sabata interlaced his fingers and flexed them until the knuckles popped. Grant kept his voice calm even though anger was building inside him.

"And if I trade?"

Javier lowered his eyes.

Doc Cruz let out a sigh.

Sabata answered. "He will kill you both. As a message."

Grant let the rage subside, holding it ready for when he could set it loose. "Then it's time I sent a message to him."

Javier held up a hand of warning. "He is ready for you. The soldiers—they are gathering."

"The mercenaries?"

"Si, señor."

Grant looked at Sabata. "Convoy?"

Sabata shrugged. "Not so soon. Unless, after the factory explosion…"

"That wasn't me."

"He doesn't know that."

"Then why the mercenaries?"

Sabata nodded at Grant. "You are a dangerous man."

Grant glared into space. "He doesn't know the half of it."

He looked at Javier. "No sign of the trucks?"

"No."

Grant fed all the information into his strategy computer. Professional soldiers. A walled, defensive position on the outskirts of town. An angry man out for revenge. He doubted Macready would underestimate Grant again after he'd slipped away from the mountain convoy. This would have to be a frontal assault unless he could think of something else.

"Is there a phone here?"

Javier shook his head. Grant thought about cell phone coverage nearer town. He hated mobile phones and had always told the young coppers in Yorkshire that he'd never have one as long as he had a hole in his arse. He wished his arse was sewn up now.

"Anybody got a cell?"

Sabata raised his eyebrows. "You gonna call him?"

"I'm going to call the cavalry."

Doc Cruz waved the idea away. "No coverage."

"Even in town?"

"There used to be two cell phone masts. Macready had them destroyed. He wants all calls going through the exchange."

"And he controls the exchange?"

"He controls everything."

"But he can't block calls."

"He'll know where you're calling from."

Grant thought about the only place he'd heard a phone being dialed: the Los Pecos Bank and Trust. Just down Avenue D from Macready's compound. Too close for comfort. Then he thought about where the call had been placed.

"Sixto's."

This time nobody objected.

THIRTY-FOUR

FRESH MEAT AND TRANQUILIZERS. Grant wasn't looking for car spares and didn't plan on entering the fenced compound at Sixto's, but he couldn't trust old Pedro not to bark. The guard dog might have wagged its tail and smiled at him before, but dogs have a way of changing their allegiance after dark. It was after dark now. Quarter to eleven. A cloudless sky. The moon was finally up.

Grant padded across the road and bypassed the gas pumps. Sixto's was locked and dark. Gilda's Grill stood empty; that thought spurred him on. The roller shutter doors of the mechanics' bays were closed. Moonlight glinted off the scrapped cars in the compound. Bright spots and shadows.

The dog was hiding in the shadows.

Grant heard the low growl off to his right. He waved the drugged meat in one hand and made soothing noises. He'd never owned a dog. He wasn't sure what sounds would calm old Pedro. In the end it was the meat that made the difference more than the low whistles and soft clucking noises. The dog wagged its tail as it came towards the fence.

The meat didn't last five minutes. Grant hoped Doc Cruz hadn't overdone it with the tranquilizers. The dog hadn't hurt anyone. The others waited across the road. Grant didn't want them reminding it to bark at strangers. He supposed that meant he wasn't a stranger anymore.

Ten minutes later, Pedro curled up and went to sleep. Grant signaled the others and turned away from the fence, then stopped. He looked through the wire at the scrapped cars. A junkyard for motor spares. He thought about the other junkyard—the Absolution town dump. The old-timer with a keen eye and an arsenal of weapons. A sniper's rifle would be perfect if Grant had to take that shot again.

He brushed the thought aside and went to the sales kiosk. The office was dark, the only light coming from the electronic bug fryer above the door. Purple light drew flies towards it like moths to a flame. Another thought crossed his mind. Even with the guns he could get from the old-timer, a frontal assault was a high-risk strategy. If he could draw them out, it would be better. Draw them to the flame. Make them easy targets.

He glanced over his shoulder at the gas pumps. There were no fumes hanging around like a hazy mirage, but that was an easy fix. The pumps weren't locked. Like Scott Macready had said, nobody steals from him. He wondered if that attitude applied to the security of the office. He checked. The door was locked. Ah, well. Nothing worth doing came easy. He scanned the front of the building for CCTV cameras. None. Then he checked the door for alarm sensors. None. This was a trusting town. Nobody wanted to go up against Macready.

Doc Cruz jogged across the forecourt and stood wheezing next to Grant. It was the second time the doctor had been out of breath by the time he'd joined the English cop. The two stood looking at each other for a moment, twinned by sadness and a sense of purpose. This was the beginning of payback time.

Grant kicked the door open.

Then he heard the low rumble that changed everything.

"DAMN. WE SHOULD HAVE come straight to Sarah's."

Grant closed the door and moved into the shadows, away from the window. Moonlight meant the shadows were towards the back of the office. That was good. The telephone was towards the back of the office. The bad thing was his assumption that Macready would have gone straight over to the motel after the explosion. The dull, rumbling vibration meant Macready was busy, and not just preparing to defend against Jim Grant.

Doc Cruz crouched behind the glass-top counter. "You might still have been too late."

"I might not have."

He took Cruz's hand and laid it on the countertop.

"Feel that?"

The vibration hummed through the glass. Cruz nodded.

"Trucks."

Doc Cruz slumped into a chair behind the cash register. "Tony said it was too soon."

Grant went to the phone and waited. He scanned the forecourt. There was no movement. Sabata was waiting in the pickup with the others. Lights out, hidden among the scrub and cacti across the road. He thought about Sabata's analysis. It held water given the limited information available. Under normal circumstances it was too soon for another convoy. The factory explosion and Grant on

254

the loose meant these weren't normal circumstances. The smuggling operation was exposed at the moment. That situation was time sensitive. Capture Grant and kill the witnesses, and it could be business as usual. Until then…

"Macready's closing it down. One last shipment to keep the partners up north off his back. They must carry a lot of clout."

"What?"

"Power. I mean, he thought they sent me as a hit man."

Doc Cruz laid a hand on Grant's forearm. "You are a hit man."

Grant let out a sigh. "I was a typist."

"In the army? After the shot?"

"For the rest of my service. I never fired a gun again."

"Ever?"

Grant thought about Snake Pass in Yorkshire. Boston and Los Angeles since he'd come to America. He held out a hand, palm down, and quivered it.

"Not much."

Cruz leaned forward and locked eyes with Grant.

"This would be a good time. There are still good people in Absolution. People who would help. People who can get weapons."

Grant shook his head. "People who could get killed."

"They are getting killed now."

"Not most of them. Most of them are getting by. Dying is forever."

"Then what are you going to do?"

Grant considered that.

"Something massive."

The rumbling vibration grew louder. It was difficult to gauge what direction, but Grant already knew. The athletics track outside

Macready's walled compound. He counted the minutes in his head. Remembered how long it took for the trucks to park up in formation. When he thought it had been long enough, he clicked his fingers.

The vibration stopped.

The mercenaries would be climbing aboard and getting ready to leave on the slow drive through town, then south towards Adobe Flats. Scott Macready had fucked up last time. This was a bigger deal. Grant was willing to bet that Tripp Macready would be in charge.

The gas pumps stood mute on the forecourt. Maybe Grant wouldn't need a flame to draw the moths. The moths were leaving and wouldn't be back until dawn. That left Grant plenty of time to prepare a sunrise surprise. He picked up the phone and began to dial from memory.

Doc Cruz pushed the chair back from the counter.

"Are you still calling the army?"

Grant nodded in the direction of the staging area.

"Those are the army's trucks. No point ringing Fort Stockton. Somebody up there supplied them."

"Who then?"

"Somebody who can go around the side."

The phone rang three times. Then John Cornejo answered.

THIRTY-FIVE

"Do the Texans know shit keeps blowing up around you?"

Cornejo's voice was calm and friendly. Nothing like the suicidal ex-marine whom Grant had met on the subway in Boston. Or the man caught in the explosion at the John B. Hynes Convention Center.

"Doesn't seem to have done you any harm."

Cornejo chuckled down the phone.

"You know what they say. What doesn't kill you makes you stronger."

Grant leaned against the wall with the phone to his ear. "That's not what you said when I met you."

Cornejo went quiet for a moment, and Grant thought his attempt at humor had overstepped the mark. Cornejo had been a damaged man until helping Grant had given him renewed purpose. Maybe reminding the marine of that was a bit insensitive. The voice that came back on the line was a long way from depressed.

"If I'd known you were gonna get me blown up, I'd have said a lot more."

Grant smiled in the shadows.

"I dare say you would."

Cornejo got straight to the point, with a twist. "So, what's going on? You don't come round. You never call."

Grant's smile became a grin. "Don't go all *Brokeback Mountain* on me."

Cornejo chuckled again. "I'd call you a top man, but you wouldn't like it."

"Top man is good, isn't it?"

"Not in America. Means the man who gets on top."

Grant feigned shock, making a shivering noise down the phone. "Pitcher, not receiver?"

"Hole in one."

"Golf jokes now. In snooker it's called going for the difficult brown instead of the easy pink."

"We play pool over here."

"Good for you."

The conversation was light and chatty. Two ex-servicemen catching up over the phone. It was nice to hear a familiar voice. Grant made a mental note to meet up when he was back doing Boston PD duties. It felt good to still be in a disciplined service. Lots of ex-servicemen became cops. It maintained the continuity of being part of a uniformed body. He made another mental note to retrieve his badge wallet from Scott Macready. There were other things he wanted to discuss with the Macready pup too, when he could get him alone.

Cornejo turned serious. "Okay, Jim. Let's have it."

Grant adjusted the phone at his ear. "You've never been much fun since you got your laces back."

"Don't know why they took 'em. Nobody hangs themselves with shoelaces."

The fact that Cornejo could joke about his suicidal tendencies suggested he was fully recovered. That was important. It was also the reason Grant had called him. Because the army didn't reinstate ex-marines who were still likely to kill themselves. Grant tested his information.

"I hear you're back in the service."

Cornejo sounded wary. "Not in. More around the edges."

"VA liaison?"

"A bit more than that. Reward for saving Senator Clayton."

"Couldn't have gone to a better man."

"That's true. Now, what do you want?"

Grant checked his watch to see how much time he had. The white band of skin against his tan stood out in the dark. The watch was somewhere in the scrub and rubble off the mountain road. He glanced at the wall clock above the counter. Just after eleven o'clock. He couldn't do anything until the trucks left. He reckoned that Macready was too busy to be monitoring calls made from Absolution but didn't want to take the chance. The Texan had plenty of people working for him. Delegation was a key part of management.

"You've got access to the defense department. Right?"

Cornejo didn't dodge the question. "I liaise with them all the time. Yes."

Grant nodded even though Cornejo couldn't see him.

"Good. This is what I need."

SILENCE FILLED SIXTO'S OFFICE when Grant hung up. Starlight through the window silvered the counter and the cash register.

259

Everything else was in shadow, apart from the bug zapper above the door. As if to prove the point, a fly zapped itself on the grid. The noise sounded loud in the hushed atmosphere.

Doc Cruz coughed politely. "You think that is going to work?"

Grant felt like he'd been holding his breath. He let it out now. "Depends on how long it takes him to convince the brass."

The doctor rubbed his chin. "And what are you going to do in the meantime?"

Grant smiled in the darkness. "Suit up and get in the game."

Doc Cruz saw the smile and reciprocated. "Now you sound like an American."

Grant flexed his aching muscles. Everything hurt.

"Don't Mexicans play baseball?"

The Mexican nodded. "And football. Not soccer. That's for over-priced prima donnas."

"I'm with you there. There's only one man overpriced in Absolution."

"Macready."

"And it's time to bring on the pain."

Doc Cruz moved along the counter towards Grant. "I meant what I said before. There are still good people here."

"That's what I'm counting on. After."

"Not after. Now. You cannot fight him unarmed."

Grant thought about the old-timer at the town dump. The exploding rat and the sniper's rifle. The propane gas bottles and the boarded-up mobile home used as an armory.

"I won't be unarmed."

Pilar Cruz's father looked worried.

"You cannot do this alone."

Grant looked him in the eye.

"I won't be alone."

There was a low rumble like distant thunder. The trucks were starting up. Grant laid a hand on the counter and felt the vibration as the convoy began to move out from the athletics track. Minus the two army jeeps that were now burned out at Macready's factory. In five minutes the convoy would be through town and heading south towards Adobe Flats. He looked out of the window, but the junction was hidden from view.

The rumble grew louder. Vibrations shook the clock on the wall. The sound of distant thunder. A storm was coming. Grant was going to make sure of that. He turned back to Doc Cruz.

"Because as soon as they've gone, you and Sabata are going to help me."

THIRTY-SIX

PREPARATIONS FOR BATTLE ALWAYS include three things: supplies, personnel, and location. Not necessarily in that order. You could add a fourth, enemy forces, but Grant already knew about most of them. The mercenaries protecting the convoy and the skeleton crew covering the hacienda. Grant would get more info about the skeleton crew when he scouted the location. The battlefield would be Avenue D, the athletics track, and the walled compound. Macready's Alamo, only with the boot on the other foot. This time the invaders were the good guys.

The personnel were already sorted. Doc Cruz, Tony Sabata, and whoever of his friends wanted to pitch in. Grant turned down Doc Cruz's offer of help from the townspeople. Like John Wayne in *Rio Bravo,* he only wanted professionals or people already invested in the conflict. Grant ticked personnel off his list. That only left supplies.

He hoped the old-timer at the dump didn't have an itchy trigger finger.

The battered metal sign was still rusty and full of bullet holes.

ABSOLUTION
TOWN DUMP
By Local Ordinance

Even in the dark some of the holes looked fresh. The moon painted the desolate wasteland an unearthly blue. The harsh light made the rust patches look like dried blood, black and congealed and leaking from the bullet holes. The sign rattled against the wire fence as Grant slipped through the gap.

He stopped at the edge of the shortcut and held both hands in the air.

"Hey—there in the shed."

No reply.

Grant risked a couple of steps towards the mobile home. The hanging basket swayed gently in the overnight breeze. Even at this time of night, the breeze was warm. He wondered if it was ever cold in Texas.

"Hey—shithouse rat eyes."

The breeze dropped. The basket stopped swinging. The mobile home was in darkness. No lights inside. No lights covering the town dump. Something swooped out of the night sky, then disappeared. Then something else—bats. Three or four of them. Grant didn't know you could have bats without trees for them to hang from. He guessed he was wrong. The bats swooped and dipped and didn't come anywhere close to bumping into him. They spent a couple more minutes playing around the town dump, then moved away. The night became still again.

Until the door creaked open.

And the rifle barrel poked out of the opening.

"This ain't no shed."

Grant moved into the open so the old-timer could get a clear view. "And I'm no rat. Just want to make that clear before you get all rhetorical on me."

The old-timer lowered the rifle and came down the steps.

"It's clear. All the rats in Absolution work for Macready. From what I hear, you're off his Christmas list."

"Me and the cat. And Hunter Athey."

The old-timer grumphed a response that could have meant anything but Grant took as being disgust. Maybe a hint of sadness. The old man leaned the rifle against the garden chair.

"Heard about that too. Living around Macready, I sometimes think the dump is the cleanest place to be."

Grant stood in the clearing in front of the makeshift home. "That'd mean you're just the person I need to see."

He nodded at a duplicate sign nailed to the caravan wall beside the door.

ABSOLUTION
TOWN DUMP
By Local Ordinance

"Does that make you the local ordinance?"

The old-timer puffed out his chest and straightened his back. "That makes me Josiah Hooper. Most people call me Joe."

Grant waved a hand towards the rifle.

"Well, Joe. How'd you like to do a little target practice?"

Forty-five minutes later, Grant was loaded up with supplies. If the wooden chest he'd examined at the factory looked like pirates' gold, then Joe Hooper's armory was a treasure trove. It was better stocked than most gunsmiths. There were handguns, shotguns, machine guns, and hunting rifles. The handguns ranged from revolvers to semi-automatics. The machine guns were mainly for show, their firing pins removed, but the hunting rifles were as mean as a junkyard dog. Full bore. Telescopic sights. Sniper's rifles in all but name.

Ammunition was more of a problem. The firearms were lovingly restored castoffs salvaged by a man with nothing but time on his hands. Some had been in Hooper's store for decades. Some looked almost new. The one thing Hooper wasn't equipped to restore was ammunition. The secondhand armory carried a certain amount just so he'd have something to sell but not all calibers for all weapons. That limited Grant's choices.

In the end he took the safest option: a five-shot Smith & Wesson .38 snub-nose police special. Plenty of ammo and the least likely to jam. He also selected a worn and scratched pump-action shotgun and a hunting rifle without a telescopic sight. He preferred to aim along the barrel. He wasn't planning on being far from his target.

That was Grant's firepower organized. Sabata and his crew didn't need anything. They'd already shown a propensity for firearms at the Kosmic Kowgirl Kafe. Doc Cruz didn't want a gun. Grant could understand that. He hated guns himself. Had done ever since he'd taken that shot in a desert township many years ago. He had to admit, though, that his aim was better than his typing. He wasn't planning on typing tonight.

The rest of Grant's supplies were hard and heavy and took up too much room. The gas bottles were too bulky to carry, and the handcart that Joe Hooper used to move them around the propane store could only take two or three. Grant tapped one of the familiar blue gas bottles. The ping echoed through the night. He nodded for Sabata to reverse his pickup into the yard.

Personnel. Check.

Supplies. Check.

Now it was time to scout the location and enemy strength.

"She is inside with the Macready pup."

Javier seemed like a million miles from the old Mexican Grant had first seen behind the counter at Sixto's. Having worked for Macready all these years, it appeared the prospect of payback was giving him a new lease on life. He wasn't even out of breath after climbing the stairs to the bell tower in the white stucco church with the powder blue steeple.

Grant scanned the battleground from the highest point in Absolution, at the junction of Avenue D and North Third Street. The nearest place to God, some people thought. Grant didn't believe in God, only the best place to view the layout and finalize his plan. The charges were set, gas bottles placed at strategic points around the compound, and instructions given. This was Grant's last chance to run through it in his head before doing one more thing.

Rescuing the girl.

"How many men?"

Javier crouched between Doc Cruz and Grant. "Two that I could see. Three including the pup."

Grant took that as an estimate. He reckoned at least four plus Scott Macready. The main force would be protecting the convoy because that was the obvious target, but old man Macready was too wick to leave the hacienda unguarded. Moonlight threw the street into sharp relief; a pale blue expanse with pitch-black shadows. The moon would be a problem. It was like a searchlight covering the perimeter. The only shadows Grant could hide in were from the derelict buildings across the street. From there it was open ground all the way apart from the sports stand next to the athletics track.

Grant looked over his shoulder. The distant horizon was obscured by a cloud shoulder building in the south. Some of the clouds looked dark and heavy. A flicker of lightning forked the ground. The storm was still a long way off and moving slowly, coming this way. There was no thunder. Not yet. Overhead, above Absolution, a smattering of loose clouds acted as vanguard to the approaching storm. One fluffy white cloud drifted in front of the moon, and the street went dark. Just for a minute. Then the pale blue light came back. That would be Grant's window of opportunity when the time came.

Grant patted Javier on the shoulder.

"Thanks. Go join the others."

The Mexican nodded and went back down the stairs. The bell tower fell silent. The town below waited. Grant could feel the pressure from the weather front building, but his internal pressure was zero. He relaxed. That was always his way. A few deep breaths and a flexing of muscles and he would be ready. It was his greatest strength, being able to remain calm under pressure. There was more at stake this time, though. After his shortcomings all those years ago.

Rescue the girl.

Not shoot the girl.

Doc Cruz sensed Grant's indecision. Pilar's father leaned against the wall and let out a sigh. Whatever happened today, the town his daughter had grown up in would be changed forever, for good or for bad. He spoke to Grant's silhouette.

"I do not blame you. For what you did."

Grant's shoulders slumped. "I blame myself."

"Pilar wouldn't blame you either. Otherwise she wouldn't have asked you to return her stethoscope."

Grant turned towards Doc Cruz but didn't speak. He'd thought he was past all this. The recriminations. The pain. The past was the past. He only ever looked forward while living in the here and now. The here and now today was rescuing Sarah Hellstrom and punishing Tripp Macready.

Doc Cruz spoke in a whisper. "You have come to the right place to seek absolution."

Grant shook his head. "Justice. There is no absolution."

Another cloud obscured the moon. Briefly. The first sounds of distant thunder rumbled in the south, a long way off but creeping north. The two men looked out across the town with the prophetic name. Doc Cruz nodded towards the hacienda.

"Then go save the girl. And forgive yourself."

ABSOLUTION

There is no peace. Only acceptance. Then you move on.

—Jim Grant

THIRTY-SEVEN

THE TORN PATCHES OF cloud were becoming more regular. They drifted across the moon like a hand in front of a torch. One minute it was bright, the next it was dark, and then it was bright again. Grant crossed Avenue D during the next eclipse and was hunkered down in the derelict building opposite by the time the moon came out. He scanned the other buildings on the edge of town. All empty. All heading towards rack and ruin. Macready had obviously bought them for the same reason he'd bought the houses en route to Adobe Flats. No witnesses. A firebreak around his own personal Alamo.

The crumbling walls and tattered rooftops let the night sky in. Stars twinkled overhead. They glinted off the broken glass in the windows. A desert town in hostile territory. The more things changed, the more they stayed the same. He glanced towards the church. There was movement at the base of the steeple. A car door slammed. An engine started up.

Grant nodded to himself.

Time to move.

Another cloud obscured the moon. Grant scurried from one building to the next until he was opposite the athletics track. Still hidden. Still ready. The moon came out and bathed the open ground in frosty light even though the night was warm. Grant slung the rifle strap over his head and across one shoulder. He hung the shotgun across the other. The straps looked like crisscrossed bandoliers. He tucked the .38 into the top of his sock and pulled the trouser leg down to cover it. Stealth and secrecy were required now. He wasn't planning on shooting anyone until later.

The moon went in.

The lights went out.

Grant darted across the street while darkness hugged the town. There was no avoiding the little puffs of dust that followed each footstep, but he hoped they were hidden by the complete absence of light. Anyone looking this way would have to adjust to the dark— not an easy task when the moon kept coming out or hiding behind the clouds. He reached the sports stand before the hand came away from the torch. The compound wall became pale blue stucco. The narrow door at the rear stood out like a rectangular domino.

He was ready.

The best way to sneak into an enemy position was if the enemy was busy looking somewhere else. Diversion. Even with just four defenders, it was better if they were otherwise engaged. The engine grew louder, and Doc Cruz's car sped across the open ground towards the compound gates. For a moment it looked like it was going to veer off to one side, but then it steadied even though there was nobody driving. Grant heard raised voices inside the compound. Shouts of alarm.

Then the car crashed into the gates, and Grant made his move.

THE BACK DOOR WAS wooden but not as solid as it appeared. He remembered it feeling dry and brittle from before, when he'd been led towards the trucks waiting on the athletics track. It was hinged to open inwards. One good policeman's kick broke the latch and splintered the frame before the sound of the car wreck stopped echoing around the compound.

The barbecue pit was dark and silent. The tables were empty. This was a long way different from the pre-action picnic Macready had thrown for his men. Tonight his men were on the road, protecting the final convoy or running towards the front gates. Doc Cruz's car was small and lightweight. It hadn't even dented the heavy wooden gates. It had burst into flames though, and dry wood and fire don't mix.

Grant counted two men opening the gates while a third pointed a fire extinguisher at the burning car. He skipped round the side of the barbecue pit and found the back stairs to the balcony. He didn't know the layout of the house but the bedrooms would be upstairs. Scott Macready, being the lily-livered punk that he was, would be holding Sarah in the bedroom.

The balcony ran all the way around the hacienda. The warmth of the night played in Grant's favor. Several windows were open. Some of the rooms had patio doors; half of those were open a crack. Only three had lights on inside. Keeping low behind the balcony wall so the men in the compound couldn't see him, he checked the nearest room first. It was a large, ornate bedroom with flowing curtains and a king-size bed.

The room was empty.

Grant crept along the balcony to the next room.

This one was smaller—a guest room. A bedside lamp threw light across the double bed, but there was no movement inside. The curtains had been tied back so they didn't sway in the breeze. The door to the landing was partly open to let the air circulate. A narrow wedge stopped the door from banging—not something you used in an occupied room.

That only left the third room.

Grant could hear voices coming from inside. Low and inaudible, not light and chatty. No laughter. Just tense voices, like a captor and his captive. Grant moved back against the balcony wall and sidled along until he had a view into the master bedroom. He knew that's what it was even before he got a good look inside. The size of the room told him that. Lace curtains hung from the windows. They were fastened to the patio doors. It obscured Grant's view but not as much as it blinded the people inside.

One of the voices did most of the talking—the familiar Texas twang of Scott Macready. The other voice fell silent. Grant couldn't tell where it was in the room. Macready was easy to pinpoint. Front and center in the middle of the room. At the foot of the bed with his back to the balcony. That implied something Grant didn't want to think about. Sarah Hellstrom had been held prisoner too long for nothing to have happened. Scott Macready wasn't a patient man. He thought of Sarah as his own personal property. The bed was an elephant in the room. No matter how hard you tried to ignore it, it was always there.

Macready was tucking something into the front of his jeans.

That was enough for Grant. He crossed the balcony, threw a quick glance around the bedroom, then opened the door and slipped inside.

THE DOOR BANGED JUST enough to get Scott Macready's attention but not so loud it would alert the guards in the courtyard. Macready junior yanked his zip up and spun around. Fear dilated his irises and flared his nostrils. His hands were shaking.

Grant pointed at the front of Macready's jeans. "I knew a kid once, got his dick caught in his zipper."

He took two paces into the room. "Because of faulty Y-fronts." He stopped and scratched his head like Columbo.

"Do you have Y-fronts over here? Underwear with an inverted Y panel that you can take a leak out of without dropping your pants?"

He stood facing Macready.

"Anyway. This kid. He's wearing a pair of Y-fronts that had gone a bit saggy. His todger was poking out of the slot when he pulled his zip up, and…yipes. Zipped his foreskin into the teeth."

Macready didn't move. Grant feigned a shiver.

"Enough to make your eyes water. Kid had to go to hospital to get himself untangled. Blood and foreskin everywhere. Nurse just yanked the zip down."

Grant stood to his full height and relaxed his arms.

"I guess that's why Levis brought out 501s. You know—the jeans with a button fly instead of a zipper. There being so many dicks in Texas."

Macready blinked as if slapped. Grant doubted if anyone in Absolution had called the boss's son a dick. The dick remained mute. He finished tucking his shirt into his jeans and fastened his belt, then stood still in front of the bed.

Grant raised his eyebrows.

"There was an upside. Nurse took twenty minutes rubbing cream into my cock. Opened my eyes, I can tell you. And I never wore Y-fronts again. These days I find it's best to keep my tackle where it belongs."

His eyes turned hard as he glared at Macready.

"You'd better not have been putting yours where it doesn't."

Macready glanced at the bed. Grant followed his gaze. The bedding was untidy and strewn across the bed. The pillows were dented in the middle. An uneven hump was hidden under the covers. The hump twitched. Grant took one step forward and punched Macready as hard as he could in the stomach.

The wind went out of the Texan like a pricked balloon. He dropped to his knees, holding his stomach. Grant rubbed his knuckles. He didn't like using his fists. There are more bones in the hand than almost any other part of the body. Hit something solid and there's a good chance you're going to break your hand. Grant usually used leverage and safe striking surfaces—the heel of the palm or the point of the elbow. He dialed back the anger. Control was the key. Grant rarely lost control. He was annoyed at himself for losing it now.

Macready looked up at the Yorkshireman.

"You're gonna pay for that."

Grant let out a sigh.

"In dollars or pesos?"

Macready tried to keep the pain out of his voice without success. He did manage to smile though. The smile didn't reach his eyes.

"In zippered dicks."

He barked a laugh at his own joke.

"When my father gets back."

Grant leaned over Macready and patted him gently across the face.

"Well, he's not home now. So where's her clothes?"

He nudged the hump in the bed.

Macready's smile became a grin. "Whose clothes?"

Grant nudged the hump again. "Don't be a dick. Sarah's."

The dick clambered to his feet, still holding his stomach. "Probably still wearing them."

The hump shifted and threw the covers back. The naked woman lying in the bed wasn't Sarah Hellstrom. It was the petite Mexican waitress from the barbecue. She pulled the bedclothes up to cover her breasts. Macready didn't give her a second glance.

"Strapped to the front of the truck."

THIRTY-EIGHT

THE ROOM FELL SILENT. Grant had devised contingency plans for various scenarios, but this wasn't one of them. The main plan involved gunfire and explosions, two things guaranteed to cause harm to a human shield strapped to the front of a truck. Grant ran through the timings in his head. It was over an hour to dawn. The convoy would be on its way back. The first explosion would be the gas station at Sixto's—to push the convoy into the crossfire out front of the walled hacienda. Propane tanks and sniper fire would take care of the rest.

That had been the plan when the trucks only contained Macready's men. With Sarah Hellstrom thrown into the mix, that plan was too dangerous. Grant needed to call it off and come up with something else.

Scott Macready finished rubbing his stomach and stood up straight.

"What's up? Cat got your tongue?"

Grant leveled his gaze on the young Texan.

"You don't have a cat no more."

Macready looked far too confident.

"There's always plenty of mousers."

Grant felt the short hairs bristle up the back of his neck. Something was very wrong here. He glanced through the patio doors. It was still dark outside, but the first hint of blue was lightening the sky. The disturbance in the yard had subsided, the car fire extinguished. There was no sound of footsteps racing up the stairs to aid the boy Texan, and yet Macready didn't look as worried as he should have been, confronted by an armed man who outweighed him by fifty pounds.

The woman on the bed pushed backwards, out of the way.

Macready flexed his shoulders like a cocky schoolboy.

Grant quickly scanned the room. It was just the three of them.

"There's always plenty of mice."

The Texan smiled.

"This is Texas. We don't have mice."

Grant relaxed his arms.

"Same as you don't have moss?"

Macready looked confused.

"What?"

"Too dry."

"Too big. We don't do anything small. The rodent problem in Absolution is bigger. Big and hairy. Rats and Mexicans."

Grant tried to remember which strap he'd shouldered first without looking. The shotgun or the rifle. The one he needed now was the shotgun, and he had a feeling he'd be needing it very soon.

"I'm not Mexican."

Macready held out his hands, palms upwards, and shrugged.

"There you go then."

Grant hooked his thumbs into the straps as if they were braces. He ran them up and down until they reached the crossover in the middle. The shotgun strap going one way and the rifle strap the other. The shotgun strap was on top. Good.

"I had to tell the old-timer at the town dump I'm not a rat."

"You didn't tell me."

"Same answer though."

"You're a rodent. Poking around where you don't belong."

Grant eased one hand farther up the strap.

"Among the trash and underbelly, you mean?"

Macready's face turned to stone.

Grant got ready to move.

"Because if that's the case, then I'm the biggest rodent you ever saw."

Macready clicked his fingers. Grant unshouldered the shotgun but wasn't quick enough. Three doors opened at once: the hallway, the adjoining bedroom, and the balcony. Two men came in through each and two more materialized from behind the curtains. All armed. All pointing their guns at Grant.

The girl yelped.

Macready's smile broadened.

"This isn't what we call a Mexican standoff."

The old Mexican from Sixto's had been wrong. Not two men plus Macready. Eight. Rough hands snatched the shotgun. The rifle was torn from his shoulder. Grant needed to distract them from finding the .38 in his sock. He whipped round and jabbed an elbow into the nearest face, then blocked a handgun that was swung at his head. Two more men caught him from the sides. A blow to the side of the head made him see stars. A sharp downward kick to the back of his leg collapsed him to the ground. Nobody fired. This was a controlled situation. They didn't need to.

Macready leaned over him.

"You can't drop off a cliff from here."

His eyes turned to flint.

"But you can drop."

He nodded, and a sledgehammer blow took Grant out.

THIRTY-NINE

GRANT WAS GETTING TIRED of waking to a world of pain. At least the pain this time wasn't all-encompassing. It wasn't debilitating, and it wouldn't slow him down when the time came. That time was coming soon.

Dawn broke over Absolution, Texas, like the last rays of sunshine on a condemned town. Hard, bright sky overhead belied the danger ahead. North, east, and west were as hot and sharp as any other day, just a smattering of clouds scurrying across the sky in the stiffening breeze. South was a wall of bruised cloud and lightning as the storm front approached. Grant could see it through the window of his cell. Not a cell in the true sense of the word—there were no bars on the windows or shackles on the walls—but he was a prisoner just the same.

He reached for his ankle.

The .38 had gone.

So much for trying to distract the gun thugs from a thorough search. That left him unarmed and defenseless in a three-window room at the top of the hacienda. Some kind of office or day room with two chairs and a carved wooden coffee table. It had good light through the windows and a brilliant view if you liked desert plains and dust clouds.

That pricked Grant's interest. Not one cloud of dust but two. The first coming from the south, just ahead of the approaching storm. The second from the north, farther away. The wind was whipping the dust clouds sideways, away from whatever was causing them. The same wind that was rushing the storm towards Absolution. It would be touch and go which hit town first; maybe all three at once. That would be a confrontation to match the one between Santa Anna's army and the defenders of the Alamo. The mission that became a fortress. The fortress that became a shrine.

Absolution was going to be a shrine for somebody.

Grant was determined it wasn't going to be him.

He peered down from the window. Avenue D was deserted. The church steeple stood out against the tattered sky. The derelict houses across the street were in shadow from the sun hanging low over the eastern horizon. The athletics track stretched to the edge of town. The Christmas Mountains were faded blue humps in the distance. Somewhere to the south, Adobe Flats and the hills of Big Bend National Park were hidden behind a curtain of rain clouds and rolling thunder.

The plan had fallen apart. Grant wasn't in a position to change it. He had to trust the good men of Absolution to do the right thing. He had to trust that Doc Cruz had been right when he'd said there were still good men who lived here. For now that boiled down to a Mexican coyote, an old-time sniper, and a small-town doctor. Not much of an army to combat the Macready empire.

The army. Grant replayed his conversation with John Cornejo. He hoped the ex-marine had as much influence as Grant gave him credit for. Convincing the authorities that something was rotten in Fort Stockton was a big ask. Getting them to do something about it would be harder still.

He squinted at the dust cloud to the north. If Cornejo had succeeded, then that should be a detachment of MPs coming to the rescue. If he'd failed, then it would just be Cornejo and whatever friends he could rope together. It was impossible to tell from this distance. Grant turned his attention to the cloud trail to the south. A five-truck convoy coming hard and fast. Was it a bigger cloud than Cornejo's? Hard to say. The only thing for certain was it was a lot closer than the cavalry.

Footsteps sounded on the stairs outside the door. A key rattled in the lock. The door was flung open, and three men stood in the opening. Grant threw one last glance at the dust cloud hitting the edge of town, coming past Sixto's soon before crossing First Street into Avenue D.

Two guards stood in the doorway, one with Grant's shotgun and rifle slung from his shoulder. They didn't speak. They didn't need to. They flanked Grant and led him downstairs.

Doc Cruz's car was a smoldering wreck beside the front gates. The courtyard was empty. Two men stood guard at the open gates, and three more were spaced out across the patio on either side of the barbecue pit. The other three were with Grant. They led him down through the hacienda and out of the front door. Scott Macready stepped out behind him, his cowboy hat pulled low over his eyes to show how tough he was.

"Hold it there."

The guards stopped. Grant turned to face the Macready pup.

"Morning, junior."

Macready's eyes twitched. "Ain't gonna be a good morning for you."

"I didn't say it was good. Just that it's morning."

The Texan tried hard to sound like a badass. "No. It's payback time."

Grant took a deep breath and relaxed his arms. He put all his weight on the balls of his feet, ready to move quickly. If the boss's son was going to make a play it would be now, while he had three mercenaries backing him up. The cowboy hat was so low over his eyes it was almost comical. He glared at Grant through slitted eyes. Grant stared back, his peripheral vision keeping tabs on the guards to either side of him. Macready didn't move. Grant nodded. A staring contest was all the cowboy was going to engage in. His father was coming home. Seemed like Tripp Macready wanted Grant all to himself.

Grant looked at the Stetson and then at the storm clouds bruising the sky.

"I hope that's an expensive hat, 'cause I've seen cheaper ones go soggy in the rain. It'd flop down over your head like a foreskin on a limp dick."

There was no sudden lunge, so Grant continued. "And you know what happens to foreskins."

He made an upwards zipping motion with one hand.

"Zzzzip."

Macready blinked under the brim of his hat. If he hadn't been so tanned, Grant reckoned he'd be blushing. To cover his embarrassment, he barked an order to the guards.

"Take him out."

One guard pushed Grant towards the patio steps. All three walked him across the courtyard. The main gates were open. The breeze was strengthening into a wind. Dust swirled in tiny spirals across the parched earth. A broken window shutter banged in one of the derelict houses opposite, and an empty shopping bag tumbled across the road, a tumbleweed in all but name. Grant approached the mouth of the compound. More of the street came into view. Despite the wind he could hear the rumbling of trucks driving through town. He could feel the vibration coming up from the ground. The convoy was here.

Sixto's. Anytime now the petrol fumes would be ignited and the gas station was going to explode—a misdirection intended to force the convoy into the crossfire. Trouble was, the crossfire could be deadly for the woman strapped to the front of the truck.

Grant counted the seconds. He listened to the approaching trucks. He threw a quick glance to the church steeple overlooking the killing ground. Checked the position of the propane tanks strategically placed along Avenue D. Anytime now all hell was going to break loose, and Grant was going to be standing right in the middle of it.

The convoy turned off First Street and drove up past the Los Pecos Bank and Trust. It passed through the shadow of the church and came straight towards the Macready hacienda. Five heavy trucks with big tires and canvas backs. The canvas flapped in the wind.

A military jeep pulled out from behind the last truck. The army must have loaned him another one—better this time because it had a fold-down canvas roof across the back. Tripp Macready sped the jeep to the front of the convoy and held up a hand.

The trucks stopped.

The swirl of dust was whipped away by the wind.

Grant stood in the middle of the street in his tattered orange windcheater and waited for the explosion at Sixto's, already delayed from the original plan. He held out his arms like Jesus on the cross and took a deep breath.

Nothing exploded. Nobody opened fire at the propane tanks. Grant lowered his arms and looked at Tripp Macready. Seeing him driving an army jeep wasn't the only surprise. Grant checked the front of the lead truck. Sturdy ropes had been fastened to each corner of the cab, one for each leg and arm. To stretch Sarah Hellstrom like an X across the front of the truck.

The ropes hung loose.

Sarah wasn't fastened to the front of the truck.

She was sitting beside Tripp Macready in the jeep.

FORTY

THE ENGINES WERE TURNED off. Five trucks but not the jeep. The jeep's motor sounded puny after the throaty rumble of the trucks. It was barely audible above the sound of the wind and the flapping window shutter. Sarah Hellstrom looked relaxed in the passenger seat. Not handcuffed or tied up or in any other way restrained. She was a guest, not a prisoner. Grant felt disappointed.

The mercenaries disembarked and formed a loose circle around Grant. Tripp Macready swung his legs sideways and got out of the jeep. He looked at Grant, threw a glance towards Sarah, then focused on the Yorkshireman again.

"Don't look so surprised. It's a small town. We all have to get along."

Grant nodded. "And I'm a rodent. I get it."

Macready stood in front of Grant. "A lizard. Isn't that what you said?"

Grant smiled.

"*Rango*. The Johnny Depp lizard Western. Yes."

"The stranger in town."

Grant finished the line.

"And strangers don't last long."

Macready tilted his head as if considering Grant.

"Except you ain't a stranger no more."

He held his arms out like Jesus on a cross. "You're the Resurrection Man."

He lowered his arms. "I remember you now. From the TV news. Boston, wasn't it?"

"Jamaica Plain."

"You're a long way from home. Yorkshire or Massachusetts."

"It's a small world."

"And this is a small town."

"You've said that already."

"Just wanted to emphasize the point so you'd understand. I'm not the bad guy here. I'm the guy that provides for the good folk of Absolution."

Grant nodded in the general direction of town. "Doesn't seem like everyone agrees with you."

Macready nodded. "And that's exactly why I need to set an example."

He made a come-hither motion with both hands, and two mercenaries broke off from the circle.

"Send them a message." The mercenaries stood on either side of Grant. "That strangers aren't welcome."

Macready put his hands in his pockets. "They don't last long. Me, I'm here to stay."

Grant glanced across the street, then looked Macready in the eye. "You said I wasn't a stranger."

"Play on words. You're a rolling stone that gathers no moss."

Grant looked at Sarah. She flinched at the ferocity of his stare. Macready ignored the interplay.

"Passing through. Only you aren't. Not anymore."

He leaned forward for emphasis.

"You should never have got off the train."

Grant weighed up time and numbers. Time was running out and the numbers didn't add up. There should be more mercenaries than the few forming the circle around him. He glanced across the street again at the derelict buildings that looked so much like another desert township fallen on hard times. The shutter banged again. Loose canvas on one of the trucks flapped in the wind. Nobody opened fire from the cover of the buildings. Nobody set off the explosions around the killing ground.

Macready followed Grant's gaze, then shook his head.

"Don't go getting your hopes up."

He held a hand above his head and gave a curt wave.

"There ain't no resurrecting you from this."

THERE WAS MOVEMENT IN two of the derelict buildings. Hunched figures shuffled into the open with their hands behind their heads. Bigger men herded the figures towards the trucks. The missing mercenaries.

"Your friends chose the wrong side."

Sabata, Doc Cruz, and three others crossed the street, betrayed and captured. Grant looked at Sarah and let out a sigh of defeat. How could she do this to her own kind? Fellow citizens of Absolution. She lowered her head.

The prisoners were corralled between the first and second truck, out of the wind and away from Grant. The mercenaries holstered their weapons. The threat had been neutralized. Grant ignored them. He couldn't take his eyes off Sarah, the first helpful face he'd seen after he'd arrived and the last person he expected to stand up for the Macready clan. She rubbed her wrists. The tiny movement caught Grant's eye. He focused on the rawness just above the joints. Rope burns. Then he looked at the ropes still dangling from the cab of the lead truck.

Macready saw the look and nodded.

"I'm not stupid. Leaving her strapped across the truck wouldn't look good coming through town. I cut her down at Sixto's—where you planned on starting your little welcome party."

Grant snapped his eyes back to Macready. Sarah Hellstrom didn't know about the welcome party. How could she? She'd been taken long before he'd discussed it at Javier's house on the edge of town. The old Mexican who was supposed to have set off the first explosion at the gas station.

Grant saw Macready's eyes turn towards the main gates. Grant turned around. Javier walked through the gates with hunched shoulders and a protective arm around his daughter—the waitress from the barbecue. The girl in Scott Macready's bed. He walked her down the street without meeting anyone's eyes.

Macready broke the spell.

"It's amazing what a man will do to protect his daughter."

Grant saw Doc Cruz shudder but wasn't thinking about the irony in that remark. He was wondering how much Javier knew of the overall plan they'd discussed in the old Mexican's kitchen. Not all of it but enough. He knew who would be helping and where. He had helped place the gas bottles around the ambush site. Grant didn't check to see if they were still there. They either were or they weren't. He doubted if Macready had had time to remove them. He'd been on the road all night, and his son had been bed hopping.

Josiah Hooper. Grant tried to remember if Joe had been mentioned in any detail. He didn't think he had. The sniper was Grant's ace in the hole. The sniper and the cloud of dust racing south along Iron Mountain Road. Grant forced himself not to look up at the bell tower to see if the rifle was still pointing in his direction.

Macready pulled out his own ace in the hole.

"And don't go thinking your call to Boston will do you any good."

Grant felt a chill run down his spine.

Macready smiled.

"That's a long drive across big country. This ain't like the movies. Cavalry don't always get here in time."

Grant relaxed. That last remark told him Macready might know about the call but not what was said. The cavalry wouldn't be coming from Boston. If John Cornejo had convinced the authorities, it would be coming from a lot closer, bringing thunder from the north just as the storm front was bringing it from the south. The meeting point would be Absolution, Texas.

Macready did that double wave thing again, and two mercenaries stepped towards Grant, weapons holstered to free their hands.

"Now it's time for that example I was talking about."

He indicated the front of the lead truck—"Shame to waste a good rope"—then reached into the jeep and pulled out a machete.

Grant flinched. Not at the prospect of being cut but at the confluence of memories and reality. Derelict buildings and a dusty street. Local militia and a man with a long knife. If he was angry before, he was furious now. He relaxed his arms so the men wouldn't have anything solid to grab hold of. He flexed his knees.

A sudden gust of wind whipped sand around his feet. The flapping canvas went into frenzy. Something blew over in the nearest building across the street. The circle of mercenaries threw their hands over their eyes. The two nearest Grant were too late. Sand and grit stung like tiny needles. They turned away from the wind.

Macready stepped back, head down.

Grant slitted his eyes.

Nobody heard the engines breach the edge of town from North Eighth Street.

Everybody saw the compound wall explode in a ball of gas and flame.

FORTY-ONE

THE RULE OF THREES. The storm. The sniper. The cavalry. The perfect trifecta. The wall of rain entered Absolution from the south. The cavalry came in from the north. The old-timer who spent his days splatting rats took aim again, and another gas bottle exploded. In the building nearest the trucks this time.

Grant thought he heard a raised voice shouting in the wind. "Don't like that, d'ya? Yer little fucker." That last bit might have been his imagination.

The first part of the trifecta to arrive fired again: a third gas bottle blew a hole in the sports stand, triangulating the convoy's position between balls of fire and clouds of smoke. The rain wasn't here yet. The cavalry hadn't arrived. For now it was Joe Hooper and a handful of prisoners. The distraction gave the prisoners room to maneuver.

Grant was first to move. While the two guards were still shielding their eyes, he stamped down hard on the back of the nearest leg. The knee buckled and the man went down. Before he hit the ground, Grant snatched the gun from his holster and shot the second man point-blank. Two guns now. Then everybody was moving.

The crippled guard tried to unsling the shotgun from his shoulder. Grant stamped on the broken leg and grabbed the straps. The shotgun came loose but the rifle was tangled in the fallen man's arm. The circle of mercenaries broke and darted for cover. Sabata elbowed one of the ex-soldiers in the face, and Grant fired at the other two guarding the captives. They scattered. Doc Cruz dropped to his knees. Sabata took the guard's gun. Three guns and a shotgun between six. Still outgunned and surrounded.

Another gas bottle exploded among the wooden barrels and water trough at the gates. One of the barrels disintegrated into a shower of whirling splinters, and the bottom hinge dropped one gate at an angle.

Grant dashed across open ground towards Cruz and Sabata just as the mercenaries regrouped and opened fire. Bullets stitched a line of dusty explosions behind Grant's feet until he dived between the first and second trucks. Ricochets echoed from the heavy wheels and punctured one tire. The truck sagged to one side, and the loaded crates shifted inside.

The final gas bottle punched a hole in the compound wall and blasted masonry across the forecourt. Dust and smoke obscured the battlefield just like any battle in any war. Bullets dinged off the side of the trucks. Sabata returned fire, but the mercenaries had taken up good defensive positions. The freed captives couldn't take good aim.

Grant offered the second gun to Doc Cruz, who held up his hands. "I can't shoot for shit."

Grant handed him the shotgun instead. "When they get close."

Cruz nodded. Grant crouched beside the rear axle and surveyed the scene. The street had become a cacophony of sound and gunfire. Constant movement distracted the eye. Constant danger kept his head down. The resurrection man might have avoided being cruci-fied on the front of a truck, but Grant reckoned he'd only exchanged one death for another. The ramshackle band was outnumbered and pinned down. There was too much open ground to the nearest cover among the derelict buildings, and the mercenaries were mov-ing around to cut off that line of retreat.

The gunshots became more sporadic. Grant risked sticking his head out for a better look. A bullet dinged off the mudguard just below the filler cap. Grant ducked back behind the wheel. He glanced over his shoulder.

"Anybody got a light?"

One of Sabata's men tossed Grant a Zippo. Grant nodded his thanks and reached inside the tattered windcheater. The lining came away easily. A long strip of beige cotton fabric with snatches of orange trim. The wind was getting stronger. Grant hoped that diesel fumes would overcome its attempts to snuff the candle. He jabbed a finger towards the gunmen and everyone understood.

Grant twisted the strip of cloth into a fuse.

Sabata, Cruz, and the other man took up positions near the wheel.

Grant nodded.

All three opened fire at once. Not aiming. One general direction.

Grant dashed out from cover and unscrewed the filler cap. It was tight and wouldn't move. He gripped with all his strength and it turned a fraction, then a fraction more, then all the way off. Return-ing fire kicked up dust around the truck, and he dived for cover again. First half done.

He paused for breath, then nodded again.

The trio opened fire, and Grant squirreled the twist of cloth down the filler tube until it soaked up diesel. He pulled it out and reversed it so he'd have a soaked portion to light. The Zippo sparked, but the wind blew it out. He sheltered the lighter with one hand and rasped the flint again. This time the flame held firm enough to ignite the diesel-soaked rag. The shotgun went off close to his ear, and the world descended into muffled silence. His ears were ringing. Gunshots were distant thumps on a woolly drum. Voices sounded like they were underwater.

The rag became a flaming torch. Bullets punched silent holes in the side of the truck. Grant signaled retreat with a wave of the hand. Nobody needed telling twice. Under a muffled barrage of covering fire, the defenders moved back two truck lengths, between trucks three and four.

Grant looked up at the church tower. Muzzle flashes showed that Joe Hooper was still firing into the mercenaries despite having no more propane to aim at. Silent gunshots blasted chunks of stucco near the bell tower. Then Grant's hearing came back full power when the lead truck exploded. The rear axle jumped off the ground. The wooden cargo bed spat planks and rivets. Gold medallions and dented goblets showered the street. The canvas covering was torn apart, and the cab flipped forward in a twist of flame and shattered glass.

The gunfire fell silent—for a few seconds. Then it returned with full force and anger. The defenders were forced deeper behind the truck. Bullets hit all around them, coming from all directions. All Grant had done was exchange a defensive position at the front of the convoy for one at the rear. Either way they were still surrounded. Still outgunned.

Then something happened he hadn't expected.

Bullet hits began to raise dust among the mercenaries—a fusillade that forced the ex-soldiers to fall back. Not from the cavalry coming in from the north. From both sides of the street.

From a source that caught Grant by surprise.

THE FACES MATERIALIZED THROUGH the clouds of dust and smoke. Grant only recognized a couple of them, but there was no mistaking where they were from. The bank teller was the most obvious shooter, having expressed his dissatisfaction with Macready at the Los Pecos Bank and Trust. The hotel clerk was more surprising, a man whom Grant had pegged as being in Macready's pocket. The rest were just average townsfolk with everyday lives—until they decided to stand up for what they believed in. Seeing a little old lady firing an antique hunting rifle would have been comical under any other circumstances. Seeing her take a bullet in the shoulder was anything but.

The rain finally arrived. Bruised clouds and darkness replaced sunshine and hard blue sky. Thunder rumbled amid the clouds. Lightning flickered in the depths. Spots of rain kicked up puffs of dust that were only slightly smaller than the ricochets from across the street. Until the rain became heavier and indistinguishable from the gunfire.

The battle raged. The clouds of smoke and dust were slain by the downpour. Everything became clear and focused. The mercenaries were taking casualties. The townsfolk were showing courage. Scott Macready was hiding behind the barrels and water trough near the unhinged gate as if they would protect him. It showed a level of incompetence and cowardice that was no surprise to Grant. One good shot would go through the barrel, the trough, and most of the adobe wall as well as dispatching the junior Macready.

The rain grew stronger. The thunder became louder, more regular, more like something that Grant hadn't heard for years. The dust cloud coming from the north hadn't been just the jeeps or trucks of the cavalry arriving. The heavy, thudding beat was as familiar as it was painful. It *thwup, thwup, thwupped* its way into his ears like an old friend from the distant past. The camouflage paint was different, and this wasn't a cargo chopper, but the military helicopter swooped into town and was the final straw for the gold smugglers and their gunmen.

Lightning flashed. The clap of thunder was so loud it made everyone jump. The helicopter landed in the clear space between the burning truck and the derelict buildings across the street. John Cornejo jumped out of the open door. Grant felt a wave of affection for the wounded ex-marine. Their eyes met briefly, but there was still work to be done.

Avenue D fell into an uneasy silence apart from the slowing blades after the engine was turned off. The gunfire fell away. Scott Macready stood up from behind the barrel and put his hands in the air. The mercenaries followed his lead. They were hired gunmen. They weren't about to die for a losing cause and an insolvent paymaster.

There was no cheer from the townsfolk. Losses had been too high. Doc Cruz became the man he had always been: the town doctor. He treated the wounded and gave solace to the grieving. Viewed from behind, he could almost be mistaken for the woman Grant had come here to honor.

Grant looked at the gun in his hand. He hated guns, even more today than most days. He dropped it in the dust and strode towards Cornejo. Then he stopped. Despite the heavy rain, the street was sharp and clear. Clear enough to see that something was missing.

The army jeep. Together with Tripp Macready and Sarah Hellstrom.

FORTY-TWO

GRANT STARED AT THE swirl of muddy tire tracks where the jeep had skidded a U-turn and sped away. The trail was short—about ten feet—and obscured by the squat bulk of the military helicopter. The rotor blades were buffeted by the wind. Gale force and strengthening. This baby wasn't going anywhere. Any pursuit would have to be ground based.

Cornejo saw where Grant was looking. "What?"

"The jeep."

Sabata noticed Grant's agitation and came over. The trio stood in the curved skid marks that looked like a question mark without the dot. The shape that harkened to Grant's first meeting with Sarah. And now possibly the last.

Cornejo held his hands out, palms upwards. "Didn't see it. Why?"

Grant shouted above the rain. "Macready."

Cornejo jerked a thumb to one side. "I thought that was Macready."

Grant turned to look. Scott Macready was being corralled with the mercenaries by a group of MPs. His hands were tied together out in front of him with strong plastic cable ties. Grant dragged him out of the crowd of prisoners.

"Where'd he go?"

Scott Macready looked like the crestfallen bully that he was. A frightened schoolboy blinking at the certainty of his imminent comeuppance. He looked dazed and confused. His mouth moved but words wouldn't come. A goldfish blowing bubbles.

Grant tried to prompt him.

"North?"

Macready didn't answer.

Sabata stood close to Grant to make himself heard. "He's just lost the final shipment. North will not welcome him."

Grant nodded. In the back of his mind he knew where this was going to end.

"The border."

Sabata indicated the truckloads of Aztec gold.

"He has friends down there."

Grant looked a plea at Cornejo. The ex-marine glanced at the helicopter, then at the storm raging overhead. He shook his head.

"Grounded."

"Damn."

Grant looked around for alternative transport. The trucks were too big. The MPs' vehicles were too heavily armored. Doc Cruz's car was a crispy critter at the gates of Macready's compound.

Sabata tapped Grant on the shoulder and held out his keys. He waved towards the derelict buildings across the street. The front of his pickup was just visible through the rain. Grant nodded his thanks and was about to cross Avenue D when he stopped. He turned on Scott Macready so fast it made the cowboy jump. Grant grabbed him by the scruff of the neck.

"Wallet."

Macready's eyes widened. He pointed shackled hands to his jacket pocket. Grant tugged it open and pulled out his badge wallet. He flicked it open to see the Boston PD credentials.

Sabata noticed the set of Grant's jaw.

"You planning on arresting him?"

Grant clenched his teeth.

"Not likely."

He closed the wallet and put it in his back pocket. He took a deep breath, then jogged to the coyote's pickup. South towards the border. A route he'd taken before. He doubted Tripp Macready was going to make it that far. He doubted the Texan intended to. Not yet.

Grant got in and started the engine. The tires spat mud as the pickup did a U-turn back along Avenue D. Heading south through town towards Adobe Flats.

THE RAIN EASED ONCE Grant crossed the railroad tracks. Not as torrential but not exactly dry yet either. Daylight struggled to lift the dirty green smudge of cloud as the storm ran its course. The aftermath was just as gloomy, stretching south as far as the eye could see. Dull and gray and wet as a Yorkshire weekend.

Damp enough to grow moss.

Slick enough for a rolling stone to gather none.

Grant was a rolling stone; Sarah Hellstrom had told him as much. He was passing through, not putting down roots. A stranger. Strangers don't last long. Wrong. This stranger had inverted that saying. It isn't the stranger who doesn't last long; it's those he comes

303

up against. The gas station at the factory was damaged beyond repair. The hacienda compound was breached. The gold shipment had been seized and the mercenaries neutralized. Scott Macready was in custody.

Not bad for a rolling stone.

Not good for the man he was pursuing.

A kidnapper and a braggart. A killer of cats and defenseless old men. A man Grant was desperate to meet again so he could pull the final tooth from the jaws of the Texan empire. The man in black. Tripp Macready.

Grant squinted through the windshield. The wipers were struggling to clear the screen. The road was a vague suggestion in the uneven landscape. There was no trail of dust to follow. There was no dust cloud following Grant. In the wet and stormy conditions there was no dust at all. The buttes and mesas were darker smudges on a horizon defined by smudges and sky. The sky was dirty and green, like a bruise that was beginning to heal. There were no breaks in the clouds. The wind pushed them across the sky like stampeding cattle.

The pickup followed the track. Hard-packed dirt that was now slick and muddy. Still hard but not good if he had to brake suddenly. It was so dark his headlights scythed through the rain like searchlight beams. It was the one thing that gave him hope he'd be able to see Macready once he got nearer. The Texan would need his lights on too. Taillights would stand out like shiny red beacons in the storm-ravaged day.

The road suddenly fell away in front of him. Grant slammed the brakes on. A bad mistake. The pickup slewed to its left and picked up speed. Like the skidpan at training school, Grant turned into the skid and took his foot off the gas. He dabbed at the brakes. Graded braking. The pickup stopped two feet short of where the road dipped into the dry gulch he'd crossed before.

The gulch wasn't dry anymore. The riverbed had become a raging torrent, carrying scrub and cacti with it. Rainwater from the hills of Big Bend National Park blasting through the watercourses of West Texas. Strong enough to sideswipe a battered pickup. Powerful enough to carry away an army jeep. Question was, how long had it been this deep? And had Tripp Macready already made it across?

Grant stared through the windshield at the edge of the road. It was impossible to tell if there were any tire tracks; the rain had washed them away. He looked out of the side windows. The track didn't deviate. It was cross the river or bust. He tried to remember if there'd been any turnoffs on the way. There weren't any. He'd have remembered from his previous trips.

Something flashed in the distance. Not lightning. The storm had eased, and it was now just heavy rain and strong winds. It was something red. Grant screwed his eyes up and focused on the distant horizon. There it was again. A double tap of red, there twice then gone again. A driver feathering the brakes so he didn't skid like Grant had done.

Grant let out a bark of satisfaction. He looked at the river again. There was only way to find out how deep it was. He steered for the middle of the slope and eased the pickup forward.

THE WATER ALMOST TORE the steering wheel from Grant's hands. It buffeted the pickup and threatened to lift it off the riverbed. The front tires bit into the sand and gravel bottom. The water level crept up the side of the cab, at the bottom of the door as Grant left the riverbank.

Grant held firm and drove slowly.

Three feet out from the riverbank.

Six inches farther up the pickup's door.

A surge turned the front wheels. Grant forced them back straight.

Three more feet.

Six more inches.

The river was getting deeper.

Three more feet.

Six more inches.

Halfway up the door now. Water leaked into the cab. Any deeper and the pickup would float away downriver. The load bed was empty. There was no extra weight to hold the pickup down. Grant forged ahead.

Three more feet.

The bottom leveled out. The water held steady halfway up the door. Grant pressed his foot on the gas. Forward momentum stabilized the wheels. A bow wave threatened to come over the radiator grill and hood. More speed. Steady acceleration. No sudden movements that might dislodge the traction the tires had built up.

Point of no return. Heading towards the opposite bank. Climbing out of the depths onto a gentle slope of silt and rock. The tires skidded once, then bit. Grant headed for the flat section of riverbank that he'd driven up twice before, both times in drier conditions. Low gear and steady movement kept the tires firmly grounded. The pickup came up out of the river dripping water from every orifice. Grant found the road again and put his foot down.

The pickup followed a gentle slope out of the arroyo, then the road crested between two crumbling buttes. He stopped on the brow of the hill. The road continued down the slope to the final stretch of flatland before the foothills of Big Bend National Park.

The small group of buildings at the bottom reminded Grant he'd arrived at Adobe Flats.

The red brake lights in the distance told him he wasn't alone.

FORTY-THREE

THE RAIN HAD STOPPED. That was the only good thing. It was still gloomy and overcast. The wind still whipped the clouds across the sky. The windmill atop the well still creaked as it spun like a Spitfire's propeller. Or a helicopter's rotor.

Grant pulled into the turnaround in front of the burned-out hacienda and parked. The jeep was angled towards him next to the well. Open ground lay between them like a showdown at high noon. Grant turned off the engine and got out of the pickup. Tripp Macready got out of the jeep. He was alone. There was no sign of Sarah.

The smell of burned wood was stronger after the rain. Like cigarette butts in a wet ashtray. It was as if the fire had only recently been put out. As if Macready had only just torched the house that Pilar Cruz grew up in. The desert smelled different too. Grant couldn't put his finger on it. Not as dry and parched. That much was obvious. What wasn't so obvious was Macready's intentions.

Grant took two steps towards the Texan.

"Nice of you to wait."

Macready didn't move.

"Well, I figured you'd be coming. Why put it off?"

"You reckoned this was the place, huh?"

"It's why you came to Texas. Right?"

"It's where I came to visit. Not why."

"To see a broken-down Mexican you'd never met before."

Grant could feel his pulse beginning to race.

Macready turned the screw.

"Father to a fallen hero."

Grant clenched his teeth but kept quiet.

Macready noticed the muscles of Grant's jaw tense and knew he was winning.

"I've been doing my research. So you came to Absolution looking for peace."

Grant flexed his neck one way and then the other. He took a deep breath and let it out slowly. He slowed his heart rate. Relaxed his muscles. Refused to let Tripp Macready wind him up. Keeping his voice calm, he took a step towards the surly Texan.

"There is no peace. Only acceptance. Then you move on."

Macready hardened his stare.

"I'm from Texas, and I am not so accepting. And you are gonna pay."

He stepped away from the jeep, the machete hanging loose from one hand. He began to twirl the blade in a sweeping arc. Slowly, like a martial artist going into his warm-up routine. The cutting edge was bright in the gloom. It stood out against the man in black's clothing.

Grant didn't take his eyes off Macready's stare. The twirling blade was a secondary consideration. If he was going to attack, the first sign would come from the eyes. Grant used his peripheral vision to check the jeep and the surrounding area. No movement. No Sarah. That was worrying.

Grant took another step towards Macready and tried to buy some time.

"One thing I've got to say about Texas. The welcome has been consistent."

He hooked his thumbs into his belt, fingers covering the heavy buckle.

"About as friendly as the one those Mexicans got who visited the Alamo."

Macready moved sideways, away from the well. The machete began to twirl faster. Smooth and deadly.

"They weren't invited."

Another step sideways.

"And neither were you."

Grant didn't sidestep in the opposite direction. He moved towards Macready. The secrets of facing a man with a knife were to either keep your distance or get in close, inside the fighting arc. Keeping your distance meant you were safe from being cut, but it didn't get your man. Grant was like the Mounties. He always got his man. Deft fingers unbuckled his belt.

"How do you know?"

The twirling blade stopped.

"I know Doc Cruz didn't invite you."

Grant let the belt fall open and shrugged the tattered orange windcheater off his shoulders.

"His daughter did."

Macready tightened his grip on the machete.

"That must have been just before she died."

He smiled.

"You're not having much luck with girlfriends, are you?"

Grant noticed the rope for the first time. Fastened to the back of the jeep and extending to the well. Stretched tight.

Macready nodded.

"I've been researching Yorkshire too. Want to know what I learned?"

GRANT FORCED HIS EYES away from the rope. Thunder rumbled in the distance to the north as the storm moved on past Absolution. The clouds overhead were still moving fast but weren't as dark as before. There was a hint of brightness in the sky. There was nothing bright about the confrontation at Adobe Flats. At this stage, keeping Macready talking was the best defense. Grant kept his voice soft and even.

"If you wanted the recipe for Yorkshire pudding, you should have asked."

Macready's voice feigned friendliness but couldn't disguise its hard edge.

"There's more to Yorkshire than Eccles cake and Yorkshire pudding."

"Eccles is in Greater Manchester."

Macready dismissed the interruption with a wave of the machete.

"But you've got a dark side. Over there in the English countryside."

Grant kept his dark side under control. Not prepared to unleash the fury until he was certain where Sarah was. Macready used the machete as a pointer, punctuating each piece of information with a little jab of the blade.

First jab.

"It was the training ground for the 7/7 bombers. Bradford University teaching them how to blow up trains and buses in London. I bet they didn't advertise that as part of the curriculum."

Second jab.

"You had that American who shot the cop at Christmas."

"Boxing Day. David Bieber. The American."

"Still an English cop killed by an American. A bit like here."

"Cats and old men for you."

"I'm not finished yet. I want you to feel at home."

The hard edge still behind the conversational tone.

"What was Yorkshire's biggest claim to fame, do you think?"

A rhetorical question. Grant didn't answer.

"Got to be the Yorkshire Ripper, wouldn't you say?"

Grant was getting worried for Sarah now, if Macready was going to use Peter Sutcliffe as inspiration for punishing Grant. Grant kept quiet. Macready did not. The Texan made sure Grant got the point.

"Killer of prostitutes and loose women. How many was it?"

Grant kept half an eye on the rope while focusing on the machete.

"I didn't count."

Macready pointed the blade to his stomach, then made a gutting movement.

"A lot. Between 1975 and 1980. With a hammer and a knife."

He carefully ran a finger along the cutting edge.

"Makes you feel kinda homesick, don't it?"

Grant wrapped the windcheater around his forearm for protection and flexed his shoulders. He scrutinized the gleaming length of the machete. It was clean; there was no blood. If Macready had wanted to make a point using the ripper, he'd have left Sarah's blood dripping from the blade. That meant he hadn't cut her yet. He'd made his intentions clear, though. Mentioning the man from Hanging Garden Lane was just setting the scene. The Texan was going to gut Sarah like a fish, and he wanted Grant to know about it beforehand. That's what Grant reckoned from all this talk.

Grant was wrong.

Macready sidestepped some more, already halfway around a semicircle from the jeep. Grant didn't mirror his movements. This wasn't two boxers in the ring sizing each other up before closing in for the fight. Grant took two paces towards the twirling machete and raised his covered forearm as protection. He brought his other hand across his waist. This was going to happen soon, and it was going to happen fast. Grant put added steel in his voice.

"You going to shit or get off the pot?"

The blade stopped spinning. Macready stood still. He feigned disappointment.

"There's no need for that kind of talk. I haven't got to the good part yet."

He glanced at the blade, then back at Grant.

"I could never do that to Sarah. I'm just pointing out that Yorkshire isn't all it's made out to be. All that rain. It must cultivate the inner darkness."

He held a hand out, palm upwards.

"But it's stopped now, so let's talk about that other Yorkshire legend."

Grant waited.

Macready drew the moment out before speaking again.

"The Black Panther."

Grant knew where this was going and what it meant for Sarah. "In the '70s. Robbed post offices."

Macready nodded.

"Shot people."

The clouds slowed in their race across the sky. They began to thin and let watery sunshine filter through. The hacienda brightened in the background. The windmill atop the well slowed down. Grant looked towards the jeep, still dripping water from its river crossing. He spoke almost absentmindedly.

"Branched out into kidnapping and ransom."

Macready looked pleased that Grant had made the connection.

"Kidnapped Leslie Whittle in 1975."

The sun broke through the clouds and shards of light glinted off the jeep, picking out the weave of the rope all the way to the well. The rope thrummed with tension. Macready nodded.

"And hung her from a wire in a drainage shaft."

FORTY-FOUR

GRANT MOVED FAST BUT not fast enough. He darted towards the jeep. Macready blocked his path. Two quick swipes of the machete forced Grant back. The fancy twirling movements were over; this was the business end of the knife fight.

Grant couldn't stop Sean Connery's voice playing in his mind. "Just like a wop. Brings a knife to a gunfight."

He might just as well have said, "Just like a tyke. Brings a folded coat to a knife fight." Except Grant didn't just have a folded coat. Using his free hand, he pulled the belt out of its loops. He dangled the heavy buckle almost to the ground and swung it gently from side to side.

Macready didn't look worried. He feigned a lunge with the machete.

Grant didn't react to the feint.

Macready jerked his head towards the well.

"She's on a ledge halfway down."

He put one hand around his throat, tilted his neck, and stuck his tongue out.

"One slip and she's gone."

He straightened up and swung the blade in a narrow arc in front of him.

"You know how that worked out for Leslie Whittle."

Grant knew. Leslie Whittle had been hung down the drainage shaft by a wire around the neck. Her hands were tied behind her back. Her feet barely held firm on a narrow ledge halfway down. Neilson aborted the ransom pickup atop the well, and the police didn't do a full search until the following day. Leslie must have slipped off the ledge. She was found dangling in the void.

Macready saw the recognition on Grant's face and smiled.

"Of course she was down there longer than Sarah has been. So far."

He swished the machete. Twice.

"You could save her. If you can get past me."

Another swish of the blade for effect.

"A one-man mob with a machete."

Grant focused on Macready's eyes, but he was conscious of the rope. He could practically feel the tension pulling the weave tight. The rope jerked—just a small movement but enough to send shock waves racing through Grant's body. The rope settled down again. It didn't stretch tighter. She hadn't fallen off the ledge, but she was moving. That was dangerous.

Macready continued to push Grant's buttons.

"A bit like your other girlfriend. Only you can't shoot this one."

That was enough. If Grant had kept the gun, he'd have shot Macready and saved the girl. Absolution for having killed the woman he loved. Instead he began to twirl the belt, the heavy buckle swishing through the air. Macready knew he had the upper hand. No point bringing a belt to a knife fight. He flashed the machete in two crisscross swipes intended to open Grant's chest. The second swing had a longer follow through. Too long.

Grant unleashed the belt. It wrapped around Macready's knife hand, and Grant tugged down hard. He moved inside the fighting arc and stamped on Macready's knee. The leg buckled. Grant slammed the heel of one hand into Macready's throat, and it was game over.

Macready dropped to the ground, coughing blood.

Grant snatched the machete and dashed to the well.

The wind finally dropped to a gentle breeze. The clouds became thin and wispy. The hot Texas sun was burning them off like mist on a summer's morning. Adobe Flats was transformed by the downpour. Parched foliage that had looked dry and brown now burst into life. Vibrant greens picked out the surrounding countryside, and spots of color blossomed around the foot of the well. Desert blooms that had just been waiting for sustenance. Like flowers growing on graves in a hot, dusty township halfway around the world.

Grant hoped the well hadn't turned into a grave.

He grabbed the wooden cover and flicked it open. Pipes from the windmill ran down the center of the shaft. The windmill blades squeaked as they slowed in the breeze. The rope was tight across the stone rim. Grant could feel it throbbing beneath his hand. He leaned forward and looked over the edge.

Sarah Hellstrom was a shadowy presence six feet down the shaft. Sunlight beating across the turnaround didn't extend more than a few feet into the well. Grant could make out the rope and the pipes and the top of Sarah's head. The noose had pulled tight around her neck, but that was the extent of Macready's knot-tying skills. The cord he'd used to fasten her hands dangled from one wrist, unpicked by deft fingers and sharp focus. The focus didn't extend to being able to untie the noose. Her weight at the end of the rope meant there wasn't enough slack. She reached up with one hand but missed the rope and almost fell off the ledge.

The rope twanged like it had before, vibrating all the way to the jeep. Grant doubled over the retaining wall and shoved a hand out but couldn't reach. Sarah teetered on the edge of slipping. Grant did the only thing he could: grabbed the rope and tugged. Sarah regained her balance, but the rope tightened around her throat. A gurgling death rattle echoed up the shaft.

Grant shouted into the void. "Still."

The sound of his voice calmed Sarah down. The choking lack of air did not. Her face was bright red going on purple. Her cheeks were puffed out like a blowfish. Soon her tongue would swell and protrude. There was no time. Grant anchored his feet as best he could at the base of the wall and leaned into the darkness.

"Reach up."

Sarah raised one hand, careful not to overbalance. She couldn't look up to see where she was reaching. Grant stretched down. The hands groped for each other but were two feet apart. Grant stretched even farther.

His left foot slipped on the sandy ground.

Shock sparked through his system, and he jerked backwards.

Sarah whimpered, the sound echoing up the shaft.

Grant caught his breath and changed his footing. Legs apart for a more solid base. He slipped one end of the belt through the buckle and pulled it all the way to the end, forming a manacle just big enough for Sarah to slip her wrist in. He wrapped the loose end around his fist and leaned into the well again.

"Okay. Try again. Slowly. Slip your hand through the loop."

He was talking just to calm her down, the sound of his voice giving her reassurance. It was obvious what she had to do. The end of the belt dangled above her head. Without looking up she found it with one hand and slipped her wrist through the loop. Held tight and grabbed the strap with her other hand too.

Grant took the weight with his right arm. Muscles screamed in his shoulder. As soon as he felt she was secure, he swung the machete at the rope where it stretched over the wall. The blade was sharp. The swing was heavy. The twang of the rope snapping sounded loud in the silence.

"Now turn."

Sarah didn't need telling twice. She turned to face the wall of the shaft and used her feet to find grips on the way up. Grant braced his legs and pulled. She came up three feet. He leaned back from the wall and pulled again. Another three feet. Sarah held onto the top of the retaining wall, and Grant leaned over and grabbed the waist of her jeans. One final tug, and she tumbled headlong over the wall.

Grant fell back and sat on the ground. He let out an explosive breath, then loosened the noose from around her neck. The rope had bitten deep, leaving a burn scar that would take months to heal. The belt came loose from her wrist. Her eyes watered as she gasped for air. She coughed and retched and was sick on the flowers around the base of the well.

No one else was coughing.

That was Grant's first thought.

Then Sarah found her voice.

"*Jim.*"

Grant spun around too late. The machete wasn't on the ground where he'd dropped it. It was swinging at his head in a killing arc.

SUNLIGHT GLINTED OFF THE blade. It slashed downwards towards where Grant was sitting. Not from very high because Macready was sitting too, his broken knee twisted at an ugly angle. The razor edge had become serrated where it had struck the stone wall when cutting the rope. It wasn't any less sharp as it sliced through the orange windcheater wrapped around Grant's upstretched arm. Blood seeped through the cut. Pain flared.

Grant rolled to one side and spun his legs to face the threat. Standard practice when an officer was on the ground facing a hostile force in a riot situation or a pub fight. Police training school had contingencies for everything. He didn't remember them teaching him how to defend against a machete attack. Get in close. That was all he could think of. Inside the fighting arc. Easier said than done when you were on your back and down to one arm.

The blade swung again. From high to low in a chopping motion. Grant flick-rolled in the opposite direction. One swift movement followed by a straight-legged kick to the chest. His foot slammed Macready backwards. The Texan twisted but his shattered knee couldn't follow. He let out a scream and snarled at Grant. Speckles of slaver dripped from his lips. His face was red. He looked like a rabid dog. He tried to bring his arm back for another strike, but Grant lurched to his knees and gained the higher ground.

The machete arm was in the middle of the backstroke. Grant caught the wrist before it could swing forward. He pulled Macready's arm straight and slammed his elbow down on the Texan's forearm. It snapped just above the wrist, and the machete fell to the ground.

Grant darted forward and whipped the belt around Macready's neck. He knelt behind the Texan and caught the other end of the belt. The cords of Macready's throat stood out as the belt tightened.

Sarah shuffled back against the well. Sunlight haloed around her head. The bright little flowers at the base of the well stood out in another glorious Texas morning. Not flowers on a desert grave. New life in a desolate land.

Grant squeezed tighter. Macready had killed Hunter Athey and tried to kill Sarah. Not to mention the cat. This wasn't a man who deserved mercy. This wasn't a man who would see the inside of an Absolution jail cell. Sometimes justice was more than following the letter of the law. Grant turned his back on Sarah and locked one arm around Macready's neck. He grabbed the Texan's head and prepared to administer summary justice.

FORTY-FIVE

They didn't talk on the drive back to Absolution. Grant concentrated on keeping the pickup on the road with only one hand. Sarah concentrated on resting her throat, still sore from the hanging that almost cost the waitress her life. That's what they told themselves, but the silence spoke volumes. Tense and spiky and full of hidden meaning.

The sun rode high in a hard blue sky. The storm was past. The fallout was still evident. For practically the first time since Grant had arrived on the *Sunset Limited,* the Texas wastelands showed color other than desert sand and pale blue sky. Green blossomed everywhere. Not exactly the garden of England greenery, but considering the scorched earth he'd experienced the last few days it was a riot of color. Strange plants had sprung up along the roadside. Flowers bloomed. Even the cacti looked bright and green instead of sad and lonely.

The river level had dropped as quickly as it had risen, the water already soaking into the parched landscape. The pickup negotiated the watercourse with ease. The tires had no problem climbing out of the other side. Grant was surprised to find that the dust trail was back in his wake. Not another car following him this time but simply the shadow that followed everything in the desert wastes. It felt good. Like an old friend coming back to join him.

Absolution lay ahead. Grant wasn't sure if he deserved it. The town was just a row of uneven rooftops breaking the smooth lines of the horizon. Smoke hung over portions of the town—straggly wisps that pinpointed the aftermath of the gun battle and Macready's compound. The entire street would be a crime scene. Sheriff Al Purwin would have his hands full sorting that mess out. He'd need lots of help from outside agencies. No doubt Avenue D was a hive of activity. Cornejo's MPs would be able to provide initial scene preservation, but the investigation would need a leg up from nearby towns. There would be lots of questions and lots of paperwork. Grant wasn't feeling up to that just yet.

He crossed the railroad tracks and paused at the junction with First Street. Left towards town or right towards Sixto's. He glanced at the fuel gauge. Nearly empty. He couldn't return Sabata's pickup with a dry tank. He turned right, away from the inevitable questioning, and headed towards the gas station and the diner.

Grant's dust trail hadn't gone unnoticed. By the time he pulled onto the forecourt, the reception committee was waiting.

THE BULLET-RIDDLED SIGN AT the roadside still read

ABSOLUTION, TEXAS Est. 1882
Pop. 203—Elev. 4040
Welcome/Bienvenidos

But the welcome was friendlier than last time. John Cornejo and Doc Cruz stood in Sixto's doorway. Old Pedro wagged his tail in the fenced scrap yard, apparently recovered from his drug-induced rest. An insect zapped itself on the bug catcher, sparking purple light above the door. Dust swirled around the pickup. Grant turned the engine off and got out. He nodded at Cornejo.

"Can you debug the windshield while you're at it?"

The ex-marine crossed the forecourt and stood beside the gas pump.

"I thought you'd show up here."

Grant indicated the filler cap.

"Running on empty."

Cornejo looked at Grant's battered face and the makeshift dressing that was oozing blood down his arm.

"You certainly are."

"Know where I can find a good doctor?"

The tone was light to cover the seriousness of the situation. Typical cop-speak that transferred to all the emergency services and the military. Gallows humor. Bury your feelings deep. Doc Cruz wasn't in the military. He wasn't a cop. He was a country doctor who had just treated injuries no man should ever have to see. Combat was a brutal activity. A cut arm and scarred face were small potatoes.

Cruz walked straight past Grant and helped Sarah out of the pickup.

"Oh, my child."

He examined her neck but she waved him away. The doctor looked hurt by the rebuff, so Sarah put her arms around him and squeezed. He hugged her in return. Sarah fought back the tears and smiled.

"I'm okay."

Doc Cruz shook his head. "No, you're not. But you will be."

He gave her another hug, then turned towards Grant. "You saved the girl."

Grant couldn't hide the gravity of his thoughts. They were written all over his face. Hard eyes fought to overcome the emotion.

"This time."

Doc Cruz rested a hand on Grant's injured arm. "Both times. Consider yourself absolved."

Grant let out a sigh. "There is no absolution. Only acceptance. Then you move on."

"Then move on in peace."

Cornejo joined them but kept quiet. He understood that this was a private moment, but there were things that needed resolving. Grant shrugged it off and glanced at the ex-marine. Cornejo raised his eyebrows.

"Macready?"

Grant's face hardened. He looked across the pickup at Sarah, and she stared back. Neither hard nor soft; nonjudgmental. Almost. She gave the gentlest of nods. Grant jerked his head towards the cargo bed. Cornejo walked to the back of the pickup and dropped the flap. A crumpled tarpaulin was humped up in one corner. Cornejo gripped the edge and pulled it to one side.

Tripp Macready blinked into the sunlight. His neck was unbroken, but his nose was not. One eye was swollen shut. Summary justice in the field. Grant flicked open his badge wallet. Cornejo barely glanced at the Boston PD shield.

"Did you read him his rights?"

Grant smiled.

"I haven't quite got my head around the Miranda warning, so I gave him the Yorkshire version. I think he understands his rights."

Doc Cruz stretched Macready out on the load bed and began to do what he did best. Look after people. It was what Pilar Cruz had done too. Now that the stethoscope had been returned, Grant felt he could move on. Cornejo brought him down to earth.

"When you've finished galloping around the country, you going to do some real police work back in Boston?"

Sarah turned away and took a deep breath. Grant saw the movement and knew what it meant. Rolling stones gather no moss. He cradled his arm and looked at Cornejo.

"I'm not fit to travel. Need to rest up a bit first."

Cornejo nodded and turned away. Grant went to Sarah and grimaced in pain. Looking for the sympathy vote. He lowered his voice.

"I could do with a coffee, though."

Sarah didn't smile. "Diner's closed."

Grant held her gaze with his. "But I know the owner."

Resistance crumbled. The faintest of smiles feathered her lips. "Latte?"

Grant nodded. "Two sugars. No lid."

THE END

ACKNOWLEDGMENTS

Once again I find myself thanking the people who helped make this book possible. They didn't write the words, but they helped guide them towards publication. My agent, Donna Bagdasarian, as always. Nothing more needs to be said. Terri Bischoff and Midnight Ink, thanks for believing in me. And my editor, Rebecca Zins, for a bang-up polish job. My final thanks go to the readers. Without you there would be no books. I count myself among that number. Without reading there would be no writing.

The following excerpt is from

SNAKE PASS

The forthcoming book from Colin Campbell.
Available April 2015 from Midnight Ink.

21:50 HOURS

Jim Grant was pissed off long before he got to Snake Pass on Thursday night. Before the snow began to fall and the entire world decided to shoot it out at the Woodlands Truck Stop and Diner. He was already pissed off three hours earlier when he parked his patrol car across the mouth of Edgebank Close and turned the engine off. Ravenscliffe Avenue stretched out behind him like a nighttime runway with half the lights missing. Ravenscliffe woods bulked up against the night sky beyond the houses in the cul-de-sac. He was four hours into his ten-hour shift, a half-night tour of duty that started at six in the evening.

Being pissed off meant he wasn't going to make it until four.

PC Grant adjusted the stab vest under his uniform jacket and drummed the fingers of his right hand on the steering wheel. He stared at the house at the end of the short, stubby street. He looked calm and relaxed and completely un-pissed off on the outside. That was one of his strengths. It was why Sergeant Ballhaus had made him a tutor constable and why the fresh-faced young constable in the passenger seat didn't know to keep quiet.

"But isn't that unethical?"

"What?"

Constable Hope was carrying on the conversation they'd been having for most of the shift. Being eighteen years old and in the first six months of his service meant he didn't know when the subject was closed.

"Ignoring a crime just because you're off-duty?"

"I'm not saying you should ignore it. Just don't go charging in waving your warrant card with no radio and no backup."

"But your warrant card gives you authority as a police officer throughout England and Wales."

"Doesn't give you shit-all in a pub fight with no baton and stab vest."

"But—"

Grant held up a hand for Hope to be quiet.

"Case in point. Young copper I knew goes for Chinese down at Mean Wood junction. Pubs are shutting. Lot of drunks ordering takeaway. Trouble brews. A fight ensues. Young copper whips out his warrant card and orders them all to cease and desist. What do you think happened?"

Hope tried to keep the hero worship off his face. Listening to a legend of the West Yorkshire Police recounting tales of derring-do was like manna from heaven for the young probationer constable. He answered with a question.

"They didn't cease and desist?"

"They did not. He got the shit kicked out of him and spent three days in the hospital. The riot he provoked wrecked the Chinese and two shops on either side of it and put everybody on double shifts for a week. Point is, drunks fighting each other are par for the course.

Serves 'em right if they've got sore heads and a few bruises the following morning. It's no big deal."

"What about theft?"

"What about it?"

"Should you ignore a theft?"

Grant let out a sigh. This kid never gave up. It was one of the things Grant liked about him. He could be exasperating at times, though.

"Judgment call. Another example. Inspector Speedhoff was down at the supermarket with his kids, aged two and four. Spots some dickhead nicking citric acid for his drug habit. Wades in to make an off-duty arrest. What do you think happened?"

Hope smiled.

"He got the shit kicked out of him?"

"In front of his kids. They had nightmares for weeks. Citric acid isn't exactly the great train robbery. Let it slide. Or if you feel strongly, tell the store detective. But don't go wading in without communication or backup. Off-duty is off-duty."

The engine purred. Exhaust fumes plumed into the cold Yorkshire air. The cul-de-sac was quiet. The house at the end of the street was mostly in darkness, apart from a light in the upstairs landing. Hope displayed why he was a prospect for the future and had been paired with Grant.

"Don't you think we should communicate for backup before we go in?"

"We're not off-duty."

Grant smiled at his protégé.

"And it's only an address check. We won't need backup."

Grant turned the engine off and looked at the house through the windscreen. Hot metal ticked and popped under the bonnet as the engine cooled. The veteran had been here many times before, but he examined the front of the house again anyway. Standard procedure before going into action, address check or not.

The house was a run-down three-bedroom semi, the left-hand half of the pair across the end of the cul-de-sac. The front aspect had a wide living room window and a narrow front door. Above them were the main bedroom window and the smaller spare room. Round the side of the house there was only a kitchen window and the upstairs landing window. The one with the light on. Kitchen door was in the rear aspect, hidden from view, but Grant knew what it looked like. Upstairs was the rear bedroom and the bathroom at the top of the stairs.

Lee Adkins could be hiding in any one of those rooms.

Grant stopped drumming his fingers and got out of the car. Hope got out of his side too. Both closed their doors quietly, making barely a click. The boy had smarts. Steam bloomed around his head in the cold night air as he waited for Grant's instructions. Standard deployment for a house search was one covering the back in case the suspect tried to escape. An address check was much more low-key. It didn't matter if someone jumped out of the back window. Except this wasn't really an address check.

"Go cover the back. You remember what I said?"

Hope nodded.

"Stand at least six feet away from the house at the corner so I can see two aspects at the same time—the back and the side. But I thought this was just an address check?"

Grant pulled his black leather gloves on.

"Always best to be on the safe side."

"Everyone knows Lee Adkins lives here."

"Intelligence is only as good as the last time it was checked. You have to constantly update it. I'm updating it tonight. Now, get round the back."

Hope's shoulders sagged.

Grant was sorry he'd sounded so harsh. It was nothing personal. He just didn't want the young lad with him when he went in. Some things you don't need witnesses for. Some things you don't want to burden your probationer with. He watched Police Constable Jamie Hope walk down the side of the house and disappear into the gloom, then took the bloodstained bus pass out of his pocket. The shaved head and surly eyes of Lee Adkins stared out from the plastic wallet. The blood smeared across the plastic wasn't his.

THE SLAP ACROSS THE face knocked Sharon Davis off her feet in the foyer of the Rugby Club on Harrogate Road. The second slap wasn't a slap at all, it was a punch, and it was probably the blow that broke her nose and closed one eye. She kicked out in vain. Lee Adkins stepped in and thumped her three more times while she was on the floor. She stopped crying out after the second punch.

The club reception miraculously emptied. The few customers waiting to pass through into the lounge bar vanished. The old-age pensioner manning the signing-in book behind the counter went into the office. Nobody witnessed the assault. That's what the old man told Jim Grant when he responded to the report of a disturbance twenty minutes later.

Grant crouched beside the shivering mass of blood and flesh that had once been the prettiest teenager on the estate. Nineteen years old going on ninety. Grant comforted her as best he could until the ambulance arrived. She feigned memory loss but Grant knew she wouldn't point the finger at the biggest thug on Ravenscliffe. The burgling, drug-dealing scumbucket Lee Adkins. Everyone was afraid of him. Everybody knew he was Sharon Davis's boyfriend.

After she'd been taken away, Grant let Hope take the report from the old man. A barebones affair that would be needed to write off the IBIS log back at the control room. There was enough evidence of an assault to record a crime, but with nobody willing to come forward as a witness and a complainant who was refusing to name her assailant, the statistics boys on the third floor would want to downgrade this from a Section 47 assault to a noisy disturbance. Meet the target figures for reducing violent crime.

Grant made enquiries in the office. The CCTV cameras that covered the club inside and out weren't recording tonight. There'd been plenty of recordings the night the club got burgled three weeks ago. That didn't surprise Grant. He'd been trying to nail Adkins for eighteen months, but you couldn't get a conviction without evidence or witnesses. Holding the estate in a grip of fear was the best protection the thieving bastard could have got. Except tonight he'd made a mistake.

The plastic wallet had been lying under Sharon Davis's crumpled body. Grant had picked it up when she was being carried to the ambulance. He flicked it open now while Hope finished taking the report. The cardboard bus pass was sealed inside the plastic. The shaved head and surly eyes stared up at him from the photograph. Lee Adkins' face was covered in blood, the fresh redness smeared across his image. Grant slipped the wallet into his pocket and smiled. He could sense a tactical address check coming on.

Grant closed the plastic wallet and put it back in his pocket. Hope was now safely out of the way. The house was still in darkness apart from the light from the landing window. Grant flexed the fingers inside his leather gloves and took a deep breath. He let it out slowly, the cloud of vapor hiding his face for a moment, then strode down the garden path towards the front door.

He threw one last glance to make sure that Hope hadn't snuck down the side of the house. Some things you don't need witnesses for. It was an adage that Lee Adkins lived by. Grant was simply using the villain's strength against him. He raised his heavily booted foot and kicked the front door open.

22:00 HOURS

ADKINS WAS IN THE bathroom. Grant could see the light through the open door at the top of the stairs. Not the landing light, the bathroom light spilling out onto the landing. The front door smashed backwards against the side of the hallway, its frame splintered to oblivion. Shards of wood stood out like porcupine quills around the lock. The house was clean and tidy, in contrast to the drug addicts' homes that Adkins supplied. It smelled of soap and air freshener. Radio traffic squawked on Grant's shoulder, the rest of the shift going about its business, unaware of the drama unfolding at number 5 Edgebank Close.

Grant flicked the hall and landing lights on and took the stairs two at a time. Speed was key once you'd forced the breach. Speed and light. He didn't want to be stumbling through the shadows with his target holding the high ground. He might have been here many times before, but you had to expect the unexpected. The roller skates on the stair bed or the tripwire across the risers. He reached the landing before the front door had stopped quivering.

Adkins stood up from the sink, his face dripping water.

Grant leaned on the bathroom doorframe.

338

"Cut yourself shaving?"

The water swirling down the plughole was pink. Splatters of red dotted the washbasin. Adkins held a white towel in one hand, the knuckles stained with Sharon Davis's blood, the towel painted in the stuff. Grant leaned forward, turned the tap off, and put the plug in. He snatched the towel out of Adkins' hand.

"You missed a bit."

He indicated the blood splatters on the side of Adkins face. He'd beaten the girl with such ferocity that the blowback had spread way beyond the knuckles that caused the damage. Blood that would tie him to the assault and prove the case if Sharon Davis hadn't been too frightened to bring a case against the burgling drug dealer. Grant made a snap decision. The blood on the towel and Adkins' knuckles would be enough.

He whipped his free hand up and grabbed Adkins behind the head. The leather glove snatched a handful of hair and slammed the burglar's face down into the sink. His nose and lip exploded. One eye swelled shut immediately.

"How do you like it, fuckface?"

Adkins was about to reply but Grant smashed his face into the sink again.

"That was a rhetorical question."

Adkins' knees buckled, and he flopped to the fluffy beige carpet that was now speckled with fresh blood. Grant was thinking clearly. He saw the drug dealer kneeling on the floor and the stripped pine bath panel in the background. He'd tried to get a search warrant for this house a dozen times but couldn't get the paperwork past the magistrate. There had never been enough evidence to prove that Adkins was involved with all the crimes he was involved in. The spoils of those crimes were hidden in this house. The drugs and the money.

Grant back-heeled the bath panel.

"Oops."

The top of the panel opened slightly, leaving a two-inch gap. The preferred hiding place for drug dealers ever since the toilet cistern had been exposed on too many TV shows. Grant heard footsteps charge through the front door and made another snap decision. He didn't want Hope getting caught having to lie about Adkins' injuries. He pressed the transmit button on his shoulder.

"Stop resisting."

Adkins threw Grant a confused look from the bathroom floor.

Grant kept his finger on the transmit button and spoke into the open mike.

"Put the weapon down. Don't—"

He turned his face to one side and head-butted the wall. The porcelain tiles cracked and cut his forehead. Releasing the transmit button, he reached down and grabbed Adkins' right arm, twisting it behind the fallen burglar's back. The footsteps bounded up the stairs. Grant could hear Hope shouting into his radio.

"Officers need assistance. 5 Edgebank Close."

He didn't need to say urgent. Jane Archer knew that an officer-needs-assistance call was always urgent. The radio controller relayed the request over the airwaves, and every copper in Bradford stopped what they were doing and headed towards Ravenscliffe. That's the way it worked on the frontline. Grant felt a pang of guilt at setting that in motion but was already looking at the bigger picture.

Jamie Hope burst into the bathroom.

Grant held up one hand to calm the probationer's approach. He got to his feet, dragging Lee Adkins with him. He caught sight of his reflection in the wall mirror. Blood trickled down the side of his face from an ugly swelling above the right eye.

Hope's mouth dropped open.

"Are you all right?"

The most ridiculous question but also the most obvious. Grant decided to cut Hope some slack and not fire a sarcastic reply. He simply blinked his eyes instead of nodding, then jerked his head towards Adkins.

"You should see the other fella."

Hope regained his composure.

"I can see the other fella. What happened?"

"Resisted arrest."

Hope showed again why he was a prospect for the future. He moved so that Grant blocked Adkins' view and lowered his voice.

"Arrest for what?"

Grant pointed at the gap in the bath panel and pulled it open another couple of inches. Careful not to disturb any fingerprints that would prove Adkins had opened the panel before. The rolls of banknotes were barely visible through the gap, but the bags of white powder stood out even in the dim bathroom light.

"Eureka."

Hope proved he had a sense of humor to match his smarts.

"Wasn't that to do with water displacement in the bath? Not hidden drugs underneath it?"

Grant wiped the blood from his eye.

"Calculating weight by measuring displaced water. Something like that. I'll bet there's enough weight in there to send this little bastard back to Her Majesty's school of hard knocks."

Adkins moaned. Hope kept his voice low.

"A bit careless of him, leaving it open like that."

Grant shrugged.

"Probably got dislodged during the struggle."

Grant could see where Hope was going with this and headed him off at the pass. He didn't want the young constable giving Adkins ideas for his defense. He held the bloodstained bus pass up.

"This is what got him arrested. The rest is just good luck."

Hope nodded that he understood. Another tick for Grant's tutor report. He put the plastic wallet back in his pocket.

"I'll bet a pound to a pinch of shit whose blood it is."

"Sharon Davis."

"You win. Now let's cuff this twat and cancel backup. We only need transport and an ambulance. Just make sure it's not the one that took her. We don't want to be accused of cross-contaminating blood samples."

Hope went outside to make the calls. The blood was a moot point since Grant had comforted the bleeding Davis at the crime scene. She wouldn't make the complaint anyway. It was the drugs that would send him to prison. Grant handcuffed Adkins's hands behind his back as blue lights began to flash in the street.

22:30 HOURS

"You know as well as I do that calling it forced entry to preserve evidence isn't gonna fly."

Sergeant Ballhaus stepped back from the landing to let the SOCO get to work with the blood samples trapped in the U-bend. The scenes-of-crime officer was careful where he knelt as he unscrewed the waste pipe. He wasn't dressed in the full forensic paper suit—this wasn't a murder scene—but he didn't want to get blood on his trousers.

Grant had bagged the bus pass for DNA testing himself to at least preserve the illusion of avoiding cross-contamination. Having the samples from the waste pipe and the bloody towel booked in by the same officer who had seized the bus pass at the crime scene would make it too easy for the defense solicitor to pick holes. There were enough holes already.

Grant stood in the doorway to the front bedroom.

"Worked, though, didn't it?"

He pointed towards the bathroom.

"The evidence is preserved."

Then he nodded at the bath panel, still open a few inches at the top.

"And I'm telling you, we're gonna hit the evidence jackpot."

Ballhaus let out an exasperated sigh and glanced over his shoulder to make sure that Jamie Hope had gone downstairs. He jerked a thumb towards the bedroom.

"Fuck me, Jim. Ways and Means Act doesn't work anymore."

Grant followed his sergeant into the front bedroom. He knew he was skating on thin ice but was confident that Ballhaus was a practical copper and not the pencil-pushing desk jockey that most supervisors became once they were off the frontline. A shift sergeant at Ecclesfield Division was about as frontline as it got.

"Sarge. There's always a way of getting the job done. Nose to the grindstone trumps thumb up the arse every time."

Ballhaus stood by the bedroom window and looked down at the sea of blue flashing lights. The paramedics had taken Adkins away but there were still three patrol cars and the divisional van choking the cul-de-sac. It was a testament to the code of the streets. When you called for backup, everyone responded. Ballhaus appeared to fill with pride that his boys honored that code. He turned back to face Grant.

"Jim. Grow up. This is the modern police force. There are more thumb-up-the-arse types than there are practical policing types. So let's not give them anything to poke shit-fingers at."

Grant nodded his understanding.

"Okay. Let's shape this right."

He rubbed his chin for a moment before clarifying the first point.

"Entry to preserve evidence is out. Right?"

"Right. There is no power of entry to gather evidence for a crime if there is no complaint of assault. The girl isn't going to cooperate. Is she?"

Grant shook his head. He should be annoyed that Sharon Davis was unwilling to accuse Adkins of assault, but he understood her reasoning. Police officers could deal with confrontations, then go back to the safety of their own homes. People on Ravenscliffe estate had to live among the thieves and burglars. If they gave evidence against them, they were easy targets for intimidation. That was a lot to ask of a nineteen-year-old girl.

"What about entry to prevent a further breach of the peace? An officer—that's me—fears for the girl's safety. Forced entry to preserve life."

Ballhaus smiled but shook his head.

"Good try. But the girl was taken away in the ambulance. Remember?"

Grant raised his eyebrows.

"I knew that. Could have been discharged after treatment, though."

"At the BRI? You kidding? Takes three hours just to get through triage."

Grant scratched his head since rubbing his chin hadn't worked. Then he stopped and clicked his fingers.

"Okay. Evidence of an assault at the rugby club. Officer—that's me again—believes a crime has been committed, which will only be disproved when Davis declines after treatment. Officer has reason to believe that Adkins committed that crime"—he held up the sealed evidence bag with the bloodstained bus pass in it—"and pursued the suspect to his place of residence. Suspect goes into house and locks the door. The officer, in continued pursuit of the felon, forces entry in order to effect the arrest."

Ballhaus nodded his approval and finished the chain of evidence.

"After making a lawful arrest, search of any premises that the prisoner has control over is allowed to preserve evidence for that crime."

Grant pointed at the SOCO under the sink.

"Including blood on the towel and in the sink."

Ballhaus smiled.

"Eureka."

Grant held up a hand. He wasn't finished yet.

"And during that search, evidence is uncovered of other crimes, namely drugs and money pertaining to illegal supply of Class A drugs."

Now that they'd got their story straight, Ballhaus stepped onto the landing and nodded towards the bathroom.

"You know, if you fell in a pile of shit, you'd come up smelling of roses."

Grant squeezed past the burly shift sergeant and stood in the bathroom doorway. The SOCO had almost finished with the sink. Now it was time to draw his attention to the bath panel.

It took over an hour before Drug Squad detectives arrived at the house and took over. By that time SOCO had photographed the contraband in situ. Standard shots of the bath with the panel partly open, then with the panel removed. Then establishing shots of the sheer scale of the discovery followed by close-ups of the individual bags of white powder and rolled-up banknotes.

There were six large sealed bags of white powder, like five-pound bags of sugar only you wouldn't want it in your tea. Behind the bags was a cardboard tray containing 150 dealer bags, little self-sealed plastic baggies with individual portions ready for sale. Beside the tray were twenty-five thick roles of banknotes held together by elastic bands.

Twenty-five thousand pounds, it would turn out later.

The lead detective looked excited but weary. There was hours of work ahead seizing and labeling the evidence. Counting the money. Weighing the drugs. Making sure that the chain of evidence was observed. SOCO would have to fingerprint the bath and the panel. The bags would have to be removed and examined. They wouldn't bother with the money. Everyone who'd ever handled the banknotes would have left a trace.

This was a big find for a council estate. The value of the drugs would far outstrip the quantity of money they'd recovered. The rest of the house would have to be searched just in case there was more, but Grant told the lead detective there wouldn't be any. Adkins kept the house spotless for just that reason—so that no visiting police officers could stumble across his stash by accident while harassing the local villain. Grant should know. He'd been harassing Adkins for over a year.

The blue lights in the cul-de-sac thinned out. The rest of the shift went back to chasing the radio calls. Grant had a quiet word with his probationer. The only thing that Hope needed to be clear about was the continued pursuit from the rugby club to the house, which wasn't a stretch since Grant had come straight here after they'd taken the report. He left Hope watching the evidence being gathered in the bathroom and joined Ballhaus, who was still waiting in the front bedroom. The sergeant appeared to be having more fun than a shift supervisor normally got on a half-night tour.

Grant stood beside his sergeant in front of the window.

"Like they used to say in *The A-Team*."

Ballhaus followed Grant's train of thought.

"I love it when a plan comes together."

The only thing Ballhaus was missing was a big fat cigar.

Grant let out a sigh.

"Thanks, Sarge. It's nice to know the good guys get to win now and again."

Ballhaus was about to reply, then his face stiffened.

"Thumb-up-the-arse brigade."

Grant followed his gaze through the window.

"What the fuck's he doing here?"

Down in the cul-de-sac an unmarked Astra pulled up behind Grant's patrol car. A tall, well-dressed man got out and strode towards the house. D & C's top bulldog, Inspector Nelson Carr. With two gold fillings in his false smile.

The question was, what was Discipline and Complaints doing at the scene of a routine drug seizure?

ABOUT THE AUTHOR

Ex-Army, retired cop, and former scenes-of-crime officer Colin Campbell is also the author of British crime novels *Blue Knight, White Cross* and *Northern eX*. His Jim Grant thrillers bring a rogue Yorkshire cop to America, where culture clash and violence ensue. For more information, visit www.campbellfiction.com.

www.MidnightInkBooks.com

From the gritty streets of New York City to sacred tombs in the Middle East, it's always midnight somewhere. Join us online at any hour for fresh new voices in mystery fiction.

At midnightinkbooks.com you'll also find our author blog, new and upcoming books, events, book club questions, excerpts, mystery resources, and more.

MIDNIGHT INK ORDERING INFORMATION

Order Online:
- Visit our website www.midnightinkbooks.com, select your books, and order them on our secure server.

Order by Phone:
- Call toll-free within the U.S. and Canada at
  1-888-NITE-INK (1-888-648-3465)
- We accept VISA, MasterCard, and American Express

Order by Mail:
Send the full price of your order (MN residents add 6.5% sales tax) in U.S. funds, plus postage & handling to:

Midnight Ink
2143 Wooddale Drive
Woodbury, MN 55125-2989

Postage & Handling:

Standard (U.S. & Canada). If your order is:
  $24.99 and under, add $3.00
  $25.00 and over, FREE STANDARD SHIPPING

AK, HI, PR: $15.00 for one book plus $1.00 for each additional book.

International Orders (airmail only):
  $16.00 for one book plus $3.00 for each additional book

Orders are processed within 12 business days. Please allow for normal shipping time. Postage and handling rates subject to change.

"VERY REAL.
VERY GOOD."
—LEE CHILD

NEW YORK TIMES
BESTSELLING AUTHOR
OF THE REACHER NOVELS

Jamaica Plain

*A Resurrection Man
Novel #1*

COLIN
CAMPBELL

978-0-7387-3583-2
5³⁄₁₆ x 8 • 384 pages

English cop Jim Grant is in Boston on a temporary assignment, and his instructions are simple: keep out of trouble. But for Jim Grant, keeping out of trouble is not an option, even if he doesn't carry a gun.

First thing Jim Grant does when he lands in Boston is buy a map. Second thing is get laid. Third? He almost gets himself blown up interviewing Freddy Sullivan, the prisoner he came from Yorkshire to question.

With an uncanny inner calm and the fists of a bare-knuckle fighter, Grant leaves a trail of broken bad guys and burned-out buildings behind him. And thanks to a public standoff with a frantic gunman, Grant finds himself splashed across the evening news, tagged with a new nickname—Resurrection Man. Down-and-out marine John Cornejo and the sensuous Terri Avellone offer Grant refuge in a hostile city, but as the clues add up, it's clear the political intrigue brewing in Jamaica Plain could become bigger—and bloodier—than anyone ever imagined.

Montecito Heights

A Resurrection Man Novel #2

COLIN CAMPBELL

978-0-7387-3632-7
5³⁄₁₆ x 8 • 384 pages

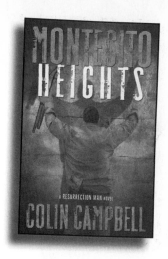

Saving a senator's daughter from LA's porn industry is one gig that needs serious discretion…but discretion is not Jim Grant's specialty. Before long, Grant finds himself busting a robbery on live television, spreading his arms wide to show he's unarmed—the same pose that earned him the nickname Resurrection Man in Boston.

The spotlight may be good for Grant's ego, but it's bad for his health. The Dominguez drug cartel is looking for him, and his work for the senator has uncovered a ring of dirty cops who want him out of the way. Helped by an ex-cop working on *CSI: NY* and hindered by a film crew that wants to make him a reality television star, Grant must tread carefully. In the city of angels, corruption runs deep, loyalty is fragile, and justice is hard to find.